Wind Drinkers

ALSO BY FRANCK BOUYSSE

Born of No Woman

Wind Drinkers

·

FRANCK BOUYSSE

Translated from the French
by Chris Clarke

OTHER PRESS / NEW YORK

Production editor: Yvonne E. Cárdenas
Text designer: Jennifer Daddio / Bookmark Design & Media Inc.
This book was set in Vendetta by Alpha Design & Composition of Pittsfield, NH

1 3 5 7 9 10 8 6 4 2

Library of Congress Cataloging-in-Publication Data
Names: Bouysse, Franck, 1965- author. | Clarke, Chris, translator.
Title: Wind drinkers / Franck Bouysse ; translated from the French by Chris Clarke.
Other titles: Buveurs de vent. English
Description: New York : Other Press, [2023]
Identifiers: LCCN 2022027285 (print) | LCCN 2022027286 (ebook) |
ISBN 9781635421729 (paperback) | ISBN 9781635421736 (ebook)
Subjects: LCGFT: Novels.
Classification: LCC PQ2702.O9845 B8813 2023 (print) | LCC PQ2702.O9845 (ebook) |
DDC 843/.92—dc23/eng/20220622
LC record available at https://lccn.loc.gov/2022027285
LC ebook record available at https://lccn.loc.gov/2022027286

They wanted to escape their misery
and the stars were too distant for them.

Thus Spoke Zarathustra
Nietzsche

Prologue

The man and the man's shadow preceded the woman along the wooded slope. He labored to advance, leaning forward, his back crushed beneath the weight of a heavy bundle wrapped in deer hide that contained the couple's belongings; shells hanging from his belt tinkled each time he set a foot down upon the earth. The woman carried nothing on her back, but a child in her arms. The child was not crying, and it wasn't sleeping either. The man walked cautiously, primarily to avoid hazards, but also because he was on the lookout for any sign of tracks that might suggest they weren't the first.

They came to the summit of a ridge. The man glanced in the direction of the valley below them, then he looked at the woman, and she at her child. Wariness swelled in the man's eyes. He wanted to continue on down the slope, and she grabbed him by the arm. Maybe she tried to dissuade him, on the pretext that something monstrous surely lay concealed in the dense tangles of vegetation, which in places revealed the dark waters of a sinuous river. Nobody knows for sure. And nobody knows whether or not he replied, or if his silent determination was enough to convince her to see what she wasn't seeing, to convince her that a dream was being born, to open herself to a great undertaking of staying put, to suppress the silent chaos of their trek. Nobody knows, nobody remembers, because in the years that were to follow, neither he nor she would think to write of their shared fate, and it has since been lost, and they have since been forgotten, no living on in myth, no true glory.

The Black Rimstone was what the place came to be called. Nobody knows who chose the name, perhaps the man, perhaps the woman. Most likely one of their descendants. For the moment, there is no need to say more. There is nothing left to be done other than allow the landscape to unfold like the blade of a knife long imprisoned in a handle etched with names and faces. This isn't so long ago. It would suffice to wind back the clockwork mechanism of time, to have its hands come to a stop at that morning hour whose moment was fixed on the liquid face of the river, to take up the story well after the arrival of that first man and that first woman, the moment when a body, reduced to a corpse, its throat slit and washed clean of all its blood, drifted along on the waters of the river, swirled and spun, dashed against the rocks, to finally be impaled on a broken branch and worn away by the force of the turbulence. To return to the river's edge, among the descendants of that first man and that first woman by its banks, and to imagine what came before with the help of what came after.

Not one bird, not one reptile, not one mammal, not one insect, not one tree, not one blade of grass, not one stone was moved by the scene. Just one man, in the crowd, felt a dull and inexplicable pain in his belly, like a wrenching prescience of his own end, a germinating of death that would give birth to a new world, driving some to leave and others to remain.

The only way to tell the story of what took place next would be to paint over the silence with words, even if words can never suffice in translating a reality, and it isn't truly necessary. And yet we must. Bear witness to the paltry and the sublime. Return to that ridge, up there, all the way up there, atop that ridge where they appeared, that first man with his burden and that first woman with her child, a few centuries ago now, that woman who cast a look full of hope across a verdant cradle that she thought had been made for them, for their children to come, and all their children's children; and that man, not unlike a beast slumbering at the entrance to its burrow, under the humble sway of worlds that lie buried beneath.

Among those present on either bank of the river, frozen like wax figures in a museum, watching a corpse reduced to the state of a branch caught on a second branch, was quite possibly, and even quite surely, the murderer.

Eyes met, elusive, stunned, suspicious, eager, or idle, all searching for a clue in the hope of writing the tale that ended with the floating corpse, trying to surmise what force had reduced it to such a state and pushed it out into the current. Guesses would be made, each man would have his own, assumptions which often overlapped, and yet none of them had the ring of absolute truth. A lack of evidence.

In the days that followed, a few men even found themselves tempted to divert the river, believing that in this way they might erase the nightmare by commanding the body to go back up the river's current and disappear from sight. They were so few in number that they very quickly gave up, returning to the herd, not wanting to owe anyone anything, not wanting to be excluded from the building of this new world. Because that's what it truly amounted to: the construction of a world from a crucified corpse that had been dumped in the river, in those decisive hours that clumped together like flies on flypaper, languid hours filled with memories fashioned in silence.

It's time now to let the words come, without trying to spare anyone whatsoever, the innocent no more than the guilty, a string of words that will disappear in the end, but that will live on as long as they inhabit our memories.

At the moment this story begins, they knew nothing yet of this world in the making, but the old world had birthed them with the unique end of sending them off into another. They knew nothing of the story still being written, but they were all prepared to tell one themselves, after their own fashion, some with a quaver to their voice, and others with enough pride to appear unaffected. And that is exactly what they did: they told a story, the one that finally brought them together, that propelled them toward a goal entirely different from the discovery of the guilty party's identity.

Who is to say today that they did not succeed?

Who would dare?

One

There were four of them, but they made one, they are one now, and they will be one forever. A single legible sentence made of four slivers of flesh, coiled, soldered together, galvanized. Four siblings, four lives interwoven, joined one to the next in a single phrase that is in the process of being written. Three brothers and a sister, born of the Black Rimstone.

When school let out, the children would head to a viaduct formed by the imposing arch that supported the railway trestle, under which the river flowed like a thread through the eye of a needle. On evenings when the weather was fair, the sun tore the surface into thousands of grimacing mouths, tattooing shadows across it in some ephemeral symbolism, one that remained in perpetual motion only to disappear at dusk, erased by an asinine god. When the weather was poor, tatters of fog unraveled in misty strips, like tiny ghosts hesitating between two worlds. Fat drops of water detached themselves from the arch, kidnapping the light as they followed the dizzying course that would lead to their death. In a great eddy beneath the viaduct, a fisherman's boat fastened to a pile smacked at regular intervals against the pier made of rectangular granite blocks. It was almost as if something was alive beneath it, giving rise to that movement that jerked at the rope, some sort of entity larger than a body, an entity without desires, unjudging, without any sense of hierarchy, just there to detachedly call attention to the hopes of man, to give the illusion that there was a time when they were not in vain.

By making their way to the river, Mark, Matthew, and Mabel were postponing the moment they would get home. There was so little for them there that they had made this place their kingdom. Luke was waiting for them already, because he no longer went to class, not since their schoolteacher had told his parents that there was *nothing more she could do for him* in a tone signaling defeat. Reunited at last, they lingered for long moments, lost in their memories, giving free rein to their emotions, each of them fanning the flames as they sat side by side, like alley cats abandoning the gutters to wander the rooftops.

With all the wisdom of her ten years, it was Mabel who first came up with the idea to bring ropes that could be suspended from the viaduct. Her brothers thought it was a splendid idea, and wondered how it was that they hadn't thought of it before her. They scaled the least steep of the arches, each of them carrying two ropes coiled over their shoulders, just like mountaineers. They reached the summit of the viaduct, which towered over the entire valley and its quarry, on the downstream side, and upriver, the power plant, the dam, and then a row of houses, which had gradually taken on the appearance of a town, but looked more like an immutable trompe l'oeil, seeing as no one was allowed to build any additional buildings, not even a chicken coop, without authorization.

The children had thought of everything. They hooked their ropes tightly around the guardrails, two of them separated by about sixty feet and two others directly opposite them. Matthew had suggested they double up each rope, to be on the safe side. They then threw a length into the void and fastened the other end around their waists. Mark was tasked with securing them, having learned a good many different knots from a book.

Matthew made his way down first, to demonstrate how it should be done. Once he had reached the bottom, he motioned with his arm. The others joined him, and the four of them remained like that, suspended in this chosen void, like spiders at the end of a silken thread, on the lookout for the arrival of the train, united in silent agreement.

As soon as they heard the locomotive roaring in the distance, the children began to scream, blending their cries into a single voice to reduce their fear to ashes and commune in a shared and immediate joy. The vibrations produced by the train as it hurtled at full speed along the rails intensified as it approached, until they reached the ropes and instantaneously passed through the children's slender bodies like a perfect wave of pure, living sensation. A feeling that they had somehow escaped the flow of time, multiplied by four. Overwhelming emotion.

After the train had receded in the distance, the kids looked at each other in silence, their bodies relaxing, keenly aware of the world that surrounded them. After a moment, Luke laughed as he began to swing back and forth. The others followed suit, laughing as well, with the feeling that even more air was entering into their lungs, but not the same air that was down below on solid ground. The river, the trees, and the sky blended together as if they were in one of those glass globes that you flip over to change the landscape.

In the beginning, they drove away the birds who were nesting under the arch of the bridge. Some challenged them, like little matadors protecting their brood, or just their territory, and this so earnestly that soon the kids got in the habit of tucking a stick into their belts with which to defend themselves, inventing secret musketeer weapons as they laughed all the harder. One bird in particular, a falcon, according to Matthew, who knew all about birds and about everything nature shared with them, almost managed to put one of Luke's eyes out, and he retained from this encounter a cicatrix on his right cheek, a battle scar of which he was quite proud and that he wouldn't have rid himself of for anything in the world, going as far as to secretly scratch away at the scar to be certain it left a mark that wouldn't fade, a symbol of his bravery. Over the course of their encounters, the birds came to accept the children's inoffensive presence. They didn't attack them anymore, no longer provoked them, brushing against them on occasion, as if to greet them, to let them know that they had become a part of their environment, that they were necessary components of its balance; and yet the birds continued to keep an eye on them.

They were still nothing more than kids defying fate, without any ambition other than those moments of absolute freedom, the memories of which they would keep until their deaths. They laughed madly in the face of the danger, never even considering that the rope might fray and even less that it could break. In turn and in secret, they each contemplated cutting their own rope, but never mentioned this to the others. If they had done so, perhaps they all would have agreed to take the plunge together. In the days that came, it would cross none of their minds that the game wasn't worth being played.

The Volny family lived in a two-story house that stood below the dam and the power plant. A narrow strip of land extending due south stretched out behind it, which they employed to grow vegetables depending on the cycles of the seasons, those of the moon, and certain other beliefs that had also borne fruit.

The house had been constructed directly upon the rock by the great-great-grandfather of Martha, the children's mother. It was a structure built of stone from the Black Rimstone's quarry, with an oak-framed roof covered in slate. Across half of the façade, the sloped roof of mismatched shingles served as a porch, and at an angle from this, the leaves of a yucca, hard and sharp as bayonets, leaned forward, battle ready. On a raised larch floor, they had placed a bench made by laying a plank across two battens affixed to the façade on one side and a crossbeam on the other. This is where, since forever, the men had sat to smoke and the women accomplished their necessary drudgery, although never at the same time.

Every year, in the fall, it fell to the men to verify that the construction was still watertight and holding fast, to replace any defective materials if required, and this before they were able to cause the slightest inconvenience. Their family wasn't a special case, this was how things went for all those who owned one of the few houses in the valley, and accordingly not a week went by in the region without the thud of hammers, the sounds of saws or any other kind of tools, as if they were in some way musical instruments to be tuned.

The interior of the Volny home was made up of an upper floor divided into five rooms of identical size, crudely furnished, with dividing walls as thin as those of a hornet's nest. Over the years, an attic became home to useless objects and a few scant mementos, which were seldom visited, and then only in secret. On the ground floor, a common room was employed as a kitchen and refectory, as no one would have thought of employing the term *dining room* upon observing the family assembled to eat in silence, as if all sharing a single mouth, with no joy in being together, or any visible desire to be so. There was also a bathroom, and a small room that had served as the grandfather's bedroom ever since the tragedy had unfolded.

When she was still alive, Grandma Lina used to tell the children that a giant spider lived within the power plant. The kids often observed spiders in nature, all sorts of them. They knew what they were capable of when it came to capturing other insects, the wealth of cruelty that they could deploy. They imagined the slow agony of their prey, without ever thinking of freeing them, not out of sadism, but because they didn't feel they had the right to influence the natural balance, and this without ever having consulted one another. It was another sort of spider that grandmother had told them about, even more merciless, according to what she said and the conviction with which she said it. She explained with the greatest seriousness that the lines they saw hanging outside of it were nothing more than its web, which uncoiled in every direction.

Aligned on each wall face of the power plant, just below its flat roof, the grime-blackened portholes well and truly had the look of a spider's eyes. A predatory mother fed by the waters of the river, keeping watch over a gaggle of philistines, who were no longer able to do without light. By illuminating their nights, she rendered

them somewhat less barbaric and somewhat more en-
slaved. The creature never came out of its lair, but when
they passed in close proximity to it, the children could
hear it buzzing away, imagining that it was spinning its
dark web without rest so as to continually extend its territory, and they stared at one another, wondering which
of them would have the courage to venture inside.

At one time, Grandfather Elie went into the power
plant every day, his tin lunch pail in hand. He fed the black
widow in his own way, so that she could continue to spit
her web out of her swollen and feverish abdomen, so that
she could continue to weave her dream of conquest well beyond the valley walls. Later, it would be up to Martin, the
kids' father, to fulfill this task, after grandfather's accident.
And then, everything accelerated very quickly. Grandmother died, without telling the kids the story's conclusion. They would discover how it was to end themselves,
before too long. They wouldn't escape. While they waited,
they fed their imagination by constructing other dreams
of conquest. They never dared ask questions of their father
or mother, no more than of the men they saw coming out
of the plant, backs hunched over, worn out, as if they had
conceded a part of themselves and it was precisely off that
which the beast fed, and not solid food, before abandoning
them to the sterile fatigue of the silent road home.

This was how the men of the valley lived, like eternal
children who had waited too long to discover a secret,
and this was how they died, having become too weak to

push open the door to the monster's lair, as if they were no longer worthy, not even honored for services rendered, powerless, the meaning of their lives smothered by the strands of the web, the excessive size of which still restrained the imaginations of the children they had never ceased to be, within the confines of their narrow adult understanding.

In truth, the submissive souls that peopled this corner of the world were all prisoners to the web from the day of their birth. And perhaps the worst part of it all was the pitiful sense of pride that was passed down from generation to generation, that of living off this creature, a status of victimhood that gave sense to their lives. No one would have thought of changing their lot, because it went without saying that there wasn't any other that was more desirable. No one could have said how long it had been that way. People vanished, tirelessly replaced by new flesh that was enthusiastic, at first, to conform to an immutable law, as if wrapped in swaddling clothes that were far too tight, in such a way that they were already dead upon leaving their mother's womb, without any hope for existence, for not having to regret their own failure. At least it was the fate promised to all, without any possible redemption, and without discriminating on the basis of race or sex. One lone fate that was endlessly made new.

There were no more illusions in town than anywhere else in the valley. Each generation sacrificed the one to follow it on the altar of the spinning goddess, because suggesting a better life would have been considered an act of high treason toward the creature. To go on, to transmit the submission and the fear, to dismember the dreams that had been glimpsed in childhood, these were the adults' sole projects. Above all, to never believe in dreams, to show no respect for them at all, accompanied by the steadfast sentiment that if they should not, it would be their greatest downfall. To accept defeat without going to war. By refusing to do battle, nothing all that bad could befall them. And yet, there remained a space lit by a diffused light, one which most of the children, even those born of the most disastrous families, had conceived of one day at the river's edge, as they tried to understand its language, its mystery, but they eventually grew up and could no longer make out the fluid sheets under which their souls slumbered, like algae clinging to an indistinct boulder. And if they happened to awaken from this illusory embrace, it was always too late.

The entire town belonged to Joyce, the spider's master. No one knew how old he was, as is often the case with people that no one saw grow up. At the time of his arrival, the town tried its best to impress, with its main street lined by hovels, its church and its square, in the middle of which flowed a fountain beneath the statue of a general, his name no longer legible on its zinc plaque.

Joyce had turned up in town one October afternoon with a leather satchel in his hand, of the sort carried by doctors, with a metal hasp that ran its length on both sides, and a small lock in the middle. No one had heard the sound of any engine that might have explained his appearance, and there wasn't yet a train station. Later, people said that he had likely come on the boat moored down below the viaduct, which no one seemed to have ever used.

No sooner having arrived, Joyce went straight toward the largest building in town, the inn in the square, which was also a hotel. A heavy curtain of velvet hung inside, preventing a view of the interior. Joyce studied the room rates posted on the glass door. He then took

a look around to make sure that he was not being observed, and counted out the money he would need to
pay for a full week.

Ten years later, as a result of multiple fruitful invest-
ments, he owned the entire town, and the main street had
ramified, like a mycelium. Each street bore his name followed by a number, with the exception of Joyce Main. They
say that he himself was the one to have erased the general's
name, so that this former hero could not block out any of
the light that was to shine on him. He had taken power to
rule over the valley of the Black Rimstone and never had
to justify himself for any reason, not even when it came
to his origins. His greatest pride lay in the construction
of the power plant, which was fed by giant turbines swept
around by the water of the river that slammed against the
dam, like the brow of a tremendous bull.

Joyce believed in no god. He thought of everything
in terms of construction, he confided in no one, and
when he spoke, it was always to fire out an unquestioned
order. He lived by himself in a seven-story building situated in the town center, which he had had built for his
use and his use alone. He changed rooms each night, he
alone choosing which one. The exits were continuously
watched over by his guardsmen and their dogs, night as
well as day. He rarely left the building other than to make
his way to his office at the plant, always going on foot,
accompanied by his bodyguards, who kept a tight rein
on their muzzled watchdogs, their ears pricked up like

arrowheads. Joyce often went unnoticed in the middle of his men, wearing the same clothing and carrying a revolver. He would arrive just before dawn. Slipping in by way of a secret entrance, sealed off by a reinforced door, he went into the large office from which he managed his affairs. He had placed a director at the head of each one of his businesses, and they turned the books over to him once a week, in that same office. Joyce selected them from the rank and file. He knew from experience that taking revenge upon life made people more merciless toward their fellow men.

The power plant was Joyce's exclusive domain, the nerve center of his all-powerfulness, and he wouldn't have left it up to anyone else to take the reins. He didn't leave his office the entire day and did not eat lunch. His ambition was his sole nourishment, an ambition that spread out in a web of works, complex and unstoppable. Joyce reigned through fear. The plant's workers almost never encountered him, but they knew he was there, hanging over their destinies. They felt his presence, caught as they were in that web, like so many paltry charms. They were wary of the spies that surveilled each of the strands, those they had identified, those they suspected. No one dared to openly complain about the salaries and working conditions. In the past, a few had stepped out of line on rare occasions, typically because of alcohol, but that hadn't gotten them any further than the cemetery. Since those days, they left the fire smoldering without blowing on the embers, out of a fear of finding oneself alone in the blaze. Nobody was prepared to sacrifice themselves, to be the one to stand up once again. The muffled angers engendered by the plant invariably ended in miscarriages, embryos drowned in the river. For anything to be otherwise, a wind of change would need to penetrate the inside of that matrix of concrete, but Joyce would have never permitted two doors to be left open at the same time.

Elie was a wizard with his hands. From the moment he began working in maintenance at the power plant, he was able to carry out all sorts of repairs, improving what already existed, inventing, innovating. His ingenuity allowed him to find a solution to any problem. He never boasted about it. The results spoke for themselves, and that was enough for him. His renown was tremendous but it never traveled beyond the plant's walls. He might have been able to make money from his talents in other ways if he had had a bit of ambition. But in that case he would have had to leave. He was never tempted while it was still possible. His dignity rested on the fact that he had found his place in the world, his part to play, or at least so he thought, right up until precisely the moment that that precarious world crumbled around him.

In those days, Elie was paired off with Sartore, a snide and lazy guy who had been foisted off on him, a cousin of the foreman, a slacker who hit the bottle the moment he woke up as well as during work hours. On top of taking care of his own work, Elie had to cover for his partner's incompetence. It was while trying to make up for one of the many blunders of that souse that Elie slipped. His right foot was caught up to the calf by one of the gear trains he had himself installed to drive the conveyor belt that fed the boiler furnace. He had the presence of mind to hit the shutoff, while Sartore stood staring at him in astonishment, petrified by the crushed foot and the flowing blood. If not for the safety switch, Elie would have surely been pulled in entirely.

When he found out about the disaster, the surgeon decided to amputate up to the midthigh to avoid any risk of gangrene. This man, a skilled physician, appeared to be so sure of himself that no one found a reason to say otherwise, and truth be told, he didn't inform anyone until after the operation was completed.

Afterward, Elie never blamed Sartore, not out of a sense of loyalty, but because of an inopportune sense of pride. Sartore only once came to the house to visit him, with a bottle of fruit brandy wrapped in kraft paper. Elie was sitting in bed, covered in sweat. A white sheet concealed his lower body, stopping at his waist. The visitor couldn't tear his eyes away from the boundary that was formed by an abrupt drop-off to what no longer existed.

"Does it hurt?" he managed to say with a stammer.

Elie didn't respond. He took the bottle from Sartore's hands and folded back the paper to expose the neck, then he began to drink in little mouthfuls without offering any to the other man, as if he wasn't even there, as if he had never been there.

"I'm really sorry, you know, I feel awful...If there's anything I can do."

Elie drank. He had never had the habit of drinking all that much. His eyes, riveted to the bottle, glazed over. The date started to dance upon the label pasted across it. If he had had enough strength, he would have swung the bottle at Sartore's face, and Sartore surely sensed that, as he took a step back, then kept his distance, his eyes glued to the bottle that continued at regular intervals to come back to rest at the spot where the section of leg was not, like a piston rising and falling.

Sartore apologized again, and since Elie still wasn't responding and the bottle was empty, he left and never returned.

Once the wound healed, Elie spent long moments looking at the stump that his memory persisted in extending, and it certainly wasn't a miracle, but the worst of lies maintained by that body that still dreamed itself whole. Later on, his strength having returned somewhat, he asked to be brought his tools and some wood. Without even getting out of bed, he set about fashioning himself two crutches. Each evening, Lina went in to shake out the bedding and sweep away the wood shavings that had fallen to the floor, took them out and threw them into the furnace and then returned, a bowl of soup in her hand. A few days later, his work completed, Elie sat on the edge of the bed and got up, supporting himself on the crutches. He took a spin around the bedroom and sat back down, tired out as if he had crossed the valley at a dead run.

Ever since, in that house, the crutches leaned permanently against either side of his chair, like two wings at rest. In the middle of the afternoon, he would grab hold of them, pull himself up, and go out. He'd meander all the way to the town square and sit daydreaming at the edge of the fountain. Often, as he turned to go, he would set to spinning around as a dog does around his shit, as if seeking a new sense of balance, then he would come to a stop, out of breath, and stare at the statue of the general towering above the fountain, frozen in his heroic charge, his sword glinting in the light, and would begin to shout incomprehensibly as he watched the clouds parading along. Passersby promptly distanced themselves from him, thinking him prey to fits of madness.

In his own way, he too had been bitten by the spider. It had cost him a leg and had extinguished what bit of a glimmer had remained in his eyes, which those witnesses worth their salt affirmed they had seen in the long-ago past. Truth be told, Elie shouted out to prevent himself from crying, and when he had run out of saliva, he sat down again for an instant to replenish his strength. Then he would go back home and shut himself away in his room, his eyes still full of moisture and rage, then of an infinite sadness. He remained hours looking at the now-empty bottle that Sartore had brought him, passing his finger back and forth across its sullied label. He never drank a drop of alcohol other than that which had come from that bottle.

The spider's curse was underway. Lina left the world six months after her husband's accident, another strand of the web that had worn thin and snapped.

Martha, as the children always called her, and never by any other name, only swore by the hodgepodge of religiosity she had learned in the Old Testament, which never left her bedside table, bristling with countless wisps of straw that served as bookmarks. She thought that her god was mightier and more just than any other, that it was her god who had set everything in motion with the creation of the world, that he sat enthroned at the precise center of the universe, that the other divinities were nothing more than avatars who arrived later with the sole intention of reigning, them too, like cuckoos wanting to take over an already occupied nest. Insidiously, she imposed her convictions on the rest of the family, reciting grace before every meal, and linking effects to causes that had been decided in high places, in very high places.

Martha had managed to bring three sons and a daughter into the world. The well had dried up with the birth of Luke. Her greatest goal as a woman had been to seat twelve apostles at her table, and her dream had fallen apart with the bellowing arrival of this incomplete son, simple of mind, so much so that, in sheer frustration, she had taken it out on the Gospels, rechristening

Simon as Matthew and Thomas as Mark, without giving anyone a chance to question her decision, under threat of dragging the entire family into chaos, as she put it, pointing to the Good Book with a finger that could pass through the ceiling.

After the tragedy, the mother little by little lost all interest in her children. She sometimes looked at the image of them frozen in a photograph that stood on her chest of drawers, and it was always with the same incomprehension, the cause of her failure, the aborted memory of a great happiness stymied by a *simpleton*, as this was how she thought of her youngest.

As time passed, her readings had led her to become a distant wife, an absent mother, and the most diabolic of women. She kept her world far removed from any form of emotion, which she suspected was at the root of any lapse in faith. Martha offered them what she could. Needless to say, she didn't have the words or gestures to fill this empty void of feelings: all she could do was knead the dough, cooking all sorts of meals with an undeniable talent. Then, she served the family at the table in a specific order, her husband first, then her father, and the children, by order of arrival, always filling her own plate last. The meal completed, she lost herself in the clinical observation of plates scraped clean with contentment. A daughter of the spider, she too, in her own way, a prisoner to her own habits and to words left unsaid.

Martha held the family in the palm of her hands, and her hands were immense and terrifying. She sometimes squeezed her fingers shut, for no reason, over nothing concrete. In this way she held at bay the suffering she had taken on, made up of regrets that she piled on top of a consenting submissiveness, the only education she would ever be in a position to transmit to her lineage. She was convinced that children are conceived in order to blindly follow the first person they see, reassured by that presence which pervades them, to guide them surely toward the salvation of their souls, a promised land beyond the earthly world. She thought that was enough. She thought that for a long time.

And yet, in the saddened and tender look that she cast upon her children on rare occasions, it was possible and even worth considering that she wished for them a different future, one unlike her present, but she always restrained herself from fostering in them any human ambition whatsoever. A mother in spite of it all, a status that was at the root of everything she was and, above all, everything she had never dared to become. No one had taught her how to be anyone else. She had never seen a cherry blossom bloom on the branch of an apple tree, especially in the deep of winter. That was the image that inevitably ended up springing to mind whenever she began to dream.

After Elie's accident and the death of Lina, Martha could no longer tolerate having her father around the house. She came to hate him, reducing him in her mind to the vulgar state of an animal without utility, a bug that is best put out of its misery by sheer indifference. His daughter's attitude seemed to wash over the old man like water across a bay leaf, far too crafty to fall into her trap. He had thick skin, and other fish to fry. He thought there would be a day when the situation would come back to haunt her, perhaps when she would see him lying on his bed in his Sunday suit, his hands clutching a branch of box tree and hair plastered to his forehead by a bit of holy water. In any case, the treatment Martha inflicted upon her father didn't prevent her from putting on a good showing at church, where she forgot that her god was everybody's god, the god of the strong as well as the weak, that of the poor, the scorned, the sinners and the infirm. She had always worked things out with God before, she wasn't quite ready to change her tune now.

The children's father, Martin, left on foot early each morning, after having swallowed big hunks of bread soaked in egg yolk almost without chewing. He always wore royal-blue overalls with a pocket over the stomach in which he kept his pack of cigarettes, emptied over the course of each day, and a battered waterproof lighter that he refilled once a week, on Sunday mornings; he carried the ever-present tin lunch pail with his noon meal in it, its handle in the bend of his elbow, and smoked the length of his journey. He, too, had answered the call of the spider. To see him walking along no matter the season, at dawn and at dusk, it was as if he never seemed to wonder about it, having entered the world with his head down, without hopes or desires. It was just too easy for him to turn out that way. He was of course a child of the spider, but also of a war.

He thought back on it often. Time had passed, but it didn't change anything; the war came back to him, whether asleep or awake. Looking out at the multitude of ships that filled the horizon, Martin had imagined that it would be enough to impress the adversary, who would turn tail without further ado, but the enemy was prepared to hold its position, whatever the cost.

Martin witnessed the great military landing from a distance, and yet even from afar, the spectacle was fascinating, remarkable. At first. Then, the remarkable turned to horror, into a day that was accursed and blessed at the same time, where so many souls reeking of ruined flesh set to roaming. Martin saw men running along the beach, firing blindly, first of all to win, but most of all to save their skin. He was part of a small detachment of about twenty men. None of them took action. They couldn't even look at each other, out of fear of that they might perceive a glimmer in the eyes of another, a sparkle of heroism. Flat on their bellies atop a dune, flabbergasted by what was before their eyes, ravaged by fear at the sight of the corpses and the wounded, they let their allies and the enemy sort things out. If they had been more audacious, or more insane, they would have joined in the combat and would certainly not have returned; they would have become the sort of hero of which history keeps the memory alive until the end of the memorial service.

This had been the way of things since the dawn of time. Men sent other men to fight each other, as if that was somehow one of the laws of nature. Nothing ever changes, thought Martin, stretched out in the sand, and nothing will change, no more for the men than for the women, at home waiting for enough men to return so that they could repopulate the devastated world, an idea passed from mother to daughter, a tale of regenerating the lineages, of adding blood to blood.

Returning home without a scratch on him, Martin was suspected of desertion. And so he began to haunt the world at peace; he attended the celebrations, paraded among the companies of survivors, none of whom spoke his tongue, and he kept his own glued to the roof of his mouth so that the images of horror didn't slip out in spite of himself. And so he went quiet to prevent that from happening, letting himself be slowly devoured by a rage that he held in so that it wouldn't come pouring out at whoever it was that happened to be in his way. His wounded knuckles testified to blows rained upon stationary surfaces, trees or rocks. For a long time, he hoped that that would suffice.

He found work at the quarry, initially as a laborer. He left his parents' home and rented an apartment in town. A few weeks later, he encountered Martha during the village's annual celebration. They had gone to school together without ever having paid much attention to one another. That evening, it was she who made the first move, inviting him to dance, and he didn't know how to dance. She tried her best to teach him. Her partner's clumsiness made her smile, as if she was already decided on showing him everything she knew that he did not. Later, he accompanied her back to her front steps. She kissed him, and then ran off, turning to close the door of her family home. Once he had returned to his place, Martin quickly forgot about the kiss, thinking it to be just a bit of fun.

After that evening, when Martin was leaving work, Martha took fate in her own hands by placing herself along his road home. She had an obstinate way of getting her hooks into him, allowing her long legs to show from beneath her pretty flower-print dresses, in the days when she had long legs and wore pretty flower-print dresses, simpering like a cat that was looking for something to rub up against. In those days, Martin didn't have the mental strength to resist. His physical envelope had certainly returned safe and sound from the war, but he would never again find everything he had left behind, not even on Martha's lips, and not between her thighs either. In truth, he didn't even know what it was that he had lost back there, and so he let himself be reeled in, absent and consenting at the same time, with the cowardly feeling that any other woman would have done the trick. The opposite did not hold true, according to what Martha later confided atop a bed of spring grass bright with stitchwort flowers that had the look of tiny white suns, after a much-needed and liberating tryst. She had planned it all ahead of time, ever since she had seen him sitting on a bench the evening of the party, imagining the sort of man she'd make out of him later, this man to whom she would never leave the choice of becoming anyone else without her.

I knew it was going to be you, she told him.

You couldn't have known.

Sure I did.

And what if I hadn't come back? he asked coldly.

You did come back, she replied in a way that let him know she would always be a step ahead.

He smiled bitterly, then lit a cigarette.

This is what I escaped those bullets for, is that what you're saying?

There was never a bullet meant for you.

Do you really believe what you're saying?

Martha and Martin, they sound almost the same.

If only that was all that counted.

It was our destiny.

And you don't feel as if you forced it a little bit?

Martha didn't have anything to add, holding that same look on him, one that hadn't changed what it was saying since the beginning, a gaze made of an unshakable conviction that served as love, a word that neither he nor she had ever heard spoken.

Later on, when Martin lay at Martha's side, as he thought back on their conversation, she seemed a stranger to him, and he felt anger that she had never permitted him to think of her in any other way, without ever daring to reproach her for it, without even being able to imagine a way of loving her.

But in that moment, with their sweat not yet dry, Martin wanted to believe in the miracle, precisely because of that conviction that had filled her stare, much stronger than any that might have been contained in the books he had read during the war thanks to Corporal Duval, a student of literature who had belonged to the same company. Duval had always had books stowed in his kit. The two men had immediately hit it off after the assault that was to decide the victory. Despite their clear-cut differences, which Duval didn't give a damn about, they were able to find themselves in the shared solitude that only reading a book can provide. Duval thought literature, he breathed it at all times. They discussed afterward. Martin the instinctual, Duval the academic. The other soldiers steered clear of them. At first, they watched them strangely, as they flipped the pages of magazines from which beautiful naked girls smiled at them, frozen in sensual poses.

And then Duval was gone one morning at dawn, strewn about in the pale light in tiny bits, mixed in with the pages of the copy of *Martin Eden* he had been carrying in the pocket of his fatigues, having set off a mine. From that moment on, Martin believed that literature was solely responsible for Duval's death, that it had killed him just as surely as the mine that had blown up in his face, that by thinking too much about books, a man forgets where he's putting his feet, that death prowls all over their pages. He swore that he would never read another book in his life, and that he would protect his family, whatever the cost, from that lethal activity, a mission that would form the basis of an education that would cost his children dearly.

The sun passed behind a curtain of trees. The lights of the stitchwort went out and the green of the grass grew hard. Martha took a tissue from a pocket of the dress that lay abandoned next to her, moistened it with saliva, and without a trace of modesty wiped away the semen that had flowed along the insides of her thighs. Then she pulled on her panties and her dress, and perfunctorily fixed her hair. She put her shoes back on and remained there a long moment, sitting, looking straight ahead. Martin watched her with the unpleasant feeling that he could no longer go back, that he had never possessed the strength.

You have nothing more to say?

I've nothing more to say, she replied, instinctively caressing her belly.

If someone had asked Martin who he would have liked to be, what he would have done differently, he likely wouldn't have known how to respond, other than going back to a beach in Normandy to run down a dune, or perhaps making his way into one of those devilish books to let himself be devoured or smothered between its pages. He could remember his last reading, completed just before Duval died. The book spoke of isolated soldiers in the far reaches of a desert awaiting an enemy's hypothetical attack. For Martin, that wait would have been a wonderful diversion, no responsibility other than staring at the desert sand stretching as far as the eye can see, and maintaining one's rifle in perfect working order.

Once he was back in the valley of the Black Rimstone, Martin had set to waiting as well, but for what, he did not know. Not sufficiently on his guard. Not wary enough. Fate had turned toward a wife, then four children. Martin wasn't one of those fathers who was proud of his family; for that matter, if he had had the choice, he surely would have climbed back up into the warmth of the balls that had spawned him if it would have allowed him to avoid having to take the lead. He would have been much wiser to leave the responsibilities of progeny to someone else, but that would have been to ignore Martha's decision.

For him, the true sea change had come after the birth of Mark, the first of his children. Irreversibly, husband and wife became the two strangers that deep down they had never ceased to be. Martin never tried to forge links with his wife, and neither did she with him. They had missed so much, they understood it was pointless trying to face up to the quantity of missing things they would have had to make up for. There had never been the slightest connection between the two, beyond that clumsy dance step from a night of celebration.

Martin never knew what to do with his children, without even speaking of raising them, but even just how to look at them, how to speak to them, how to move in their presence without appearing absent or threatening. They had weighed heavily on him since their arrival into the world, and it got worse as they grew older.

Blood was the only word on Martin's tongue. "Blood is all that we possess, it is all that we will ever possess, the only thing that we're ever in a position to offer so that the name we carry with us continues to live on in this valley. They say that it's the same color for everyone, but never forget that ours is darker than other people's blood and we'll never be able to hide that," he repeated over and over. And he stopped himself from adding that he wasn't sure whether or not it was a good thing, for it to live on. He thought he knew a thing or two about the blood that flowed within and without, but he was still a way off from having explored all the possible avenues.

In the face of the slightest misconduct, Martin could find no better way to put his sons back on the straight and narrow than by wrapping a strip of leather around his hand, leaving a substantial piece hanging down at arm's length as if he were a retiarius. He would stay like that for a few seconds, as if deep in thought, as if it were possible for him to reevaluate his decision, while the child turned around, pulling aside his clothing to expose his underwear, so that the whip had more bite. It didn't matter the transgression, or its severity. Martin would begin to strike, absent from himself, and he would only stop once the first drop of blood beaded, as if it were a symbol. He would then remain motionless, scrutinizing the tangle of stripes that had the look of a game of pick-up-sticks inlaid into the tender flesh, then he would look at the lash hooked around his hand, gleaming with lymph, secretly trying to justify the excessiveness of the punishment, to connect it to some mistake that he wasn't perhaps remembering. Once he had collected himself, he would accord the guilty party permission to return to his bedroom, and off the son would go, grimacing from the pain, and ashamed.

Martin regretted nothing. He saw in his children obedient animals incapable of rebelling. One of the reasons he continued on like this, hoping that someday one of the boys would finally face up to him, defying him in man-to-man combat, was because he would never hit Mabel. He thought that a girl would never be man enough to come to his aid. He awaited the moment of confrontation impatiently, that moment when he would accomplish what patient words and gestures would never manage to get across, precisely because kindness and patience were, in his eyes, marks of submission to a nature that was cruel, and that his role on earth, and maybe his only one, was to thwart that kind of eternity, whether or not he needed to pay the price in hatred or in damnation.

The punishments began the day Martin surprised Mark reading in his bedroom. He went into a mad rage, hastening to punish his son, crying out that he didn't want to have to do so ever again. With each blow he repeated that writers are all just dangerous liars, criminals who have never known anything about real life, that there was nothing good to be taken from them, adding that he knew what he was talking about. Mark wasn't entitled to any further explanation. He gritted his teeth, counting the strokes, and yet swearing that he would never give in to his father's rage. Afterward, the brothers came to be subjected to the same punishments for each mistake they committed, so that it couldn't be said that Martin preferred one son over the others. The first blood had been enough to enact a common rule.

Over the years, the family maintained a precarious equilibrium, cemented by fear and indifference. Disorder set in after Elie's accident, as if the old man's lack of balance had spread to the rest of the family. Martin took his place at the plant, mechanically taking up the torch without being concerned about who was passing it to him. Once he had returned home from work, he sat down at one end of the table, opposite his father-in-law, and began to smoke as he followed his wife around with his eyes, waiting for the moment when she wouldn't be able to avoid him any longer, before promptly fleeing her gaze, as if he had been looking for something to save him within her, something that he knew all the same he would never find.

Martha, Elie, and the children would long remember the day when he turned up late to dinner with a gun in his hand, he with his fear of firearms. The plates were already filled with steaming stew. He slowly took a first lap around the table, and on the second, he took aim at his children one at a time, Mabel included, without saying a single word, his eyes as if they were soaked in oil. He never had any intention of pulling the trigger. He meant to show them that life can end without any advance warning, to give them a bit of electroshock, to open the kids' eyes, he who had never dared to open his own, so that they would strive to come through life in a more dignified way than their father had. For Martin, the die was cast. Each of them tried to convince themselves that it was just a cruel joke, something he had just come up with, that the weapon wasn't loaded, but nobody made a sound, out of fear that the slightest word would be enough for him to pull the trigger. The children would have voluntarily offered up their bare backs rather than having to be spectators to that scene. They had never seen their father in such a state, calm and cold, and wondered how far that moment of insanity would lead him, to what extreme. None of them would have accepted the sacrifice of any of the others. Martha remained paralyzed, incapable of reacting, searching through her memory for a similar scene from the Holy Scriptures, but her mind too muddled, she found nothing to which she could refer. At the end of what seemed like an eternity, Martin answered one of the questions that they were all asking themselves. He withdrew two cartridges from the barrel, lined them up neatly on his place setting, and left. They heard a great noise from outside, then he came back in, the rifle in his hands, broken in two and held together by its strap. He sat down, lay the rifle across his thighs, and began to eat as if nothing had happened. They would never see him touch a firearm again.

Martha got up, trembling, went over to the stove, and grabbed onto its metal edge as she gasped for breath. The grandfather had watched the situation with a detached look, and, after it was over, he continued to fix his gaze on his son-in-law, even defying him with his milky-white stare, asking himself whom Martin would have chosen to kill with only two cartridges. The answer was most likely those he had not targeted.

Joyce left a strange impression on people, as if his appearance was unable to imprint itself on their memories, leaving them helpless when it came to describing the mask that was his face. His desire for anonymity seemed to be essential to his survival. He never wore costly clothing or jewelry, he owned no luxury vehicle, nothing ostentatious, and he moved about in an odd way, as if detached from the mechanism that enabled him to walk, simply preoccupied by departure and arrival as far as moments and not as places.

Plainly, everything led one to believe that this man was absent from himself, and no one would have been able to suggest how long it had taken him to arrive at such a state, whether it was in his nature, whether some sort of supreme effort had presided over it, or some tragedy. Anyone would think that he felt himself beyond any human projection, so as to not offer anything to his *fellow man*, so that he didn't even take the risk of considering them in order not to be tempted to recognize some part of himself, even the most negligible, a reflection in a cracked mirror.

Joyce was not enlisted during the war. No one knew why. At the end of the conflict, he sent forth a pack of his bloodhounds in search of the most beautiful girl in the town. A few days later, he entered Sorenson's hardware store, to whom he leased the premises. He was accompanied by four of his sentries and his attorney, who was named Salmon, was always dressed to the nines, and had a thin leather briefcase wedged under one of his arms. He had the look of someone who knows things that others do not and never will. Salmon asked the customers present in the shop to leave at once, and they all complied obediently.

Next, Joyce began to silently explore the vast room, cluttered with its many items stacked on shelves or even piled on the floor. Standing behind a wooden counter covered in marks that looked as if they were the tracks of animals along the clay bank of a river, the hardware store owners watched Joyce as if turned to stone, without comprehending why he would be paying them a visit in person, if it wasn't to terminate the lease. Salmon looked like a deeply focused actor waiting for the moment he would walk out onto the stage, the moment that his employer would give him his cue.

Joyce took a silver watch from the pocket of his worn leather jacket and compared the time with that shown on the pendulum clock mounted on the wall behind the couple. Aggravation was visible on his face.

Your clock is two minutes slow, he said.

The Sorensens turned in unison, looked at the clock, then looked at one another with astonishment.

What are you waiting for? continued Joyce, staring at them stiffly.

You want me to move the minute hand forward, is that it? asked Sorensen.

Two men who are not on the same time cannot discuss important things.

Very well, sir.

The shopkeeper couldn't imagine what important things they might really have to discuss with one another, but he dragged a chair over under the clock and clambered up on it. He unhooked the clock and turned the gear, advancing the large hand by two minutes. He fumbled several times in sliding the eyelet over the mounting nail and repositioning the clock at the level, then he stepped down off the chair and put it back.

That will do, said Joyce.

He spun himself around in a full circle.

Your daughter isn't here?

She's busy in the storeroom taking inventory, replied the shopkeeper.

Go get her for me!

Sorensen nodded his head toward his wife. She hesitated an instant before she hurried into the back of the shop. She returned a few seconds later, followed by a young woman who was taller than her by a head.

Joyce examined the new arrival coldly. They had not lied to him; the girl was of an exceptional beauty. He didn't bother looking at her any longer and raised an arm in the air. The attorney stepped toward the Sorensens and opened his attaché case, taking out two sheets, which he set down on the counter.

What is your daughter's name? asked Salmon.

Isobel, the man replied.

With an affected motion, the attorney pulled a pen from a pocket inside his jacket and wrote the name on each page, on a line that had been left blank, and then he presented the documents to the shopkeeper.

You only need to sign the contract in duplicate, he said, pointing out the correct spot with the tip of his pen.

Sign what?

I'm marrying your daughter, said Joyce.

But...

Salmon, read them the terms of the marriage contract!

Mr. Joyce hereby commits to provide for his future wife's needs in their integrality and allocates an annuity to her parents. If, notwithstanding, said spouse does not succeed in giving him a son in the five years subsequent to this arrangement, the contract will be deemed null and void and she will be deprived of any form of inheritance. Consequently, her progenitors will equally be divested of their annuity.

The Sorensens observed their daughter awhile. They didn't ask her opinion. She represented an unhoped-for solution, and had become the incarnation of their good fortune, an architectural marvel that was finally judged by its true value. It took Isobel some time to understand the situation, but she offered no resistance, at first because the thought of no longer having to slave away at the hardware store was a personal blessing for her, and then because Joyce was a good-looking man, and above all, extremely rich.

The same day, Isobel broke off her engagement to Mario Ciotti, a young man of Italian stock, and madly in love with the beauty. When he heard the news, he drank away a great part of the following night, then he made his way to the building where Joyce lived to hurl all sorts of craziness and provocation at him. The neighbors heard shouts and barking, but nobody dared to look out their window. After a few minutes, the shouts and the barking died out and the calm resumed. The young man was found the next morning near the landfill at the edge of town, stretched out on the refuse, a pistol in his hand and his skull exploded by the impact of a 9 mm bullet. Mario held the pistol in his right hand but was left-handed. Lynch, the lawman that Joyce had under this thumb, declared the case a suicide and paid a visit to the Ciottis with an envelope full of bills that Joyce offered to help compensate, as much as possible, for the pain of their son's loss. Sipping from a glass of water, he spoke of sadness, of the devastation of heartbreak, and of booze.

Joyce and Isobel's marriage was celebrated in the Sorensens' shop four days after their first encounter, and the day after Mario was buried. The young woman entered the building across from her husband's for the first time. It was understood that they would never live under the same roof and that Joyce alone would have the right to visit her, whenever he wished.

After the wedding, Isobel was quick to regret having slid her foot into the glass slipper. Joyce had made every decision and would always make every decision. She was authorized to go out on Tuesdays from two to four o'clock, with a full escort. On these occasions she paid a brief visit to her parents, then went to buy a few books to pass the time that she almost always spent by herself in her gilded cage, aided by a housekeeper who also served as cook. Isobel was forbidden to mix with the rest of the population, even to address anyone whatsoever, with the exception of shopkeepers. In any case, no one wanted to speak to her anymore, ever since she had married Joyce. Mario's mother had taken her to task in the middle of the street, not long after Mario's death. The poor woman was unceremoniously fended off by Isobel's bodyguards. The two following Tuesdays, Isobel didn't leave home.

At her husband's request, Isobel accompanied him into town once per year. She stood at his side on a stage that had been set up in the town square during the inauguration of the festival of lights that had been established by Joyce himself. Other than these rare excursions, she remained confined to her apartments, vast and comfortable though they were. She read; she also learned to embroider, to use the right color thread, to follow the pattern point by point, everything that was expected of her.

Joyce would occasionally go across the street in the evening, to possess his wife, and then he would promptly leave. She was slow to honor the contract. Perhaps this was the way her body had found to rebel, but the obstacles of the body cannot always resist the repeated assaults of its own nature or that of an insidious willpower.

Isobel brought a son into the world five years after the signature of the contract, while her husband was considering repudiation. Joyce would always remember the date, because it was exactly ten years after the dam and the plant had been constructed. He had always wondered from how high up his creations would be visible.

With the birth of Helio, Joyce believed that he would found a dynasty. The day of the child's birth, Joyce was brought the bawling little creature that had come out of Isobel's stomach. He didn't want to take him in his arms, sickened by the look of the newborn and by his insistent desire to be heard and to be recognized, surely, to take up space and time without ever having earned the right. And so Joyce swore to himself that he would never have another child, if this was all it amounted to. After, he often dreamed that his wife bore him another. A nightmare, during which he carried away the infant to hurl it from the top of the dam so many times that if the river was to one day dry out in his dreams, he would discover a great pit full of tiny matching skeletons. Apart from that dream, he refrained from impregnating the woman again, as she could never offer him more than cries and tears, nothing that measured up to his blood.

As for Isobel, she finally found the meaning of her life in that delicate little soul, whom she cherished. He didn't look like his father, and she promised to always work to make certain that his mind and spirit were never contaminated by his frosty genetics. She would educate him to that end, hoping that one day, when Helio was big enough, they could leave together.

The Volny children avoided the stale air of the family home. They never broke with the ritual at the viaduct. Still united by that unbreakable bond, over time they came to develop different temperaments. In spite of his father's interdiction, Mark never stopped reading books in secret, most of the time under the covers, by the glow of a flashlight, after which he would silently recite entire passages while suspended from his rope. The forest, the river, and all the animals who lived there held no secrets from Matthew, his internal language in perpetual expansion; for a long time it was what counted the most to him. As she grew up, Mabel's beauty became one of those miracles that one can never get used to; at a very early age she learned to explore her body, to devote herself to pleasure, to cultivate it and make it spring forth, first by way of simple caresses, before she grew aware of the power she held over the young men of the region, and the benefits she could take from this. Luke was filled with limitless admiration for his brothers and sister, and he often lost himself in strange reveries that he didn't yet dare to reveal to them; with patience and a great deal of attention, the others learned to make sense of his meandering ways, to respect this brother of theirs, to love him without restraint.

It had been Elie who had started to call Johnna "May belle," since she was born in the spring, and this had quite naturally transformed into "Mabel."

Mabel, now that's a proper girl's name, he would say to Martha, not like that Johnna that you went and fished out of your Scriptures...

They aren't my Scriptures, and there are other examples.

You can tell anyone else whatever you want, but not me. John, that's a boy's name, no two ways about it.

It isn't up to you to decide.

At the very mention of the name Mabel, Martha would fly off into a wild rage. When she turned to Martin to back her up, insisting that he say something in favor of her choice, he went off with a shrug of his shoulders. At first, Elie wasn't conscious of just how much the provocation represented an act of blasphemy to his daughter, but quite quickly, he came to delight in it with endless pleasure. But apart from him, no one would dare contradict her in her presence, although in secret no one missed the chance.

Elie loved the boys and adored his granddaughter. He didn't want her to become like Martha, such a bigot, resigned, inhibited, her heart as dry as a dune swept by a wind of grudges and regrets. Elie hated what his daughter had become, already dead without knowing it. The old man was waiting for the right moment to make Mabel understand this, before it was too late.

Mabel had recently turned fourteen. Her mother had sent her to fetch her grandfather for dinner. She found him in the square, sitting at the edge of the fountain as he often was at that late hour, lost in thought, his gaze fixed on a reflection that he never managed to make sit still.

You have to come eat.

Elie tilted his head slowly to the side and looked at his granddaughter without moving, with a hint of a smile, then he turned back to the fountain and cupped a hand beneath the stream of water that flowed from the copper pipe.

Look! he said.

What am I supposed to be looking at?

The water flowing...What is the first word that comes to your mind?

Mabel considered it for a moment.

Source, she said.

A smile spread across the face of the old man, satisfied at having brought Mabel into the realm of his own thinking.

Exactly, he said.

And you, what word do you think of, Grandpa?

The smile disappeared immediately.

Life, he said without hesitation.

Next, he motioned to the far side of the fountain.

Do you see that pipe below the surface?

I see it.

That's the overflow outlet that makes sure that it doesn't brim over on the other side.

I know what it is, an overflow.

Elie let a few seconds pass by.

Me, I never knew to plug it in time.

The old man cleared his throat, turning away to spit before he once again took on a look of solemnity:

You don't have to be like them.

To be like whom?

Your mother and father, you don't have to be like them, he said, sweeping the surface with the edge of his hand, as if he was gathering up the crumbs on a table.

I don't understand.

Follow me!

Elie got up, ignoring his crutches, but leaning against the stone edge of the fountain.

Wait, I'll help you, said Mabel.

No need.

He made his way around the fountain. Mabel followed on his heels. Once he was before the overflow, Elie took his granddaughter by the wrist and placed the palm of her hand over the pipe, as if it were a suction cup, and held it in place until the level rose and the water flowed over the edge.

Do you understand now?

I don't know.

Life, you have to let it overflow as much as it wants to.

Elie released Mabel's wrist. She instinctively withdrew her hand, and the water went back to rushing into the pipe with a sucking sound. The level of the water in the fountain went back down. The old man weighed the impact of his demonstration in his granddaughter's eyes, then he drew a long stream of air into his mouth and let the words take seed and blossom before he let them out:

You, you're like the sun, you shine every day, and no one is aware of what a miracle it is.

Elie's voice sounded strange, full of gentleness but also firm. His gray-blue eyes were like two twin planets surrounded by fog, resting in two deep pockets that were intended to hold in any overflow, which he only permitted to brim over when he was alone.

Don't expect anything from this place. Your dreams, they're never going to come knocking at the door. You're going to have to go elsewhere to shine, you won't have any other choice . . .

The old man broke off. He gathered a bit of saliva in his mouth and went on:

And you have some, do you, dreams, I mean?

Mabel remained silent a moment, then she placed a hand on her grandfather's. The one on the bottom was coarse and fissured, the one on top soft and determined.

I do, she said with self-confidence, as if she had already reflected on the question before.

It was the truth. Mabel did have them, dreams, a whole mess of dreams that all had freedom as a common denominator. Later on, her memory of this conversation would have the effect of an insect bite, one that somehow allowed her to express some of the confusions of her longings.

That evening, during dinner, Mabel looked from her father to her mother. This father who had told her how to behave ever since she was born, and this mother who represented what she was going to become if she didn't do anything to prevent it, two crushing defeats face-to-face, two condemned people devoted to becoming her executioner. She fired a complicit look at her grandfather and picked up her fork, holding it like a pencil over the plate covered in mashed potatoes. Usually, she drew swerving paths with the tines, but this time, she traced a perfectly straight line, never taking her eyes off her grandfather, that kindhearted man who was going to lead her to make the most of her time.

Martin had always felt a weariness, ill-adjusted to a world that all the same he would never want to leave prematurely. Evenings, after he left work, he started to hang around The Admiral, the only bar in town. The barkeep's name was Roby. Staying away from the house as long as possible seemed to him the best thing to do. He didn't mingle with the regulars, and the regulars were careful to avoid him. He sat at a table at the back and ordered his beers by raising his arm. With a distracted ear, he listened in on the more loquacious odysseys, odysseys of the sort where the men succumbed to seductive sirens that just happened to appear, if you were to believe them. The tales fed off each other, rarely changing from night to night, and the sirens metamorphosed into goddesses and the goddesses into whores, whom they on occasion went up to join in a room upstairs.

Martin, too, had encountered a siren, not long after the birth of Luke, that tragic boy with his anomalous intellect. He had looked upon the creature from the deck of the vessel that was his pitiful existence. He hadn't even needed to tie himself to the mast to resist her call. And yet the siren sang wonderfully, drawn by Martin's gloomy

gaze, the mysterious cloud that hung over him, his silence. Ever since Martha, he had been wary of women, of
their song, of their ways of seducing a man. He would be
annoyed with himself later for not having made any effort to go over and join the siren. Perhaps if he had done
so, he would have felt like turning other pages, to use his
hands for more gentle caresses, to once again become
that clumsy hero who had been put to death on that bed
of grass with his deepest acquiescence. As a last resort,
seeing that he refused to jump into the water to join her,
the girl had tried her best to clamber up onto the deck so
she could push him overboard, but nothing came of it,
Martin was too far lost in himself to consider another
defeat. And off the siren went to sing for another.

It had already been quite some time since Martin
had set aside his desire, desire in any form. He carried
with him permanently a visceral fear of committing the
same errors.

When it came to speech, Martin was like a land sur-
veyor lost in the deep virgin forests, never knowing where
to set up his theodolite to plot out a coherent path for
his words. There was, however, a man, an old sailor, big
like a sperm whale, who night after night observed this
strange fellow, always sitting alone at his table and never
seeming to pay attention to anyone else, not even to the
two spies in Joyce's employ who were paid to keep an eye
on the customers and listen in on their conversations. He
sized him up for a long time before deciding to leave the

group that always gathered around him at The Admiral
to hear of his extraordinary adventures. He approached
the solitary man holding two beers, set one of them on
the table before Martin, the other in front of himself, and
sat down, straddling a chair, his arms dangling. Then he
lifted his glass and drained it. Martin glanced up at the
intruder, then lowered his head with a sigh.

You not drinking? asked the sailor.

I'm capable of paying for my own beers.

That's not the question.

I don't need any company.

The man stretched a hand out over the tabletop.

I'm Gobbo.

Martin didn't react, and the sailor withdrew his hand.

You've nothing more to say?

Martin still did not move.

Were you struck deaf all of a sudden?

Martin locked his eyes on those of the sailor, picked
up the beer, and drank.

Is that good enough? he asked, setting the beer back
down on the table.

I mean you no harm.

And I don't want any trouble.

I'm not looking for any either.

And what is it you're looking for, exactly?

Just to talk a bit, that's all.

Martin slid back on his chair.

And what good would talking do us?

I get the sense that you have interesting things to say, said Gobbo, tapping his nose with the end of his finger.

It seems like they miss you. You should probably re-join them, said Martin, looking across the bar, where a group was watching them intently.

Gobbo turned around, then back to Martin.

I made a bet with them, I told them that I'd manage to get you talking. Go on, don't let me down.

You can just tell them that you managed it.

You'll have to help me a little bit more.

What is it that makes you think I have anything to tell?

Just intuition. So go on, let's try and see what we get, just this once!

Martin drank again and let a long moment pass by before deciding to play along so he could get the farce over with more quickly.

Gobbo, that's a nickname, I suppose?

Actually, it isn't. If I told you where it came from, you'd never believe me . . .

The Merchant of Venice.

With that great surprise, a smile lit up the seaman's face.

You see, I wasn't wrong about you. You're not like the rest of them, said Gobbo, motioning to the group behind him with his thumb. It was my father who had the idea to call me Gobbo, he was a professor, always had his nose stuck in one of his books. *The Merchant of Venice.* He even forced me to learn it by heart.

Gobbo broke off, and shadow again covered his face.

He began to fiddle with the bottom of his glass, making it dance like he was playing with a hula-hoop.

I suspect that by the end he couldn't tell the difference between them and the real world, he added.

Books are worthless.

And yet you seem to know a few of them.

That's ancient history.

Tell me about it, I've got all the time in the world.

Not me.

Gobbo raised a hand in front of him.

I didn't mean to rush you.

It's okay.

The two men remained silent a moment. When Gobbo continued, the tension was visible on his face.

I spent four years on the ships. I never kept in touch with anyone and it was just fine by me. When I was at sea, I often ended up thinking of my parents. I decided one day that it was time to go home. When they saw me come ashore, they reacted as if I had just left the day before. My absence hadn't changed a thing: my father and his books, my mother and her silence. And so I left again two days later, thinking that what helped my father to live would end up having his hide, and that my mother would watch it happen without doing a thing.

You're right, as far as words go, said Martin straightaway.

Right in what way?

They can kill.

The sailor looked at Martin with curiosity.

How was it that you came to know Gobbo, the other one, I mean?

The silhouette of Duval arose in Martin's memory.

I don't want to talk about it.

Gobbo didn't insist.

I think I understand better why it is that you stay quiet so much of the time, he said in a sardonic tone.

And why's that, do you think?

I suspect that you couldn't stop talking if you got started.

After that first encounter, Martin found himself with Gobbo at The Admiral every evening, after he had finished his day at the power plant. A bit of calming de-compression, necessary before he returned home. Gobbo left the guys he used to sit with to join Martin, which led to some jealousy. He talked about his voyages. Martin listened without seeking to untangle the truths from the falsehoods, never confiding at all himself.

You never speak about yourself, said the sailor one evening.

That's likely because there's not much to tell.

Have you got a family?

I have one.

Children?

Four.

That's important, family. I've never really had one.

Gobbo scowled the way a hobo might as he prepared to spend the night under a cardboard box.

We're not reliable, us men, we think that the world can keep on spinning without us giving it a hand, he said as if he was talking to himself.

Martin offered no response. He didn't help the world keep turning either, his own world. His children didn't know him any more than he knew them. Living under the same roof doesn't change anything. His family was made up of strangers, and he had never done anything to change that; maybe he had even gone out of his way so that it didn't turn out otherwise.

It's in our nature, continued Gobbo. We all need some sea air at one time or another. God wouldn't have created the oceans and the seas, if not...

The sailor leaned forward over the table.

Same goes for women, he added, lowering his voice.

I'm not the adventurer here.

Adventurer..., replied Gobbo, distantly. For a long time I thought there was nothing more beautiful than a boat pulling away from the port, and nothing worse than a cozy little home.

And that's not the case anymore?

Perhaps there's no bigger adventure than having a family.

And what stopped you from having one?

Gobbo fixed his gray eyes on Martin's.

Your turn to buy a round, he said.

A crow was picking away at the body of a dead jack-
rabbit, and some magpies were attempting to
force it to beat a retreat so they could claim the carcass
for themselves. The crow moved forward and back on
its feet as if it were walking. Black blood dripped from
its beak, and the magpies hopped around it, spreading
their wings and squawking to impress it. Matthew was
watching from the other bank of the river, sitting on a
large flat rock adorned with a variety of incrustations,
which gave it the look of an ancient shield abandoned
after a battle between titans. He wondered whether
some sort of evolution had made it so that certain birds
move about by placing one foot down after the other,
like humans, while others cannot, forced to hop along
the ground using both feet at once. The magpies ended
up taking the match.

Matthew turned away from the spoils, lit a cigarette,
and watched the river, slowly piercing the surface with
his gaze, with deference, his hand mechanically coming
and going to his mouth for the time it took the cigarette
to be consumed. Matthew had been smoking since he
was twelve, with the kind of practical application that

ended up making it pleasurable. And there was no better place than the river, and that rock, to sit and enjoy it.

Each morning, he went out to bring in the lines he had put down the night before, equipped with steel leaders that were tied to the roots. He knew where to sink them, and all of this came before his first cigarette. He brought in eels, occasionally freshwater cod; he never went home empty-handed. He knew the river by heart, all of the spots that teemed with fish. He had long thought that the river represented an inexhaustible supply, as long as it is taken care of and that one takes from it only what one needs to feed oneself. But over time, the catch had grown less abundant. The cause of the increasing scarcity of the harvest was that not everyone saw things the same way he did. A bunch of scum-suckers of the worst sort were emptying the river by jolting it with electrodes connected to powerful batteries, and sometimes with explosives.

Matthew often found dead fish that had come up to the surface too late to be gathered up by the poachers, floating along the banks, rarely bottom-feeders, mostly trout, the rainbow on their bodies tarnished and their eyes like dirty ivory marbles. This carnage made the young man livid with rage. And so he would get down into the water to collect the cadavers, then cover them over with a big stone at the water's bottom, as much to hide them from his view as to give them a tomb that was as dignified as possible. Thus the river was strewn with gravestones that were invisible to the eyes of others. A giant cemetery inside a lacustrine city.

Matthew gave himself an hour before rejoining the rest of the family for breakfast. A ritual established during his time in school and which continued after he was taken on at the quarry.

He finished his third cigarette, got up, and stuffed the extinguished butt in his pocket alongside the other two. He then took out his knife, verified the position of the safety catch, and set to cleaning the fish, throwing the innards into the water as he went, which quite promptly became a feast for the crawfish. He always finished with the eels. Their long, thin bodies looked like irrigation pipes made of black rubber, nothing terribly inviting at first glance, but once they had been cut in segments and cooked in a stew enhanced by all sorts of spices, they would be delicious.

Matthew rinsed out one of the fish in the current, passing a finger between the edges of the incision to pull out the last bits of entrail and the various slimy parts. Large bloody and oily drops appeared at the surface, straddling the water like tiny cavaliers astride their mounts. Then he took an old brake cable out of one pocket, with a stiff iron wire at one extremity and a large loop at the other, and he slid it from one gill to the next, as if he was sewing them together, alternating burbots and eels, not to make it pretty, but for the sake of balance, then folding the tip around the loop and dipping the strange necklace into the clear water. It looked as if the serpentine bodies were coming back to life between the much larger bodies of the freshwater cod. At the river's bottom, minnows toured around in nervous groups, and stones of all sizes seemed to drift around, as if the water were standing still. The inert and the living appeared to belong to one same kingdom, the result of perfect hybridization, a subtle harmony. Matthew pulled the cable back out, raised it up with both hands and let the water drain from the fish. He had the look of a jailer hesitating as he tried to choose between one key and another. He turned his gaze for a moment down to where the river met the horizon, where the current rushed under the weeping willows, their branches dangling like long blond hair seen from the back. With one hand he grabbed his rifle, which he had leaned against a rock, and passed its strap over his shoulder. It was an old Winchester that he had bought used at the gunsmith's shop in town. He had made a one-inch stock cover out of a piece of walnut and glued it to the butt so that the weapon fit him better and he could line up the sight just right. He always carried the rifle with him when he went to bring in his lines. If, one day, he was to cross paths with one of the men who were pillaging the river, he would have what he needed to explain his way of understanding the world and make the man see reason.

It was time to go home.

E lie was smoking his pipe under the porch. The sun let off a silken light, which passed through the windows and spread around the room. Martha, hunched over the kitchen sink, was scouring a casserole with steel wool. Luke was sitting on one of the chairs. His ear glued to the radio, he was listening to a program, and his stare had that intensity one gets during a great revelation.

Jim Hockens! he shouted.

Martha jumped with a start, and the casserole clanged against the sink.

There's no need to shout like that, she said, turning toward her son.

They're talking about me on the radio.

What are you talking about now?

Jim Hockens, that's me, I'm sure of it.

It's nothing but a radio drama, good heavens.

Listen and you'll see that what I'm telling you is true.

Hush up, you silly dunce.

Dunce, that's what Martha usually called her son, as if there was something humorous about her calling her own son a dunce.

It's me, I'm telling you, for God's sake ...

There will be no swearing in this house!

Exasperated, Martha went over to the kitchen cabinet, opened a drawer, and took out a piece of paper that she shoved under Luke's nose.

You can see full well that your birth certificate reads Luke Volny. You at least know how to recognize your name when it is written down, they taught you that much, she said, shaking the paper. For the last time, that's what your name is, and nothing else.

You can make a piece of paper say anything you want, said Luke without taking his ear away from the radio.

No, you can't, because this is an official document...

So it's just official lies.

And anyway, who is this Jim what's-his-name?

Seeing that he wouldn't be able to convince his mother, Luke raised an index finger to his lips.

He went back to focusing on the tale, ignoring his mother, who had never heard any mention of *Treasure Island*, much less Jim Hawkins. Seeing that her son had calmed down once again, she went back to her task, shaking her head as if she were trying to shrug off some age-old mistake, or perhaps having realized that she had fallen for her son's game in spite of herself. Luke was still listening attentively, his gaze directed toward his mother, but he didn't see her. A corner of his mouth curled up.

Hockens! he cried once again.

Martha let the steel wool drop into the bottom of the casserole and grabbed onto the edge of the sink, as if she didn't really want to grab ahold of something, but instead was searching for the energy to allow her to flee the room, her lips pursed in anger.

Luke remained where he was to listen to the rest of the episode. Then he switched off the radio, and remained there alone in the silence of his thoughts. As if he didn't know that he was different. His mother so often repeated to him that there were things he would never learn to do, that he wouldn't even understand because he'd never manage to picture them. He couldn't do anything about what he was. He hadn't made himself this way. His father and his mother were the only two who were responsible for it. His father, actually, was even worse than his mother. Luke was convinced that if his father had been able to erase him from the family, he would have, whereas his mother bore him like a cross, playing up her role in public and cultivating her gift for hatred in private.

Damned parents, who never allowed him to do anything, not even to get a dog. Martha said that animals make a mess, that they smell bad. She couldn't even see the benefits that they could provide. And plus, the stink wasn't a very good excuse, because their house, well, it didn't exactly smell like roses. Luke was constantly assailed by one particular smell. He thought, without ever saying so, that it came from grandfather's stump, which continued to rot away. And that stench always brought back the same memory. A dead fox that he had discovered in a ditch, its skull split open right up the middle, maggots swarming about on its widespread brain, like one of those mushrooms that grow on the bark of trees. A viscous liquid oozed from the wound. Luke had looked a long time at the fox, wondering what would happen if he put the brains back in place, if the creature would come back to life, and he would have done it, too, if disgust hadn't risen up in his throat. Its hindquarters were equally torn to shreds. All that remained was a misshapen spinal column made up of pieces of bone resting end to end and growing smaller as they went. The whole made him think of a white snake stuffed headfirst into the neck of a fox. The animal's eyes were wide open and full of surprise, and surely also filled with the last thing that he had seen, maybe a car that had been bearing down on him at full speed, or the barrel of a rifle, or maybe he hadn't seen anything coming at all and it had been death that gave him that look, or so Luke thought. The fox often reappeared when Luke dreamed, running along with the big white snake attached to its back, and it was really beautiful to watch as it ran through his dreams.

Luke had begun to think of his grandfather in a strange light. As the episodes he was listening to on the radio went on, he started to suspect that his grandfather was Long John Silver, the pirate whose leg had been cut off, and not even a reincarnation, because for him, reality was nothing more than a mix of sensations and intuition. The resemblance was perfect, and coincidence was outside the scope of Luke's thinking.

From that point on, he discreetly kept tabs on his grandfather's every move. He followed him at a distance, interpreting the ritual of his daily excursion in his own way. Once he had arrived at the square, he watched him there, sitting on the edge of the fountain, and when Elie set to shouting as he looked up into the sky, Luke assumed he was calling his parrot, and that the bird with its multicolored plumage would appear in the light and come to land on his shoulder to lead him to Treasure Island. Luke watched the sky in all directions, hoping to see the bird appear at any moment.

As time went by, realizing that nothing was occurring as he had hoped, Luke began to wonder if his grandfather hadn't seen right through his plan. He told himself that nothing would come of his current approach. He thought of going to speak to him, to tell him the whole story, and hesitated for a long time, but finally did nothing.

The old man noticed this grandson, whose attitude toward him had changed. He knew he was being spied on, but he made as if nothing was going on, making sure to talk to him about this or that, and Luke came to think that his grandfather was putting on an act so he wouldn't have to share his treasure with anybody, or maybe he really had forgotten all about it.

Disappointed, Luke remained on the lookout. Other pirates were quite likely in the vicinity, obviously in disguise, and busy with their schemes. Passing for a half-wit was his cover, and much better than trying to seem clever. He had heard that clever little boys ended up with their hands fastened behind their backs at the end of a plank jutting out from the ship's rail, about to be pushed into a sea teeming with hungry sharks. The ploy would surely end up working, and the masks would come off.

Luke continued to observe his grandfather on the sly, waiting for him to make a wrong move or for his memory to return. The rest of the time he spent exploring the river, thinking that he might discover the island on his own. More than once he thought he might have found it just around a bend in the river, but usually it turned out to be nothing more than a heap of branches or at best a thin strip of land separating two arms of the river where some birds were nesting, in any case nothing that had the look of an island worthy of the name. When he saw it loom before him, he would certainly recognize it right away, and would know just where to dig for the treasure. The moment was yet to arrive, but he never grew discouraged. He would find what he was looking for, and afterward everyone would have to finally start taking him seriously.

Luke decided that the best thing to do might be to regain his grandfather's confidence so that he could get closer to Long John Silver, and that his special status as a dunce would work in his favor. As a precaution, he honed the edge of a garden spade against the grindstone so that he would be ready to dig the day he discovered the island and the location of the treasure. He couldn't stop himself from imagining what the treasure might look like, most likely made up of gold pieces and jewels, as they had suggested on the radio. Once he had unearthed it, he would give a portion of it to his sister, another to his brothers, and maybe he would even leave some of it for his grandfather so that he could treat himself to a brand-new leg. As for himself, the first thing that Luke would do would be to buy a gun so that he could defend himself against the other pirates, who would surely rear their heads at some point: a rifle like the one Matthew kept in his closet, with plenty of ammunition. After that, he would purchase a boat so that he could go down the river, then he would finally see where the current led.

Luke was hiking upriver on the right bank, ruffling the tops of the tall grass with his hands, accompanying the wind as it bowed the long blades. A cricket flew up from a fuzzy stalk of velvet grass. With a quick motion, he trapped it inside his fist and brought it up to his ear. He couldn't hear anything, but felt its feet tickling his palm and its mandibles pinching at his skin. He folded back one finger after the other, grabbed the cricket by the thorax, and held it aloft before his eyes. The insect unfolded its wings, pedaling in the void. Its large armored head reminded him of a knight's helm adorned with two feathers that had been reduced to black stems. He waited for the insect to stop struggling, for it to understand that he wasn't its enemy, that he needed to talk to it, that he would know how to decipher its language if it was willing to trust him. He asked it whether it had noticed any strange fellows around with swords, muskets, and shovels, carrying a chest. The cricket let its legs hang down and blinked its eyes, as if to signify to Luke that it knew what he was talking about. A shiver of excitement flowed all the way down Luke's spine. He thanked the insect, then asked it to show him the spot where it had observed men of that ilk. He also used the word *pirates*, telling himself afterward that a small animal likely couldn't tell humans apart by their clothing, no more than by their traits, that to it, a human must just resemble any other human. He held out his left hand, cupped, and placed the insect in it, which instantly catapulted by pressing down with its legs like they were newly liberated springs, and deployed its wings to fly off. Luke watched it go and set off hot in pursuit, running. He tripped over a stump, gathered himself up, and ran on in the same direction the creature had gone. Then he stopped. The insect had disappeared. All around him the wind was peppered with pollen and the odd mayfly trying desperately to avoid drowning.

Luke knew how to speak to the frogs, to the deer, and all the birds, and he had just managed to find himself a new ally. The cricket would help him with his undertaking. He would come back for news as often as he could.

He got down on his knees by the river's edge, looking for a moment at the reflection of his face in the gentle current as it contorted his features, then he splashed some water on it. In the distance, the sun was sliding slowly into the forest, like a gold coin into a piggy bank. The signal that it was time for him to make his way to the viaduct. He would return the next day to put the finishing touches on his new friendship, learn its language, and continue to seek the island. Now he couldn't wait to meet up with his brothers and his sister to hang from his rope. He adored the feeling of being suspended in the void, just like Jim hanging from the rear mast spying on the schemers. And what's more, you could see terribly far from up there. Perhaps the island would finally show itself.

The train had just passed. A low-hanging cloud freed the sun, which flooded the valley with its orange light.

Down there, that's it, Luke began to shout, stretching out his arm to indicate a distant point down the river.

The others stared at him, dumbfounded, as he climbed up the rope, pulling with his arms. Once he reached the top, he hopped over the guardrail, untied the knots, and then began to run toward the far end of the viaduct and on down the hillside. They saw him push his way into the vegetation and disappear.

What's gotten into him? asked Mabel.

You'd think he'd seen the Devil, said Matthew.

If that was the case, he wouldn't have been so quick to run off and join him, I would think, objected Mark.

They all climbed up as well, and stowed their ropes. Matthew took care of Luke's, then they went down to the foot of the arch, waiting for their brother to return. Some fifteen minutes later, Luke burst out of the plant cover, out of breath, greeted by his sister and brothers, who were like three statues half-eaten by the shadow of the dam's arch. Disappointment was visible on his face.

Stupid beavers, said Luke, rocking his head from side to side.

You mind explaining to us what came over you? asked Mabel.

I thought I saw the island, but it was nothing more than a big beaver dam.

What are you talking about, which island?

Luke realized that he hadn't yet taken his brothers and sister into his confidence.

Well, it's a secret that you can't tell anyone, then.

Of course, you can trust us.

Luke told them all about the revelation he had had while listening to *Treasure Island* on the radio. The others listened attentively, without ever contradicting him.

It just has to be somewhere, he added, turning toward the river.

That's for sure, said Mabel with great seriousness.

I'll never give up, I'm going to discover it and that stupid treasure too, and then...

Luke broke off, overcome by too much emotion. He turned back on the others, a jumble of words still in his mouth that made his lips tremble.

...I'll give each of you a share of the treasure...I'm going to keep enough to buy a boat so I can follow the current all the way to the sea...I'm planning on sailing all the way around the world...Maybe I'll stop somewhere before I'm done...If I come across a place where I don't feel different from everyone else...Because maybe there won't be any others, people I mean, other than you three, if you want to follow me ... Maybe that place exists somewhere, out in the water ... I have no idea where it actually is ... I don't know anything.

His lips continued to tremble after he was done speaking, and it was still the same emotion that was at the root of it, now that he had told them everything.

Mark and Matthew looked at each other, not knowing how to react. Mabel went over to Luke and took him in her arms. She, too, knew the price of dreaming.

We'll help you find your island, she said.

We'll all help you, added Mark.

Once everyone had gone to bed, Mabel joined Luke in his bedroom. He wasn't sleeping.

It's me, she said to him softly.

Luke sat up.

What's going on?

Shush.

She sat down on the edge of the bed, lit the candle she had brought with her, let a bit of the wax drip onto the slate that topped the bedside table, and stuck the candle to it. The flame danced about in the light breeze coming from the half-open window. Then she turned to her brother and began to stroke his hair.

Mabel had always been closest to Luke. The thing they had in common was always saying exactly what they thought, right when they thought it, saying what made them happy, saying what was causing them pain, what was tormenting them, without a filter and without reserve. With his brothers, Luke didn't feel as free, and it was the same for Mabel.

How do you feel? she asked.

I'm happy that you're here.

We're going to find your island, I promise you.

Then I have no doubt we will.

Mabel smiled in the candlelight, and planted a kiss on Luke's forehead. He could smell the scent of egg that came from the shampoo his sister made herself. He had always thought that it was the smell of a world that was in perfect harmony with his own.

Mabel backed away a few inches, looking at her brother with eyes that held a mixture of tenderness and gravity.

Do you trust me? she said.

I've got no reason not to trust you.

Then pull down your pajamas.

Luke hesitated.

What for?

Do what I tell you, you won't regret it.

Luke started to pull down his pajamas.

How far?

To your knees will do.

Luke obeyed, without taking his eyes off what his mother had referred to as his noodle ever since he was small, and which didn't have the look of a noodle at all at the moment.

It will be our secret, said Mabel.

What secret?

No more questions.

Mabel moved a hand over between his legs, and Luke instinctively pulled away.

Just let it happen!

With one hand, she covered the tip of her brother's penis as if she wanted to extinguish a flame. Luke felt as if he had a piece of wood between his legs. He had already felt it harden for no reason, but never this much. Then her hand slid down gently and gently moved back up and continued to gently glide up and down. Luke felt a warmth climbing up his stomach. He closed his eyes.

Are you all right? asked Mabel, slowing the movement down.

Don't stop!

Luke didn't understand what was happening inside him. He only knew that he had to get that warmth out of himself, one way or another, and that his sister was capable of helping him do so.

Mabel accelerated the rhythm a bit.

Do you still like it?

Luke just nodded his head. The warmth suddenly found a way forth, and grew scalding, but that burning was like a lightning bolt of grace that cut through the sky in the wrong direction. He thought that death was coming for him, that he was ready to welcome it, that there couldn't be any way of dying that was more beautiful than by his sister's hand. All of his life energy was concentrated within his lower abdomen, and he didn't understand where it had come from, nor what it was feeding off inside of him. And so he opened his eyes, to take what he saw with him. If he had to die at that moment, he had to take an image with him. Mabel didn't take her eyes off his penis, staring at it like a priest performing an exorcism. Luke arched his back, closing his eyes once again. He felt something surging up from the same place he usually urinated from, and he had no desire to urinate. He set free a first spurt, followed by others, less and less concentrated. He finally calmed down, and opened his eyes, surprised to still be alive. Mabel looked at her hand, which still held his member captive.

Your baptism by fire, she said after a moment, smiling.

She pulled away her fingers, covered in a sticky substance that Luke didn't recognize, a creamy liquid that looked like saliva.

What happened? he asked, frightened.

Pleasure.

I've never felt anything like that before.

There's no better way to feel like you're alive, believe me.

Can everyone do that?

Yes, everyone.

Does that mean I'm like everyone else?

No doubt about it.

Can we start again?

Mabel pulled a handkerchief out of one of the sleeves of her dress, meticulously wiped off her brother's penis, then her fingers and the palm of her hand, folded up the handkerchief and tucked it back in her sleeve.

You can pull your pajamas back up now, she said with a smile.

You don't want to start again?

Well, boys, they can't start again right away.

Ah, okay! said Luke with a glance at his weakening member, then he squeezed his fists together, trying to make it stand back up by concentrating.

You've got to wait a while for it to come back, said Mabel.

Luke relaxed.

Can we do it again later?

Mabel didn't respond. She looked at the candle, which had shrunk down by a third. The flame had grown longer; she pinched it between two fingers and pried the candle free. Darkness fell like a scythe, but the moon on the other side of the window slowly raised the veil of night, coloring in the shadows and the depth inside the room.

You'll be able to manage all by yourself, now that you know how it works.

But what if it only works with you?

It will work the same with your hand, all you need to do is think of a pretty girl.

I'll think of you, then.

If you want, until you're ready to think of another one ... You must keep this a secret, alright?

Alright, I won't tell anyone.

Luke groped around for a second before finding his sister's hand, the one that had been holding the handkerchief.

I'll never think of anyone but you, he said, the last words catching in his throat.

Tears began to flow down his cheeks. He stopped himself from drying them, sniffled, and leaning forward, a teardrop fell onto his sister's hand.

Why are you crying?

Doesn't that ever happen to you, like you cry, only the other way around?

Mabel set once again to stroking her brother's hair, focusing on the strands revealed by the faint light.

It hasn't happened to me very often, she said after a moment.

Most of the girls in the valley dreamed that they were a princess on a quest to find Prince Charming. The fairy tales they were told as children were filled with consenting victims, so much so that they ended up believing it was the way things ought to be. People were cautious not to teach them that unlike queens, princesses don't get to rule over their own lives, that they would fall asleep one day, their eyes wide open, occasionally to awaken, but only at night.

Mabel had never read fairy tales, and no one had ever told her any. Ever since she was little, she had decided to rule over her own existence, a mad ambition, a world to create, to populate, and to expand. Already a queen without knowing it. In the entire valley, there was no prince capable of subjugating her, and if there had to be a pretender one day, it would be up to her to make him king. For the time being, she contented herself with simple squires who were attentive to satisfying her desires, allowing them to be overwhelmed by the feeling that they were taking something that didn't belong to them, without her actually parting with anything whatsoever. Mabel had an eye on the distant future, perpetually in motion, elusive.

She sought out pleasure and would not rest until she
had explored it in all its forms. The consequences were
of little matter to her. She was free, and thought herself
sufficiently strong to handle her growing poor reputation, which she detected sometimes in the inquisitive
stares of people she passed in town, usually women, sour
tempered and of all ages, with their withered dreams
carefully sewn into their personal linings. But she was
strong, free, courageous, and reckless, as far as reckless-
ness is a component of courage. Mabel wanted to live the
same way she breathed, with simplicity, without having
to think about the way the oxygen entered her lungs. She
was made to avoid the shadows, to unmoor them from
their heavy foundations, and to do so effortlessly.

It was a different story altogether for her brothers.
On Sundays, Mabel accompanied them into town. Luke
had eyes only for her, walking at her side, inhaling the
air deeply in search of the eggy fragrance of her hair.
Mark and Matthew trailed behind, looking on the sly at
the other girls and their white skin, simultaneously nervous and covetous. Mabel often turned back, amused
by the awkward looks on their faces. She goaded them
on, explaining in detail how to go about kissing with
the tongue, using the image of two garter snakes intertwined in a puddle of warm water. They grew red as
they listened, but paid close attention to her advice. As
for Luke, he couldn't really see the point of stuffing your
tongue into another mouth, what good could possibly

come of it, after what she had shown him with her hand. On each of their jaunts, Mabel slowed down when they passed in front of the Brock boardinghouse—her gaze grew different and she remained quiet a moment.

As time went by, the girls didn't seem to have any more interest in the brothers than before. That lack of interest was inversely proportional to the effect that Mabel produced in men, an exponential effect, as the Devil, or God (depending on whom you asked), gradually continued to embellish her curves.

Perhaps if Mark and Matthew had had the gall to invite a girl from town out to the viaduct to show her what they were capable of, they would have seemed like less of a drag. Perhaps that girl would have no longer thought of them as a pair of hicks in hobnailed shoes, undoubtedly beneath her. Neither of them had yet come to understand that women dream of a man offering them what they have dreamed of, without saying anything of it. If only they had been able to guess in those days, things would have surely been different. But the girls continued to pass by without seeing them, and they were alright with that indifference, secretly comparing each of the girls to Mabel. Withdrawn in the same admiration, the same disconsolate longing, they both felt that at least for the moment, none of them could hold a candle to her.

The boys struggled against the excessive vitality of their bodies. Mabel never struggled. The confusion that they felt squeezed at their hearts and their failure to understand maintained the pressure. For all that, there was a sort of fraternal balance that they formalized beneath the arch of the viaduct. How could they even imagine that it would one day change? They continued to go there for a long time, even after they had both left school. No rope ever unraveled, there wasn't even the slightest mishap to regret, which would have seen their names printed in capital letters on the front page of the local paper, with a photograph as proof, taken from far enough away so that it wouldn't shock more sensitive souls. No, drama of another sort was going to come to pass one August day, drama that didn't involve a single drop of blood.

Mabel arranged her trysts for the bank of the river, always in the same location, beneath the great withered oak trees, where the undulating pole moss spread out like a monochrome-green bed, its clumps knit together like purls of heavy wool. She always arrived first, not out of deference, but because she didn't want to miss any of that first glance, blazing with desire, in the moment that they discovered her, her silhouette freed from the world of oppression.

She was the one who made all the decisions, how she was taken and how she gave of herself. She had already experimented considerably with her pleasure, first making use of a trimmed and polished and perfect piece of sapwood, alone in the alcove formed by her sheets, pulled apart by her knees, biting down on the end of a cloth so as not to be betrayed by the urgency in her throat as the pleasure grew more intense, and then flowed over. Later, she educated the boys in the ways she liked to be caressed, revealing to them the unexpected calyx that could turn her body upside down, with the finger first, then the tongue, and allowing herself to be overcome by a barbarous poetry. She hadn't found a better way to extend the limits of her own body than by sharing it with another, shaped to fit her own wants. She very quickly forgot about the sapwood. The first pleasures assuaged, she guided the hard flesh into her soft flesh, grabbing hold of that gaze that fled at first, and which she always ended up trapping in the net cast by her green eyes. Then she would let herself go to see nothing else but what was happening inside of her, panting, moaning, arching to better feel that deepest delving within her, honoring her and plundering her at once. She occasionally praised on high when she climaxed, and more often still, she blasphemed. The sounds of the water and those of her movements contributed to the liberation of the source between her thighs. This is how she was made, porous to pleasure, which came over her like a wave.

They were forbidden to climax inside her. The worst of all possible situations would have been for her to end up pregnant. The idea of wiping a brat's ass at her age was revolting to her. Her freedom was her only grail, and her renewed pleasure represented one of the multiple forms that freedom took. At any rate, she knew how the male body could get away from itself, by what means it freed itself of its shackles, like a madman from the asylum; she understood it from the changing rhythms of the flesh and from the incandescent breathing. And with a firm voice, she would then instruct him to pull out, and would begin to caress it, without taking her eyes off her caresses, as if it was no more than that, a simple caress and nothing that didn't belong to her. And then the sap would spring forth, perfuming the pole moss, the bark, and their skins. And it was another joy within her to feel alive as she watched it die each time, already dreaming of resurrection.

The current chosen one was a carpenter's apprentice who would moisturize his hands before he came to find her. She first heard the whipping sound of the low pine branches as they were disturbed, and then a heavy step, and then she saw him. She sensed what had been residing in the young man's head without him being able to get it out, what she was showing, what she was hiding. The gaps between the buttons of her dress stretched open and closed to the least movement, and with the fabric of her dress resting up above the knee, he was permitted a glimpse of the terrifying path that concealed the source of all shadows. Mabel nourished herself on the brutal transhumance of the carpenter's desires, at that moment concentrated into one single desire, which transformed him into the predictable and domesticated wolf he had become.

She turned around, placing her hands flat against the fresh moss that covered the trunk of the tree, and arched her back slightly, smiling at the river. The sun struck the slivers of silver that crested the surface and then sunk to the bottom of the water. The young man remained frozen, planted within an instant that was without materiality. He wanted to speak of a beauty of which he would never be worthy, but his lips were locked in silent worship. His belly was full of lava and his heart went silent, he couldn't hear it anymore, he couldn't even feel it. Then a wave swept away the stars, and there was nothing left but that savage night which he wouldn't even remember having traversed. He would only remember his falling to the other side of the world, where the purest of lights burn bright.

She pulled her dress up to where her hips began. He came closer, pulled her hair to the side, leaned in, closed his eyes, and breathed in the scent of her neck, remaining at a distance to revel in the moment. Without reopening his eyes, he began to caress her gently. Mabel felt his finger graze against her lips like a little water snake rippling across the bed of a creek in the month of August. She slid a hand down between her thighs to feel the rigid flesh, which she welcomed in. It came and went, slowly, pulling out sometimes to make the pleasure last, then coming back into her, trying to reach what it would never reach, what it would never manage to possess, that secret, the fire that she alone was in a position to keep going and also to extinguish, if only to better revive the embers later. She missed no part of the wave that spread through her own abdomen, clouding her sight, even cutting off her breath at the moment when she found herself back in that place where life consists of a total bond, the connection of two Siamese forces.

He pulled out then, as she had taught him. She'd never have forgiven him for breaking the pact. She

turned around, sated in the face of that feverish male-
ness. Delicately squeezed the gleaming member in one
hand, enfolding it. It was like a steel bar had come down
on the young man's lower back, and his possessed flesh
freed itself with a series of jerks, until he grew calm, his
pleasure dissipating gradually with the slow steps of the
vanquished. She continued to caress him, spreading his
seed across his hairy belly, tracing curves with her index
finger, and as it dried, the sperm looked like traces of
mucus converging upon his navel.

Later, she watched him as he got dressed, no longer
provocative at all, but moved by this envelope she had just
freed of its contents. Then he left, the low branches of the
pines whistling once again, and the universe folded back
around an ancient fire, a flame to keep burning, to cherish.

Luke was walking along the river's edge in search of the cricket. He asked the animals he encountered whether they had seen it, but none of them seemed to have made its acquaintance. He crouched down among the sedge where he had captured the insect, thinking that it might come back soon, that he only had to be patient. The air was still, and the water, deeper at this point, barely whispered. Luke stretched out. The humidity rose from the earth, spreading through his clothes, and eventually across his skin. He wasn't cold. He locked his eyes on a cloud, amusing himself by shaping it into a still-undetermined form of an animal. A strange sound rose from the other bank, repeating itself. He wasn't familiar with this cry, or the animal that might make such a sound. The animal wasn't alone—another was answering it, a more muffled voice, rougher than the first one. Luke sat up a bit, so that he could see without being seen. And he saw, and what he saw crucified the happiness he had had from being there.

Mabel was on the other side of the river, in the company of a boy. Luke had never seen him before. Even though she had already spoken of her adventures in a provocative tone, none of that existed for him, it couldn't exist. He had thought that what she had given to him she couldn't give to another. More than just her hand, she was giving what she hadn't allowed him. The sight of the pleasure that the two were enjoying together cut through his stomach, a pleasure that Luke had thought inalienable, despite what his sister had said. When the pain became too much to bear, he began to crawl through the sedge, his face to the earth, holding his breath so as to not allow himself to be overwhelmed by treacherous odors. He distanced himself and then got to his feet once he was sheltered by the bushes, and he began to run through the forest, dodging the trunks of the trees, like a pious man fleeing a curse.

Mark and Matthew had made their way to the viaduct. Luke and Mabel weren't there. They waited a long time, without a word, hoping that the others would appear at any moment to suspend themselves from the bridge with them. Disappointment gradually gave place to concern, and once night had fallen, Mark said to Matthew that they had better return home, that something must have happened. Matthew agreed, and they started back.

As they approached the house, they could hear shouts from their mother, her voice as sharp as a nail scraping across a window. They hurried over, and the first thing they saw was Mabel, at the bottom of the stairs, a suitcase in her hand and a small canvas bag slung over her shoulder. Martha was standing on the porch, raising one arm after the other, swinging them violently as if she were working a hammer, spitting out words of the sort that might be used to chase a demon back into the flames. Luke was inside the house, stationed behind the window. He was observing the scene, his hands plastered over his ears, his eyes wide open, his mouth agape and stuck to the misted-up window that caused his horrified features to disappear from one moment to the next. Elie and Martin hadn't yet returned home.

Mabel's face appeared to be riddled with little rips and tears, as if the madness her mother continued to fire at her left a mark with every impact. She turned away so she didn't have to watch. She saw her brothers then, frozen on the other side of the front gate, questioning her with their stares but not wanting an answer. She walked over to them, deploying a sad and costly smile, like an additional laceration. The boys looked each other in the eye, trying to see who would have the courage to finally speak. Neither of them was capable of saying anything to impede what was in the process of playing out, not wanting to understand what was going on between the door and the gate and the length of the straight path lined with knotweed that had withstood the never-ending back-and-forth. Not wanting to believe any of it. They remained like that, mired in their fear, while the evening heaved shovelfuls of cold night onto their paralyzed bodies.

Mabel shot a final look at her mother, without any real contempt, a look full of pity. Martha didn't take the opportunity to erase the black mark that her daughter had made within her.

Go on, get out of my sight, you are damned . . . you are damned . . . she repeated.

Mabel advanced to the gate, opened it.

I'll explain everything, don't worry about me, we'll see each other soon, take care of Luke, he's going to need you, she said to her brothers.

She didn't stop. They watched her move away into the distance in her white cotton dress, then disappear as if in a dream from which they would only awake once they, too, had passed through the gate, in the other direction, a dream that transformed into a nightmare the moment they made it inside the house.

Martha had just disowned her daughter, after Luke, mad with jealousy, had reported what he had seen at the river's edge. Once Martin got home, she told him everything. He tried to reason with her, arguing that the punishment was maybe a bit too excessive and too extreme. She asked her husband if he was on the Devil's side, and Martin lowered his eyes so that he wouldn't have to face her. The very thing his wife had been born to fight against seemed to be exactly what was in control of her at that moment. Later on, learning the way in which Mabel's departure had come about, Elie in turn tried to defend her. Martha listened to him coldly, then ended up telling him that if he wasn't happy with it, he was welcome to go live somewhere else too, or he could just die; perhaps it was the moment for him to stop being a nuisance for all of them. The old man took it in stride. His gaze passed from his daughter to his son-in-law, as if he wanted to offer them one last chance, for her to walk back her words and for him to finally stand up to her; he would have allowed him to strike her if it had come to that. Elie knew that words would do nothing more than accelerate the circulation of the venom coursing through Martha's veins. If he had imagined for one second that he could destroy her, he would surely have spoken, but it was pointless, and the silence began to poison him slowly. The moment would come when it was time to inflict a mortal wound upon his daughter, when she was least expecting it. She might drag Martin down with her, but the two of them would pay, one way or another.

From the moment Mabel left the house, Martha stopped mentioning her, as if she had never existed. It was impossible for her to forget the dishonor the entire family would endure because of her harlot actions, "harlot," a word that she was surprised she hadn't used earlier. That evening, at the dinner table, she spaced out the plates by a few evenly distributed inches so precisely that it was impossible to notice that the empty spot had been filled in this way, a small space that was multiplied to make up for a lie. In this way she thought she could remove any trace of the daughter who had never even accepted her own name. She thought that a new seating arrangement would be enough to freeze over her memories.

Elie had hoped that Mabel would take flight, but not in such a manner, not so suddenly. For Luke, Mabel's absence became even more unbearable when he realized that he was responsible. His terrible secret. As for Mark and Matthew, their sister's departure sowed strange seeds in their minds, and it didn't take those seeds long to find what was required for them to sprout in the fertile ground of a muted rage. Each in his own way, they were aware that their shared childhood had just had one of its crucial limbs amputated, and that, if they one day wanted to gain their own freedom, they would have to limp back to her.

The body's flesh is everywhere, it covers everything. The heart is a trompe l'oeil, an approximation, nothing more than a vital pump, a mechanism that is more or less well regulated, occasionally defective. We hardly even know how to locate it properly, a little farther to the right, a bit more to the left. The flesh of our bodies, however, they mingle. Hearts keep their distance. They cannot touch one another. Stretches of sand separated by a border that is guarded by one of hell's dogs. The heart is locked away, not the flesh. The flesh is free, volatile, flighty. One body's flesh feeds off that of another, grows fuller through contact with the flesh of other bodies. They dream of being bared, of shedding their skins, and having been torn free in such a way, the world will be easier to accept, like an exsanguinated cut breaking free of its sutures, a wound ceaselessly revived by the crisp, biting air of desire, in the night as well as during the day. The body's flesh begs for the cutting edge of a caress. There is no word to define the space where it spreads itself out, that vast plain where each body's flesh can strain away without any care to morality. The heart is a boring old sage. The flesh is a devilish god.

Elie was right; Mabel wasn't only one of the sun's rays, but the sun in its entirety. She bathed the family in her light and her warmth. Her brothers loved her unceasingly, each in different ways. Mark and Matthew had for a long time been aware of what her flesh called out for. They didn't judge her, suppressing their short-lived jealousy, as they knew she would return to shine for them. Mabel had built a nest within their stomachs. Her presence there was a barrier to the mixed blood of their parents, creating another blood, just for them, less dark and fuller of life.

Now that she had left, her brothers missed her terribly. They had watched her silently move down the dusty path, and as the distance grew, so had their fear. When she passed out of their sight, that fear evolved into terror in the face of the space that she had previously occupied, the earth that she had pressed underfoot, that had done nothing to preserve a trace of her. When the dust had settled, Mark and Matthew had gone into the house, as if after a staged battle during which they had fallen asleep. As for Luke, from that point forward Mabel was no longer only nested in his stomach but digging through his entrails even as she devoured his dreams.

When they were suspended over the void, Matthew and Mark's sole ambition had been to launch themselves toward a horizon that was still limited by the length of their ropes. Where Mabel was concerned, suspending herself had been no more than a step on her path toward liberation. The rope had very quickly become too short for her. She had certainly been pushed into her departure, but her greatest wish had always been to find her way to a new road, wider, one that led to her freedom.

Starting the very next day, the brothers tried to tempt fate by going to the viaduct, hoping their sister would return to them. Luke dragged his feet all the way there. He hadn't wanted to go, but the others hadn't left him a choice. He had said nothing to them of his treason.

Once they arrived, Matthew passed Mabel's rope over the railing first. It looked like the prolongment of a bell, but instead of one that calls the faithful to its proselytizing cause, its function was to announce a great exodus, the end of a world. Matthew clambered down to suspend himself over the void. The others followed suit. Dangling in the emptiness, their frenzied looks fled from the end of the rope that swung there with no one attached. The church bell in the village began to ring in the distance, and each clang subsumed the one that came before it until there was just one shared, all-encompassing echo. Then that echo faded away.

The boys one after the other turned their eyes to the top of the viaduct in the hope that they would see their sister appear, that she was going to come back to them and they would all once again be bowled over by the energy of childhood and by a new kind of rage that would push them to be more vigilant moving forward.

The hum of the plant covered over most of the sound of the water, and as it spooled between the viaduct's arch, the river looked like a twisted liquid sleeve. Luke hurt deep within his heart. A crude grin was pulling up his lips, as if he had been chewing barbwire, and his lower lip was bleeding. Mark said a prayer in his head, on the lookout for favorable signs that might appear out of nowhere. There were no signs to interpret, and the sky remained overcast. Matthew thought of what a great lie their ritual had become. All three brothers withdrew into their own pain. Into one same absence.

The train passed at the usual time, sending shivers through the ropes and the suspended bodies, but the vibrations didn't penetrate them as they usually did. Three bodies like electrical coils fallen victim to a short circuit, incapable of feeling the effects of the current, mechanisms with no power supply, just idling away. Then the train was gone, and the imperfect silence once again took hold. Luke was limp at the end of his rope, his head thrown back and his arms dangling, like a corpse hanging from the gallows. Now he was staring at the unused rope, as if trying to dissolve it, thinking that it was the only thing left to try, knowing that if he shut his eyes, he would come up with another form of treason. He straightened himself after a moment, pulled the stick from his belt, and swung it back and forth in front of him without much energy, then his motions grew slower still and he allowed the stick to fall, bounce off a rock below, tumble into the water, float away and disappear. Luke stretched his arms out as if he was on the cross, offering up his chest to the gaping mouth of the arch, and began to cry out:

Come and get me, I'm waiting, come and poke my eyes out, it's what I deserve.

No bird appeared suddenly to wage battle with him and fulfill his wish. His body relaxed, taking on the appearance of a fibrous extension of the rope. Mark and Matthew looked at him without comprehension, considering it a passing fit.

It's all my fault, continued Luke, casting a desperate look toward his brothers.

What are you talking about? asked Matthew.

It's all my fault that Mabel went away.

Of course it isn't, it's not your fault...

I saw her with that guy by the river's edge...That's why I told on her.

Luke curled himself up and began trying to unknot the rope that encircled his waist.

What in the hell are you doing? shouted Mark.

Luke continued to struggle with the knot, his gestures chaotic, impervious to his brothers' evident panic. Mark was on the same side of the viaduct as Luke; he pivoted toward him and shot his legs out, folded them back in and shot them out again, just like he would have done on the swings, propelling himself farther and farther out, as Matthew began to pull himself up his own rope as quickly as he could by arm strength alone. The first knot gave way. Luke fell about three feet and then stopped, held aloft by his second rope. He was crying, he could no longer even hear his brothers' shouts. He began to work the other knot free. Matthew flew over the guardrail and ran over to Luke's rope. Mark managed to touch his brother for a first time with the tip of his toes, with his heel the next time. The knot gave way as Mark came hurtling back, managing finally to wrap his legs around Luke's waist, then he launched his pelvis forward so that he could grab onto him with his arms, and he squeezed him tight.

Let go of me! sobbed Luke.

Catch your rope, for God's sake, and retie your knot, we'll talk about this up top.

I don't deserve to live after what I did.

Retie that goddamn knot before I lose my temper!

Luke finally obeyed. He caught the first rope and started knotting it around his waist.

It's good, said Luke.

The other one too.

Don't worry about it, it will hold.

The other one, I said.

Luke fastened the second rope.

I'm going to let go of you now, and no more bullshit, okay?

Okay.

Mark raised his eyes toward Matthew.

Go on, bring him up!

Matthew hoisted his brother up, and Mark climbed up on his own. Once they were all back together at the top, the brothers waited, gradually pulling themselves together.

Don't you ever do something like that to us again, Matthew said after a moment, trying not to raise his voice.

Luke shook his head, looking at the ground.

She's never going to forgive me, he said.

Of course she is, she even asked us to look after you.

Luke wasn't listening. Mark stared at him, touched by this brother of his who was incapable of facing the empty space left by the departure of their sister, since he had brought it about. A presence conjured up in his mind could never be enough for Luke. He wanted Mabel near him, wanted to smell her. He remembered her hand, and the sensation that had bound him to the light.

Maybe she's sorry she did it, he said, talking to himself.

Sorry she did what? asked Mark.

Luke swallowed. His fingers grabbed nervously at his pant legs, and his eyes couldn't grab onto anything. Mabel had told him not to tell anyone about their secret. He wasn't going to betray her a second time.

Do you think she'll come back?

If she doesn't come back, we'll go and find her.

Luke's scrawny body relaxed. His fingers stopped coming and going across his thighs and he stared straight ahead at the sky, which looked like a wall whitewashed with lime. His sister was not hiding behind it, merely the hope of seeing her again. Beyond the viaduct, the heat was making the air quaver above the rails and the gravel. They put away the ropes, then Mark busied himself with bringing Mabel's up. Matthew rushed over to stop him.

What are you thinking? asked Mark.

Have you ever caught anything without bait?

Luke stared at the brothers with a dumbfounded look.

And this way, each time we pass underneath it, we'll think of her, added Matthew.

Mark let go of the rope.

From that day on, the boys decided not to suspend themselves from their ropes, not until Mabel had rejoined them. Each time they passed beneath the viaduct, they instinctively raised their heads to look at the rope, as if it were some kind of conduit from which flowed happy memories. And even if it came detached one day, too worn, and even if there was no longer any reason to raise their heads, they would still raise them, because that rope, even detached, would always be hanging there somewhere under the vault of their skulls, and it would never cease to tell the true story of Mabel, which had nothing to do with the one told by the people in town, who for the most part could never hold on to anything of a life other than its mistakes and its punishments.

Well before she was driven off, Mabel had already decided to leave home. Her suitcase had been ready for ages. Her denunciation by Luke had simply precipitated things. If she had had her brother in front of her in this moment, she would have thanked him. Mabel had never shared her intentions with Matthew and Mark, out of fear that they would attempt to convince her to renounce them. They would understand later on, when they saw each other again.

As she approached town, Mabel thought back on their last trip to the viaduct. From her first moment swinging forward, she had closed her eyes, opening her mouth partway to allow additional air to pour into her lungs. In the absence of any reference points, she had had the sensation that the rope was growing shorter and that if she waited too long, she would find herself back up on the rails above with no other choices than to watch the cars pass by or throw herself under the train, to accept the finality of a destiny that was all mapped out in advance. She had decided to forge her destiny herself, in her own way, even if it meant leaving a few of her prettiest feathers behind. She had chosen freedom.

Mabel left the road, taking a shortcut, and the soles of her shoes on the narrow cinder track made a noise like biting down on popcorn. She was soon entering the square from an angle, feeling as loose and flexible as a gymnast. A headwind glued her dress to her legs and the fabric formed little ripples up her sides, the way a cuttlefish's skin forms wavelets as it swims. Elie was sitting there at the edge of the fountain. He squinted and watched her approach. She set her suitcase on the stone-covered ground, sat down near her grandfather, wet her hand in the water and rubbed it against the back of her neck. He couldn't take his eyes off the suitcase, eyes that had sunken back into their moist caverns, reddened by the glacial fires of old age.

Well, that's it, then! he said.

She didn't respond.

Do you know where you're going to go, at least?

Yes, don't worry yourself about it.

He leaned back toward the fountain, stretched out his remaining leg, plunged a hand into his pants pocket, and drew out a roll of banknotes bound together with kitchen twine. He held on to it for a moment, he who didn't have the habit of giving gifts, nor she of receiving them. He didn't really know how to go about it; she knew a little better.

Aren't you afraid you'll lose that? said Mabel.

It might just be that I'm counting on losing them all at once... Here! he said, holding the roll out toward Mabel.

I can't accept that, it's too much.

It's never too much when it's the heart that is giving, and what's more, you'll be needing it more than I do.

You never know what you're going to need.

Don't worry, I may be old, but I'm still very resourceful, you know.

I know...

So take it, and enough quibbling.

Elie grabbed Mabel's hand, thrust the roll into it, and folded her fingers around it.

You stash that away now.

Mabel stuffed the roll in the bottom of her canvas bag. Then, without mentioning a thing, they both turned to look at the overflow outlet, nestled in the shadows cast by the general's sword, as if the petrified old fossil was giving his blessing.

A cloud passed over Elie's face. His now-nonexistent leg had suddenly started to feel like a sprain that has had an ice pack left on it too long. An intense burning sensation engulfed his stump, like a warning of something he hadn't yet imagined.

Don't you go too far away, at least, he said, containing his anxiety as best he could.

I spotted a boardinghouse in town; I think they have some rooms available.

The shadow cast by the sword had grown shorter. Mabel stood up and grabbed the suitcase's handle.

Go on, off you go while there's still daylight.

Thank you, Grandpa, she said, tapping her hand against her bag.

Elie watched as she crossed to the far extremity of the square, trying to convince himself that the Mabel he was watching was no longer the one who he had advised to leave, but some other one he hoped to see blossom. A tiny floodgate gave way, and droplets spread across the lower edge of his eyes. He promptly tipped his head back. A few white clouds were sliding slowly across the sky, like row-boats suspended above an oily sea.

The Widow Brock looked Mabel over with disdain. She would need two months in advance to rent her a room in the boardinghouse, throwing the figure out with visible pleasure, convinced that the young woman would never be able to cover such a sum. Mabel took the roll of bills her grandfather had given her out of her bag. At the sight of the money, Mrs. Brock's small eyes opened wide. Mabel peeled off the necessary amount. Mrs. Brock immediately regretted not having asked for more, and her lip curled up as she grabbed the bills. She inventoried the few rights and the many obligations to which her young boarder would have to concede without discussion. These were the policies of the boardinghouse: respectability, silence, and discretion. At the first sign of misconduct, she would be back out in the street. Mrs. Brock felt it important to specify that no boys were to be allowed inside the boardinghouse. Mabel agreed to everything, and was led to a sparsely furnished room.

Flopped down on the bed, Mabel thought back over the series of events that had brought her to where she was. This spartan, little, poorly lit room represented a first step toward her freedom. She promised herself that she would climb all of the others without skipping a stage along the way, and without compromising herself. She also promised herself that she would never be indebted to anyone, in such a way that she would never have to mortgage her dreams of independence. For the first time, she felt like a woman, or at least a woman coming into being, and no longer a kid at the mercy of a time that was unchanging and unyielding. She allowed herself to enjoy the daydream for a few moments longer, then unpacked her things with a contented smile, her body hungry for the mysteries to be discovered and her heart ready to pump new blood into her veins.

Two

Everyone called him Double, because of his size. The giant was teamed up with Snake, a dwarf, all muscles and resembling a rat, a rat with the eyes of a snake. Joyce paid them to keep a finger on the pulse of the town, and there was no better place to do this than at The Admiral. Over near the bar stood a piano, its keys imprisoned by a locked keylid, which explained why no one had played it in years. As a result, they missed nothing of the conversations, even if their presence there was in reality part of the game, since everyone knew what their mission was. Snake often finished off his evenings in a room upstairs with one of Roby's girls, always the same one, whereas Double had no routine when it came to such matters.

Tensions were beginning to rise between a newly hired waitress and a worker from the power plant who was fairly calm much of the time. Double got up from his chair to put the guy in his place, but Snake grabbed him by the arm.

Leave it! he said.

Roby had already stepped around the counter to intervene. The fellow didn't insist, and returned to the back of the room, walking the length of the bar. Neither Snake nor Double recognized the new arrival, who was probably in from the valley, freshly arrived in town to make her living, and such a looker that she would have without a doubt made a dead body stand up, thought Double. The kind of girl he went for.

Snake held an arm up in the air. Roby filled two glasses. Shortly after, the girl came and set the beers down on their table and remained planted there. Snake looked at her with the beginnings of a smile, which pulled up a corner of his mouth and had a lot to say about the way in which he typically made it clear where things stood without saying a word.

You waiting for something, sweetheart? asked Double.

The money for the beers.

Double put on an exaggeratedly serious face.

Roby didn't tell ya nothing?

He told me that customers always have to pay once they've been served, that's the rule.

Increasingly amused by the situation, the hint of a smile reached its way to the other side of Snake's mouth.

Ah well, you see, Roby, he makes an exception to that rule for us.

The girl shot a glance over toward the bar.

I'll go and ask.

Before she could walk away, Double grabbed her arm with a smile.

I'm surprised that he hired a girl like you for serving . . . Serving tables, I mean! he said with a wink.

A girl like me?

With his free hand, Double stroked the waitress's arm as if he was stropping a straight razor.

What's your name?

She quickly pulled her arm back to break free and went off toward the bar without answering.

You see that? said Double.

Didn't have much choice, replied Snake in a mocking tone.

They watched her conversing with Roby, then she came back shortly after, and it was clear she was loath to do so.

Roby would like to apologize, she said cheekily.

What about you? asked Snake.

I wasn't aware that you drank on the house.

I didn't manage to catch your name earlier.

The young girl hesitated a moment.

Snake pointed a finger in Roby's direction.

Maybe you want to go ask him advice about that too.

Mabel, she said in a flat tone.

That's the spirit.

Snake promptly lost interest in her. His gaze tilted up toward the landing, where girls in various states of undress were appearing and disappearing, alone or accompanied.

Say, sweetheart, I can take care of that guy from before if you want, said Double.

Take care of him?

Teach him a little lesson, if you'd rather put it that way.

Why would you do that?

Let's just say I'm looking out for you.

It's fine.

Mabel turned away. Behind the counter, Roby moved like a nervous marionette, glancing back and forth around the room. Mabel grabbed her platter and went off to resume her serving duties. Double watched her for a good while longer, then looked back at his companion, who was still staring at the upper floor.

This isn't the time to be thinking about your redhead! he said.

The dwarf shifted his gaze back toward his accomplice, as if returning from a bad dream.

We've got time, he said.

Double rubbed the bridge of his nose with the edge of his thumb and leaned his body against the table before he spoke:

No, I don't think so. I wouldn't want him to learn it from someone else.

The Admiral was made up of a single voice, a single attire, a single laugh, and a single alcohol-lubricated gaze, a Sabbath site consecrated by the Devil and what hangs between his legs. Cigarette smoke stirred by its patrons' breathing swirled throughout the room. Martin's head was spinning. He leaned for a moment at the end of the bar, wondering how he would tell Martha that he had found Mabel in such a dive, if he should even bring it up.

Once he had sufficiently recovered, Martin set a coin down on the counter, took the beer Roby served him, and rejoined Gobbo at his table. The sailor hadn't missed a thing of the altercation that had just taken place. He took a gulp without taking his eyes off Martin, then he dried his mouth with the back of one sleeve.

Who's the girl?

Nobody.

Martin looked like a fish resting at the bottom of a polluted sea, as if the overly strong pressure prevented him from breathing normally. He put back his beer in great swigs and asked for another, which Roby brought over to him.

Since when are you interested in nobody? asked Gobbo.

Leave me alone. I'm not in the mood.

No need to get worked up about it.

Martin drank, staring off into the void.

And how about you stop avoiding the question and tell me what's going on?

I don't feel like talking about it.

Gobbo leaned to the side to better see the room.

It would seem Double is also interested in nobody, he said.

Martin began to turn his head, then stopped himself.

It's none of my business.

And yet you seem pretty edgy for someone who doesn't give a damn.

Just who do you take yourself for, really, a babysitter? blared Martin. Or the judge that this town has been missing?

Gobbo let a minute go by; his forehead had the look of an old, crumpled bedsheet.

You figure I haven't guessed that she's your daughter.

Martin tensed up. Memories surged back, stopping at the image of a cheerful little girl watching him blow smoke rings under the porch.

You should take better care of her, added the seaman.

Bloody hell, Gobbo, who're you to tell me what I ought to do? You don't have any children, last I heard.

The sailor wrapped a hand around his glass, and large veins on his forearm filled with blood. He finished his beer, put the glass back down, and the veins gradually retreated beneath the skin.

I'm not here to give any lessons, he said.

That's the only thing we're missing here.

Gobbo leaned forward, lowered his head, and then brought it up slowly, as if he were using a pry bar to tilt up Martin's gaze.

I can still give you a warning.

Martin didn't react.

Turn around!

What for?

Turn around, I said!

Martin obeyed. Double hadn't taken his eyes off Mabel. Martin immediately turned back around to face his glass and erase what he had seen.

You don't know a thing about her, he said.

Maybe, but everyone knows what that guy is capable of.

Their eyes clashed.

Well? asked the sailor after a moment had passed.

How about you buy me a beer?

You think that's the solution?

It's one that suits me just fine, for the time being.

Martin drank some more, and his sight grew cloudier and cloudier, sawing away at all of the shapes until they were a mist of filthy shavings, vacuumed up by the presence of his daughter behind him.

Much later, Gobbo's voice seemed as if it was emerging from a tunnel. Martin spat out words that he would not later remember, but which the seaman insisted on repeating back to him. After that, he felt himself lifted up, then lugged, and then nothing at all.

Double and Snake left the bar. In the street, a strange Siamese creature was staggering off into the distance, as if avoiding the glow of the streetlights under which whirled all sorts of nocturnal insects. They each lit a cigarette as they waited for it to vanish, then continued on their way back up the street. They made turn after turn, walking in silence, following the labyrinthine path that led them to Joyce's building.

They first heard the dogs whining at their approach, then a voice accompanied by the sound of a rifle breech being brought back and then forward.

Who goes there?

Put away your hardware, Astor, shouted Double as he approached the first brazier, around which three armed men stood, despite the heat, and just as many dogs on leashes.

Ah, it's you! said the man, raising his gun and propping the barrel up on his shoulder.

The building Joyce lived in was unlit, as was the one where his wife and son lived, on the other side of the street.

We need to see him, said Double.

I hope it's important, he doesn't like to be disturbed at this time of night for no reason.

We know just as well as you what he doesn't like.

Astor took from his pocket a bunch of keys held together by a small chain and moved toward Joyce's building. Double and Snake followed him. Astor used four keys to unlock the main door.

What number tonight? asked Snake.

Thirty-four! whispered Astor.

The two men entered a completely dark foyer. The door slammed shut behind them, and they heard the bolts slide back into place. Snake flicked on his lighter, and Double did the same. They advanced slowly over the parquet floor, brandishing their meager torches at arm's length, soon arriving at a wooden staircase. Joyce had forbidden any carpets or rugs so that he would hear the faintest creak. They climbed three floors, found their way into a hallway, and continued down it, passing the extinguished wall lights shaped like translucent clamshells that were placed between the numbered doors. They soon came to a halt before number thirty-four. Snake knocked four times with a second in between each one, gave his name, and spoke the word "Erebus." They extinguished their lighters. They could hear deep breathing, then some steps, and four bolts being pulled into their housings. The two men waited another ten seconds, as was the current ritual. Again, the sound of steps and an exhalation. Snake pushed open the door and stepped in, followed by Double, who closed it behind him.

Darkness ruled over this room as well. There was the sound of a switch. A lamp lit up, its beams directed on the two men, who instinctually brought their hands up to eye level. A second click, this one metallic. After a moment, they made out the silhouette of Joyce, ensconced in a leather armchair, a pistol balanced on one armrest, a watch on the other, as always.

We're very sorry to disturb you so late, sir, said Snake.

Get on with it!

Roby hired a new server. We thought we had better tell you about it right away...

What's so special about this girl?

You remember Solena.

There was a silence; Joyce covered his watch with one of his hands.

A girl like that, he said.

Even better than that.

Well, tell Roby to have her move upstairs.

We'll tell him, but she seems to have quite the attitude, said Double.

What exactly is it that you think this should mean to me? I pay you plenty to take care of such problems.

We'll do what's needed, said Snake.

Neither of the two men mentioned the altercation with the fellow from the plant.

Is that all? asked Joyce.

Yes, sir.

Well, then don't let me keep you.

Once he was alone, Joyce got up to put the dead bolts back in place and lingered a moment in front of the door, listening to the discordant sounds of the footsteps on the flooring. He went back to sit in his chair, thinking of the girl, trying to imagine her. *You remember Solena?* Once she became common property upstairs at The Admiral, no man would concern himself with possessing her, and she would no longer fan the flames of jealousy. Joyce had always done what was necessary to make sure that no one came along and disrupted the order he had established, not a woman any less than a man.

He thought back to a stranger who had arrived in town some years back, quite similar to him in certain ways, apart from discretion and distrust. At that time, the stranger had hurried to place nearly all of his money in the bank. The bank manager had immediately informed Joyce, as he owned the bank. That evening, at The Admiral, the stranger had bought rounds for the house, bragging and boasting. His drink loosened his tongue and he had gloated about how rich he was, revealing his plans to open a trading business. The customers listened to him as they drank, but not one of them alerted him to the monopoly that Joyce had put into place, knowing that others would soon take care of that.

The stranger woke up one morning in his hotel room to discover Snake and Double standing at either side of his bed. The dwarf explained to him that he ought to go back to where he had come from, or if not, that he would have to comply with the boss's rules by working for him, and that if he persisted in his notions, he would pay the price. The fellow, undaunted, asked them to leave. At that point, Double and Snake had no reason not to do so, but they waited a while longer before leaving the room.

The same day, the stranger made his way to the bank to withdraw some money to finance his acquisition of a building. The manager received him in his office and informed him, with a solemn look, that robbers had broken into his establishment during the night. Real professionals, he added, who had cleaned the place out. It had never happened before. The stranger asked how the thieves had gone about it. The manager couldn't reveal this, seeing that an investigation was underway. The man wanted to know to what degree he would be indemnified. The banker told him that as he had not taken out any insurance, he unfortunately wasn't entitled to anything. The stranger, threatening, attempted to make a scene, but the guards intervened immediately and forcibly threw him out. He went to lodge a complaint with the police. A lawman took his deposition, assuring him that he would be kept abreast of the investigation. The inquiry never moved forward. The lawman's name was Lynch.

After that reversal of fortunes, the stranger insisted on lingering in town. He was pushing his luck, and all he managed to do was spend what little money remained to him without getting anywhere at all. Out of resources, he looked for work, but it was too late. Double and Snake had warned him. All doors were closed to him. A few days later he left town with nothing more than what he had had on his back when he arrived. He was never seen again, and no one ever spoke of him.

As far as the new serving girl at The Admiral, Double would just need to have some fun with her, if she decided she didn't want to join the girls upstairs. Joyce knew the giant's reputation, all he had to do was wait a bit for her to resist. At the worst, after some appropriate treatment, no one would desire her at all.

Roby was placing the last chairs upside down on the tables when Double and Snake entered. They went over to a table, flipped over a chair each, and sat down.

Bring us some beers, tossed out Double.

Roby gave the two men a peeved look, went to draw the beers, and brought them over.

I suppose you know why we've come back, said Snake.

Because of what happened with the new girl?

Joyce would like to know your intentions for her...

The guy, he was her father.

That's not the problem.

I promise you it won't happen again.

The problem is that you've never been able to control your staff.

You can't say that!

Maybe you need us to refresh your memory.

Double was sipping at his beer, allowing Snake to conduct the conversation.

I'll speak to her, said Roby.

You do that, and keep us up to speed.

Okay.

Roby dried his hands on the rag that hung from his belt, looking at the two men, clearly ill at ease.

What is it? asked Snake.

If you both feel like going upstairs for some fun, it's on me, fellas.

Not tonight, let us finish our beers in peace.

Roby continued tidying the room. Double lit a cigarette and exhaled a thick burst of smoke that stagnated a moment before gently dissipating.

I was wondering... you know what it means, that "Erebus"? asked Double.

Not the slightest idea.

The giant thought for a long while.

I never understand anything about the boss, he said as if he had just awoken.

You're not paid to, said Snake.

You seen how he lives? He could have all the most beautiful broads in the valley by snapping his fingers, even a different one every night, if he wanted. In any case, that's what I'd do, if I had his kind of cash, instead of spending my nights alone in the dark.

You don't have his kind of cash...

And plus, his wife, she's still damned hot. I'd definitely have done her back in the day.

Shut up, will you?

Anyway, maybe it was kind of stupid to talk to him about this young one. I could have dealt with that problem myself.

Don't forget what you told me. We most certainly wouldn't be having this conversation if he had learned about it from somebody else.

Double placed a hand over his mouth before he went on:

You know what? I don't think he screws enough for his brain to function normally.

I imagine he wouldn't have everything he's got if his desire to own things wasn't superior to his desire to screw.

What kind of man doesn't want to screw more than anything else?

A kind of man unlike you, I suppose.

You should maybe think of asking your redhead to marry you, said Double, pointing a finger instinctively toward the landing.

Seeing no reaction from Snake, he belabored the point with a snicker:

And hey, seeing that one man isn't enough for her, how about half a man!

The expressions that passed in turn across Snake's face seemed as if they were driven by a notched mechanism that released features gradually, finally landing at the end of the rotation on the fixed expression of a taxidermied animal.

You make out alright with only half a brain, replied Snake coldly.

The provocation hit its target with full force. Double slammed a fist down on the table.

You know what your problem is, Snake?

I feel like it won't take me long to find out.

You have no sense of humor. You make as if you're above it all, when really, the blood that flows through your veins is frozen.

The dwarf lit a cigarette in turn, took a drag, then pulled it away from his mouth with a theatrical gesture.

Why do you think people call me Snake? he said, spitting out tatters of smoke.

Double had the feeling he had once again walked into a trap, conscious of the fact that Snake had turned the situation to his advantage, as he often did.

I really don't know why they teamed us up together, he said, crushing his butt on the tabletop, and flicking it in the direction of the dwarf, who was smiling.

You don't even have a little idea why?

You're just a lousy manipulator, that's what you are.

Kind of you to say.

Sometimes, I wonder if you aren't even more twisted than the boss.

A second compliment, that's enough already.

Go fuck yourself, Snake!

Stretched out on a sofa, with the bit of latitude he had and the diffuse light that illuminated the room, Martin let his gaze wander. Seashells of all sizes and strange statuettes rested atop the furniture and shelves, watched over by laughing masks hung from the walls. He painfully raised his head, discovering a swordfish rostrum that floated above him. The infernal dance of the alcohol he had ingested at The Admiral picked up the pace in his veins, deforming the mouths of the masks into mutely moaned complaints. He rubbed his eyes, and the seashells, statuettes, and masks began to spin around the space in all directions, like so many comets, avoiding the rostrum. Martin watched the unbelievable cosmic display, a powerless spectator. His eyelids grew heavy, and he fought to keep his eyes open. The objects faded away. A sensual silhouette appeared and came over to Martin, undulating. The traits of Mabel's face grew more and more distinct.

Whoever you are, shut off that goddamn light or I'll kill you! cried Martin.

Nobody fulfilled his wish. His eyelids fell once again, and the silhouette of his daughter was sucked into the whirling vortex of a starless night. He fell back asleep, and his memory set to cloning processions of sirens that ravaged his slumber.

In the morning, the sun's rays filtered through the venetian blinds, stabbing on their way through certain prey that looked like trophies from the previous night's carnage. The smell of coffee was floating on the air. Martin managed to unseal his lips, and the carrion taste in his mouth erased the odor of the coffee. A needle pierced his skull from one ear to the other, carrying with it the stabbing sound of a vibration, over which a familiar voice reached out:

You feeling any better?

Martin turned his head with difficulty. Gobbo was sitting in a chair, a mug in his hand.

You really tied one on last night.

What time is it?

Eight thirty.

Martin tried to sit up, but didn't make it, his body still in the grips of the booze.

Why didn't you wake me earlier, I'm going to be late for work.

It's Sunday.

Martin chewed on the little bit of saliva he had remaining in his mouth before speaking:

You should have taken me home.

I don't even know where you live, and you weren't in any condition to give me the right address.

Martin concentrated on his breathing and finally managed to sit up, his back leaning against the armrest. Gobbo got up and handed him the mug.

Here, drink this, it'll help put your thoughts back in order.

Martin grabbed the mug, drank a little mouthful, then rested the mug on one of his thighs without letting go of it.

I'm sorry, he said.

He drank again and looked around himself, noticing that he hadn't dreamed the swordfish rostrum, of which he had seen a reproduction in one of the books Duval had lent him, no more than he had the rest of the menagerie.

Some old souvenirs, said Gobbo with a world-weary tone.

The sailor grabbed the coffeepot from the table, filled a cup, and returned to his armchair, his body impaled by a ray of light.

I must have been talking nonsense last night, said Martin.

You don't remember?

No.

We'll talk about it later.

Might not be any point in that.

Gobbo took the time to finish his coffee.

You feel well enough to make it back home on your own?

Martin gently moved his chest forward and then back in a pendulum motion before steadying himself, the mug still in his hand, his gaze riveted on the reflection that had just appeared on the surface of his coffee. He was still staggering inside his head, captivated by the image, like a junkie, this face that hadn't stopped judging him during his sleep, without a word, with the demonic stare of a tawny owl perched atop its own misery. *That* he had no trouble remembering. He drank the rest of the coffee in one go, and set the mug down on the table, as if bringing down a gavel to end the bidding. At that point, he remembered the bids he had shouted from the end of the bar the night before, without having had any idea just how high Mabel was willing to go with the resentment and maybe even hatred it would take to come out the winner. And so he got to his feet, making use of the momentum to reach the door. He grasped the doorknob and remained there a few seconds, opened the door, and left without looking back.

It wasn't the fact that Martin had slept elsewhere that made Martha furious, or even that he had done so due to the influence of alcohol, but that she was going to miss Mass because of him. Because of him, she wouldn't be able to rid herself of her weekly burden like she did every Sunday, alone in the last pew of the church. Even if it was never a question of her own sins, seeing that there wasn't a more virtuous woman in the entire region.

The return trip to the house had worn Martin out. She pushed him by his shoulders to the stairs, helped him up the steps, and led him into the bedroom. Once inside, she had him sit down on the bed, got down on her knees, pulled off his shoes and his pants, then got to her feet, unbuttoned his grimy shirt, and tugged on the sleeves to get it off. Martin let her complete the task. He then fell back and curled up on the sheet. He would have liked to push back against the mute violence that he was feeling, not to be that inept man at the mercy of this woman who was preparing to leave the room. He would have preferred it a thousand times more if she had scolded him, cursed him out, and left him to his decadent ways, rather than to have her treat him like a child.

Martha looked at him a long moment, as if she were trying to conjure up some other body atop the immaculate bedsheet, even a dead one. She gathered up the clothing scattered across the floor, rolled it into a ball, and went back downstairs. She lit the stove and began to heat some water in the large tinplate basin, and remained standing there, her stare vacant. Once the water started to simmer, she pulled the basin away from the stove, throwing into it the clothes that were drenched in sweat, alcohol, and cigarette smoke, submerged them, and stirred them with the help of a stripped stick, then leaned the stick back against the oven. She then poured a little cool water into a pitcher, went back up to the bedroom, and closed the door behind her. Martin was sleeping deeply, now stretched out flat on his back. Fine droplets enshrouded his skin, like a substance meant to take an imprint of his body, to create a negative of this pitiful man, abandoned to the haughty stare of his wife. She brought a chair over to the bedside, set the jug down on the seat, went off to find some linens in the armoire, and returned to sit next to her husband. She promptly dipped a towel into the pitcher, let it drip off, and then dabbed it on Martin's forehead with an unexpected gentleness, did the same to his cheeks, worked down his torso, like a conscientious nurse taking care of a sick patient. He didn't awaken. She lingered on his stomach, tracing small concentric circles. Martin imperceptibly moved his lips, and a faint groan escaped from his mouth. Looking now at the lump in his undershorts, Martha stretched the towel out on his stomach, slowly lowered the underpants, and freed his organ. A shiver ran through Martin. She jolted back slightly, and shot a glance toward the bedroom door. Afraid that he would awaken, that someone would come in. He didn't wake up and the door remained shut. She waited a few seconds, then began to caress the penis with slow and cautious movements. She brought her hand up and down around his organ, staring at the miracle of its hardness, her entire face following the rhythm, from bottom to top to bottom to top, and her mouth looked like an old scar that was starting to reopen, something unnamable, beyond beauty and beyond ugliness, beyond humanity. A stream of air slipped out from between her teeth, and so as to not allow any sound to escape, she swallowed her saliva in little gulps. She picked up the pace. Martin was breathing more and more quickly. She accelerated still more. Soon, he tensed up, and she quickly pulled her hand away. The sperm surged forth in fits and starts, coming back down to land on the extended towel. She didn't take her eyes from the still-taut penis, from which slid a thick flow of semen. Martha washed her hands, and then returned to her husband. She made the sign of the cross and spat at the now-flaccid organ.

She folded up the towel, drenched it in the water, removed it again and wrung it out, before diligently wiping the organ clean. Once she had finished, she spent another long moment observing the satiated body, like a cadaver emptied of its own ecstasy, its substance, thinking that she was alone, which she surely was.

Matthew skirted around the base of an ancient bird blind that no one used anymore, not since a drunken hunter had found his death there by falling. Structurally it looked like an electrical tower. Two large scrap-iron weights, having served as an elevator mechanism, lay on the ground below. The young man liked to pass that way, and happily observed the progress of the ivy around the metal poles.

He then plunged into the forest and rejoined the river. Spiderwebs decorated with garlands of dew hung between the branches of the young willow trees. The current clattered away over the rocks. Matthew knew this intimate language, had learned it over the course of the seasons, the rise and fall of the water level, an equilibrium born of a grand beginning, back before man existed. He had no memory whatsoever of what the river had looked like before the construction of the dam. He had been too young in those days, but he often dreamed that one day things would return to the way they had been before, imagining an ideal Eden.

By the end of a long apprenticeship nourished by an immeasurable devotion to nature, he had learned to hear the trees growing. He never would have even considered carving anything into the bark, the way some others did to leave a trace of their emotions behind them, to persuade themselves of an illusion, thinking that such a mark would climb its way to the crown of the tree in some form of eternity, even if it wouldn't really budge an inch. Never would he succumb to such a facile act. Like Tiresias endowed with sight, the subterranean world also spoke to him, words that passed through his feet, as if he wasn't even wearing shoes, as if he had the power to return to the beginning, prior to all desire of conquest. To live in the past once again, a time well before men had misappropriated nature for their own convenience, by way of frescoes, statues, and words, to imagine themselves the creators of this beauty, where they should have been satisfied to be its guardians. Matthew didn't think it was possible to aggrandize the obvious splendor of nature. Unlike Mark, he didn't believe in art, persuaded that it was transposing the daily poetry of the world into a human project, nothing more than human. For Matthew, art had been invented by man so that he could paint death with the colors of life. He himself had never been afraid of death.

In the forest, the source of life was precisely the death of everything. It bore the name humus, a bed in which were born innumerable roots that sunk down, overlapping, bumping into, bypassing, piercing; a bed in which roamed the most primal forms, disappearing into the depths as the oxygen grew too thin; a bed in which the meticulous and opinionated decomposition of death led to life; a bed in which to awaken and to fall asleep.

Armed with twigs and branches, the river paraded before Matthew's eyes. He felt overwhelmed with emotion, as always. He pulled off his shirt. The shadows cast by the branches striped his back, and when the sun disappeared behind a cloud, their erasure revealed other stripes, these ones inlaid in his flesh, scars of different ages, his own lacerated bark, mortified layers of himself. From an early age, when his father had beaten him, he had learned to climb up and hurtle down the peaks of the pain by lightly scratching the silence with his moans. But now, his scarified back belonged to the body that was the forest. He had offered it up to the woods, an offering of ligneous muscles, of earthy flesh and invisible blood, the expression of a healthy usefulness that was eternally alive.

The wind picked up, adding a supplementary volume to the forest, much as a bird ruffles its feathers to intimidate an enemy, signifying that regardless of what men undertook against it, a few won battles would never result in its defeat. The valley contained for itself alone the past, present, and future, and had made for itself a single time, not an eternity on a human scale.

Matthew pulled off his boots and socks, his pants, and his underwear. He stood up straight, his arms along his sides, his feet resting on a bed of leaves. A wild yearning to take root, to become a tree. He felt new life teeming beneath his feet, penetrating the plants, scaling his ankles. Felt the sap climbing within his legs, like when you squeeze in a vise a branch cut in springtime. He finally belonged to this world, had become a simple filter for the subterranean forces.

Elie saw Martin cross the porch and enter the house without really noticing him. Since Mabel had left, the old man was often parked there, listless on a folding chair, his chin rested on a crutch wrapped in bandages, his eyes locked on the porch's openwork gable, above which extended a nature scene that was blurred by a growing cataract.

Afternoons, Elie never broke from his stroll, hoping to run into Mabel. *You know where to find me,* he had told her before she left. He always sat there at the edge of the fountain, lulled by the sound of the stream of water that flowed from the copper pipe, singing its monotonous and eternal song that sprang forth from the throats of the earth. When people crossed the square, they acted as if they didn't see him, and maybe they even ended up not seeing him, no more than they noticed the statue of the general. Elie remained like that, motionless for long periods, his neck extended, wrinkled up like that of a turtle, a totemic mass of faded colors, the face of an owl, with his gaze detached from himself, lost and without moorings. He slowly came out of his torpor once the sun started to hammer down upon the bicorne hat of the petrified hero.

Around that time, workers began to turn up to the south side of the square, like a distended crowd, all transformed by the avaricious spirit of alcohol and forgetting.

Then Elie went off, limping, in more of a hurry than he had been when arriving, his head bent toward the ground, which he raised only once he was outside of the town. Having reached the path, he slowed his step, trying to discreetly guess behind which tree Luke would be hiding.

The eye hesitates before harmony, roams about, wanders off, returns, never attaching itself lastingly, an infinite voyage. The eye never hesitates in the face of rupture, the evidence of contrast, drawn in straightaway and leaving behind what had previously attracted it, as if replete. Initial attraction is nothing but a vulgarity. Too much red on the lips, on the cheeks, too much makeup around the eyes; those clothes that speak in the body's place, the gait that relies on ephemeral desires.

Beauty is a human conception. Grace alone can translate the divine. Beauty can be explained, grace cannot. Beauty parades around on solid ground, grace floats in the air, invisible. Grace is a sacrament, beauty the simple crowning of a fleeting reign.

Mabel was grace incarnate, and those who gazed upon her didn't know what to do with the mystery, like looking at an ancient system of writing made up of symbols that had traversed the centuries, intended for other millennia. Mabel had no need of artifice. The eye traveled across her skin, often slowing down, oh yes, slowing, to almost fixate on one detail that took on the role of perfection, then moving away, storing away the abandoned imprint in its memory so as to find it more easily later.

Nowadays, everyone in town could look at her, when she walked through the streets, when she was serving at The Admiral. Every place she set her foot should have been transformed into a cathedral where one could go to receive the sacrament. Every day they ought to have thanked the heavens for having crossed her path. While some gave themselves over without reserve, others were already conspiring to sabotage her grace, to reduce it to something to be hated or even to be possessed.

S eated in a leather chair with large armrests, Joyce was playing with the clasp of the bag that rested on his knees, staring emptily straight ahead. He heard the bell ring for the second time. The time of day when the church spat its faithful back out. Never would Joyce understand the common need to feel considered and protected by a god, to believe oneself important enough that it couldn't be any other way. After all, they had the divine directly in front of their eyes the moment they left their place of worship: the dam, the plant, and all the rest of it. One only had to read the names of the streets to be convinced. There was no other divinity than Joyce, the traces attested to this. His name was inscribed all over the town, and that of God? Nowhere. It was he, Joyce, who had illuminated the miserable lives of the people of the town and the valley, brought the light to them, even letting it reach into their church. At the least, the people were under his heel, held under his subjugation. One day, they would all finally recognize him as the one and only creator of all things; should this not be the case, he would make them understand that he was in a position to take it all back with a snap of his fingers.

Joyce knew from experience that you can only count on yourself. If ever he began to doubt this, his own personal story brought him back to his true measure, and thus prevented him from any spiritual excess. A story that he would always keep secret. He felt that a man should know how far he can go, should push against the limits, and prove it to himself. For some time already, he had grown increasingly conscious of the fact that it wasn't enough, that you can never prove anything to yourself in the long term, that how he appeared to others was the sole fluctuating valuation of his own dignity, and yet he had always fought off their gazes.

From the moment he first arrived, he had known that it was the right place to stop and lay the first stone of his glory. Day after day, year after year, he had worked to possess it all, in such a way that nothing escaped him. His work as a builder now complete, life had lost a great deal of its salt, and the thing he had hoped would put the finishing touches on his life's work had turned out to be nothing more than an insignificant child.

Joyce thought of the street that he would have to cross to rejoin his wife and son, as he did every Sunday to share a meal together. The only weekly visit to his family. It was his greatest contradiction to find himself each Sunday opposite this overly innocent brat and this transparent wife, both of them without any ambition for their existence. This woman who avoided his eyes, who feared his every reaction, whose flesh he had desired and who had disgusted him ever since. The boy obediently sitting at the table, who trotted out "Daddy" enough times that he could fill a book, and for whom he felt no attachment whatsoever. A glimpse of two presences, the same day at the same time, nothing more. And the day had come, as had the hour.

As he watched Helio clumsily cut his roast beef, Joyce felt bitter regret at the form his offspring had taken, this child intended to personify continuity. As was her habit, Isobel was on her guard. At that moment, in Joyce's eyes, she had the look of an ancient fortress atop a rocky crag. A ruin draped in a white dress fitted to her diaphanous skin, as if cut from the same block of limestone. The notion that he might not outlive these two inconsequential beings had become unbearable to him.

What have you done to deserve being seated at this table? he said in a contemptuous tone.

Mother and son looked at one another, then lowered their eyes to their plates.

I've been working hard at school, Father.

Is that enough?

I embroidered some linens, said Isobel, her voice febrile.

Is that enough?

Isobel closed her hands tightly around her silverware as she gathered what meager force she had.

What is it that you expect from us? she asked.

Joyce chewed for a long while on a piece of meat, wiped his mouth. He appeared very calm when it came time for his reply:

Perhaps something to hate, to destroy. Perhaps I'm the sort of man who deserves that, perhaps the hatred that you reserve for me would then justify your place at this table, an avowed hatred, finally accepted.

Helio placed his little hands flat on the table.

May I be excused, Father?

You haven't finished your meal.

I'm not hungry anymore.

Joyce hurled his napkin and pointed a finger at his son.

You don't move from here until I tell you to.

He's just a child, said Isobel, fleeing Joyce's eyes.

What is it that you're saying?

Joyce's fist slammed down violently on the table. Beneath its impact, his glass tipped over and broke against his plate.

When I was his age, I was already earning my keep in the streets. That's what made me what I am today. The street taught me all I needed to know.

You should be happy to be able to spare your son that.

Happy about what? To look at you both, so useless and incapable of standing up for yourselves? If something were to happen to me, no one would ever forgive you for having become what you were never destined to be.

Isobel was on the edge of tears.

You're pathetic! he added.

I can't take this anymore, she said, breathing out sharply.

You can't take any more of this life of leisure that I buy you with my money? You'd rather be wiping the rear ends of someone else's brats while working at your parents' store?

Money isn't everything.

Yes, of course money is everything. All people think about is how to get it when they don't have any, and how to keep it when they do.

In a supreme effort, Isobel sat up straight on her chair.

Alienation has never made anyone happy, she said with the belligerence that is sometimes brought about by the pinnacle of fear.

Joyce looked at her curiously, like he was a rodent looking for a way out of a labyrinth.

Alienation, a lovely word. Tell me, he continued after a moment. You learned that word in the books that you buy with my money, I'd imagine.

Helio was huddled up on his chair, his fists clenched against his temples, and he closed his eyes.

I'm begging you, it would be better if you left. Go now, said Isobel.

Joyce got up and walked around the table. He came to a stop, planting himself directly behind his wife, placed his hands on the back of her chair, and said quietly into her ear:

Is that something you're asking me to do, or something you're recommending, my dear?...I would really like to know.

Isobel had the sensation that her spinal cord was dissolving bit by bit in acid.

I'm sorry, I shouldn't have said that.

You're not answering my question.

I'm sorry.

Stop apologizing and stand on your own two feet, for once.

Isobel leaned forward to get as far as possible away from the sound of her husband.

You were so beautiful, back when I met you...so fresh, continued Joyce, insisting on each word.

Isobel held her head between her hands and broke down sobbing. Joyce abandoned his prey. As he walked past his son, he patted him on the shoulder with the flat of his hand.

Take care of your mother, it seems that she is in need of comforting.

Joyce was about to open the door. He let out a deep sigh.

You both think that I'm a monster, don't you?

No one replied.

I'd so like to be a monster, he said as he was leaving the room.

———

Once Joyce was back in his building, he thought over what had just taken place, what he had imposed on his wife and his son, what he imposed upon himself by visiting them each Sunday. Truth be told, he found no pleasure in making them suffer so. His never-ending provocations had no goal other than to empty himself of the rage he felt for having succumbed to the path of least resistance that was the begetting of progeny, the hackneyed plan without a future that was, in his eyes, the family; his anger at the fatigue that it represented, at his wife, who had diluted his blood with her own in bringing into being this child, incapable of even properly slicing up a piece of roast beef, a son who looked nothing like his father, the spitting image of his mother, with his fine blond hair, his blue eyes, and his childish features that he would never outgrow completely. Joyce didn't hate him as one hates a human being, he hated him as an image without flesh or bone that he had contributed to creating. He controlled the town and the valley, but this small family eluded his control, had always eluded it. What ought to have counted most, he had never managed to pull it into the magnetic field of his will. Cynicism at least prevented him from succumbing to the temptation of truly pitying them. He had never been endowed with the baser emotions, and so he did his utmost to poison anything that might give rise to them, reckoning that they would be the expression of his greatest weakness.

An orphan from birth, Joyce had been entitled to nothing but contempt throughout his childhood. When he was old enough to start understanding how the world worked, he had hastened to return that contempt to others, thinking he would in that way avenge himself for a ruined childhood and push his own pain further away. Despite the failures and triumphs, he had never managed, as he knew that contempt is nothing more than a screen intended to protect someone from his own eventual collapse, and cynicism the means to reinforce that screen.

Joyce reached a room on the second floor, one in complete darkness. With one finger, he flicked on the switch. A yellowish light flooded into the bulb screwed in under the lampshade and it began to twinkle, like a far-off star stuck to the vault of the night.

No matter how much Luke concentrated as he drifted off to sleep, he could no longer make the mutilated fox appear in his dreams. Instead, it was Mabel that visited him, who came back over and over, from the moment he closed his eyes. He would have liked it if she had disappeared from time to time, for the fox to come back, in all of its sumptuous horror, but it wasn't up to him. Not anymore.

Luke couldn't get it out of his head that it was entirely his fault that Mabel had left. Mark and Matthew had tried their best to convince him of the contrary, that it had been their sister's choice to leave the house. She had even told them to take care of him, but it wasn't enough, and he didn't really believe it. His brothers didn't know the whole story.

The day of her departure, face glued to the window, nothing had escaped him, neither his mother's words, whom he couldn't see, nor Mabel, whom he could see and who wasn't saying anything. His face like a sponge, permeable to the excessive violence their mother was spitting out. He so much would have wanted to kiss his sister with that mouth of glass, to take on that violence, to spit it back, and then let it trickle down the cold glass window that was smeared with his fear. But he couldn't go backward. He had denounced her. That is what had set it all off. Even beyond his mother's rage, he was thinking about what Mabel had done with that boy, what he had thought was reserved for him, and also of the secret that she had asked him to keep, the secret that he had kept safe and sound and that had been transformed into a transgression in his head.

He had come to think that what they had done together had been a shameful act, something that you're not supposed to do when you are brother and sister. And at the same time he couldn't forget the happiness of the ecstasy, and the gentleness of afterward. When Mabel had explained to him that what girls had between their thighs was better than a hand, Luke had wanted her to show him, but she had refused. She had added that another girl would one day show him what it looked like from close up, and even how it was used, but that he'd surely have to pay her, that there was no better way to learn about it, that it wasn't a sister's role to go any further than the gentleness of a hand. He thought back to their swims in the river, regretting that he hadn't taken a better look in those days, but he had been too small then to see anything other than nothing between his sister's legs.

How to rid himself of all those contradictory thoughts and finally pull away his face, still glued to that window?

By thinking. By putting a thin layer of salve between the glass and his skin, maybe by letting Jim Hockens take over. A temporary solution, before once again being able to see the fox frolicking along in a wake of bones and blood. To become Jim and find the pirate's treasure, which would allow him to buy a ship, and also to pay one of those girls who will show you, for money, what they've got between their legs, like a schoolmistress teaching her students what is important in life.

Luke often thought back on school. And yet it hadn't been a good experience. He hadn't attended very long. The schoolmistress had said that there was nothing she could do for him. Had allowed him to sit there for a few weeks at the back of the class, just long enough for him to learn the letters of the alphabet by heart, like a parrot, but after, no one had taken the time to teach him how to use them to write the words that he heard. The symbols he saw in his siblings' notebooks fascinated him, representing well-aligned anonymous gravestones, each separated by alleyways designed for the distribution of silence. Instinctually, Luke suspected that if there hadn't been that silence, the same length as the rows of words, it wouldn't have made any sense, like a breathing out that wasn't followed by a breathing in. He so would have liked to unearth the corpses that lay beneath those tombstones, so that they would finally speak to him. Perhaps Jim Hockens would be able to look into that as well.

Luke's body had grown normally, but his head hadn't kept pace. His mother reminded him of this fairly often. Jim was his chance to get caught up, the true identity he had to assume. Jim Hockens on the lookout, capable of climbing into an apple barrel to listen to the conspirators. Luke didn't often live in reality, but Jim, he was most surely capable of facing the pirates and finding Mabel, so that she would forgive everything. He finally unglued his face from the window. Allowed Jim Hockens to take over. The right order to follow became a foregone conclusion: see Mabel again, find the treasure, and discover what is hidden between girls' legs. Three pieces to put together in order to make something of himself, to be rich in a number of different ways. Maybe they all led to the same thing, like how to end up where all four of them were once again suspended from the viaduct. After, and only after, could he take to the sea, knowing all there was to know about life.

In those days, Matthew was already working at the quarry. He was tasked with overseeing the crushing of the granite blocks torn free of the hillside by way of dynamite blasts. By the time they were sixteen years old, the men in each family had to contribute a salary to their household. Mark was hired at the quarry too, soon after Mabel's departure. Learning at school had been easy for him, and he could have gone on with his studies, but what was the point? The idea of leaving his brothers behind and abandoning his sister never crossed his mind. In any case, his parents wouldn't have wanted it. He simply requested that he have access to the school library so that he could borrow the books he would read in secret. Mrs. Loiseau agreed.

Sokal, the director of the quarry, personally supervised the recruitment process, convinced that he had no equal when it came to discerning the capacities of this person or that one, studying their words and their attitudes during the never-ending interviews, after which he announced an irrevocable verdict. He had read a few books on the subject, basic psychology, and boasted that he could get into people's heads with the facility of a dipstick plunged into a vehicle's oil pan, which, when he pulled it out, was clearly marked with the competences of each man. He had made a few mistakes over the years, but since no one had ever reproached him for it, he had forgotten those details.

Given his evident intellectual aptitude, it was agreed that Mark would be tried out in the lading service, and more specifically tasked with verifying the tonnage of the materials that left the quarry. The trial period proved to be satisfactory, and Mark was installed in a position that brought with it little difficulty, caused little fatigue, and provided a respectable salary. The laborers, who did all the work with the stone, considered him no more than a pencil pusher, and rarely spoke to him. Mark didn't care what they thought of him. His work gave him the opportunity to daydream and to make up stories.

He awaited the passage of the trucks with their loaded beds, peacefully seated in a windowed room that was attached to the administration offices, just below that of Sokal. As soon as a load arrived, he went out and compared the order form to the real tonnage, which he then recorded on a page of the logbook that permitted the establishment of precise statistics destined to produce clever progress graphs. The trucks came one after another, day after day, in long processions that reminded Mark of images of endless caravans crossing the desert, which he had encountered in illustrated books. It was by taking note of the different destinations inscribed on the order forms that he was able to envision elsewheres with names as mysterious as those he read about in his books. He had a gift for unearthing the marvelous from that mass of roaring scrap metal, capable of ignoring the simple materiality of the vehicles, forgetting the drivers, and conceiving of the fantastical beasts that were readying themselves for journeys across untamed regions. He imagined great mountains of sand and, even farther off, lands peopled by men and women with strange customs, speaking unknown languages, under the rule of some mute king with an air of divinity who received the cargo in exchange for heaps of gold.

Mark read between inspections, with an ear peeled for the slightest creak of the floor above him so he wouldn't be surprised by Sokal. Despite his father's interdiction, he also continued to read in his bedroom, refining an ideal conception of the world that would later lead him to put down his own words on blank pages. Much later on, once he had read enough, he would permit himself to do so. When night had fallen, he would tame the earth abiding by the rules of the sky, observing the stars as they communicated their eternal ends in Morse code, a luminous death, decipherable. His great secret. His internal madness projected on the canvas of his gaze. Those books that, according to his father, were home to the Devil, they saved him. Literature had the ability to sow seeds in his imagination and to spread its richness inside the valley's walls, to transform the stones of the quarry into rough diamonds, to formulate a new language that he alone was able to interpret.

A timid perspicuity made it so that he never completely abandoned himself to rest. This lucidity was like a window left wide open to a light that was his alone. Mark didn't yet know to which distant, starry reaches this light would lead him, but he hoped he would see all the beauty of it. An infinite beauty.

Before he returned home from work, Mark had gotten into the habit of taking a detour through town. Mabel still hadn't given them any news. He scoured the streets at random, looking for her, not daring to inquire with anybody.

As he walked that evening along Joyce 4, Mark heard a sound not unlike that of a pigeon taking off, and raised his eyes. Above the street floated a bunting of pennants celebrating the festival of lights, an annual celebration personally established by Joyce that marked the inauguration of the plant. A mountain breeze made the distended festoons flutter and lifted the fabric triangles shaped like grass skirts one after the other, which gave the whole the appearance of a multicolored centipede floundering in the void. Mark was struck by a gentle melancholy, like when you look at an old photograph in which the people appear to be happy and carefree. Unlike the sunshine and the bad weather that would irreversibly attenuate the colors of the pennants and even end up bringing about their ruin, the acid of time would never manage to completely wipe away the memory of his sister, no matter what happened. A memory crystallized in emotion.

Mark remained there a long moment, observing the garland, with his sister still suspended there in his thoughts. Once too much light had penetrated his retinas, it ended up blinding him. The garland disappeared, and at the same time so did the memory it had conjured up. He then threw his head forward, waiting for the contour of his shoes to be burned into the concrete sidewalk.

What are you doing here?

Mark slowly raised his head to discover his sister standing before him, or rather the phantasmic image of her that his memory had created, dressed as she had been the day she had left, the little canvas bag slung over her shoulder.

I was looking for you, he said, addressing the apparition without thinking.

You look strange.

You look real.

What's the matter with you, it's me, Mabel!

Mark went silent for a few seconds, leaving enough time for the image to vanish, but nothing of the sort occurred. Mabel let the door of the house she had just left bang shut. Mark closed his eyes and then reopened them, realizing that an apparition couldn't have done that.

It's really you, then, he said.

What did you think it was?

I thought I was dreaming.

Mabel brushed her hand against her brother's.

Convinced?

Mark smiled. He read the inscription on the sign affixed to the door: BROCK BOARDINGHOUSE.

Is this where you're living, then?

While I wait for something better.

I was getting worried.

I'm sorry I haven't given you all any news.

Mark lifted his eyes up to the garland.

We've left your rope hanging from the viaduct.

Mabel smiled sadly.

How are things going at the house?

How about we take a walk, I can tell you about it.

Not tonight, I've got a job at that bar at the corner of Joyce Main and Joyce 8, The Admiral.

Mark frowned.

I don't think I like that, he said.

It's work.

Have you seen Dad, then?

Mabel nervously adjusted the strap of her bag.

I've got to get going, or I'm going to be late.

Mark didn't insist.

See you soon? he asked.

Come by Sunday morning, we can have some time together.

And what if you were to surprise Luke and Matthew by joining us at the viaduct . . . They miss you.

We'll do that a bit later, but I'd prefer it if we could talk a bit first, just you and me.

As you wish.

See you Sunday, said Mabel.

She planted a kiss on her brother's cheek. He watched her recede into the distance, turn at the corner of the next street, and disappear. He once again heard the sound of the pennants flapping, and felt terribly alone.

Mark arrived at Joyce Main with the sensation that he was crossing an overpopulated desert, before it dawned on him that he himself was the desert that nothing could penetrate without being burnt to cinders instantaneously. He walked slowly past The Admiral and saw Mabel's silhouette through the window, but not that of his father. He resisted the impulse to push open the door. They wouldn't have let him in, he wasn't old enough yet.

He turned onto Joyce Main and set off down the road toward the dam. He left the town as the sun began to dip in the sky. Autumn was already busy changing the colors. He remembered his grandmother saying that the leaves turned yellow because they had stored up the light, which they then spat back out into the sky, so that the next spring they could color themselves once more, that the seasons were nothing more than the immutable cycle of light. Once he had arrived at the viaduct, Mark climbed up under the arch and looked at Mabel's rope, hanging as stiffly as a steel cable despite the breeze, which seemed to avoid it. His head began to spin. It was a strange feeling to be overtaken by vertigo while on solid ground, to look at a slim target whose starting point went far beyond it, because the void that kept hold of it had, in his eyes, no beginning and no end, and that inconceivable lack of reference points reminded him of his own insignificance. He was discovering what it cost to defy something he couldn't yet name as anything other than loss. He thought that the world was much more beautiful when seen from above, and that from there the vertigo was easier to accept. But there he was, and in that moment, the vertigo was working as if inverted, like when you stand below the trunk of a very tall tree. What was the point of experiencing an inverted vertigo, without the fear of falling to your death? What was the reason not to face up to it? What was the point in not facing up to one's fears?

The Admiral emptied out at midnight, which was cur-
few time. Double and Snake remained seated. Martin and Gobbo walked past them. The seaman eyeballed
them with insistence. Double asked him why he was
looking at them like that. Gobbo did no more than narrow his eyes and continued on his way with no reply. As
he was about to push open the door, Martin shot a glance
at his daughter. She was busy wiping down the bar with a
cloth; she raised the hand that held the cloth and wiped
her forehead with her arm. The white fabric fluttered in
the air, like one of those makeshift flags that announce
a truce. Then she continued to polish the counter. She
didn't see her father exit, raising her eyes just after the
door banged shut. Once they were outside, Gobbo asked
Martin if he wanted him to wait.

Wait for what?

Good God, Martin, I think I like you better when
you're drunk.

At those words, Gobbo set off down a side street, and
Martin down another.

Snake made a motion with his head toward Roby,
who went straight over to speak to Mabel. The young

woman then briefly looked over toward the two men at their table and went on with her task. Seeing that she wasn't obeying, Roby grabbed her firmly by the elbow and led her over to the table, despite her resistance.

Have a seat, said Snake.

I've just finished my shift, I'm tired.

Don't worry, it won't take long.

Double leaned to the side and pulled out a chair. Roby gave Mabel a shove toward it. She dropped onto the seat and rested her hands flat atop her dress. Roby went back behind the counter.

You like this job? asked Snake.

It pays the bills.

That's not what I asked you.

Mabel looked at the dwarf with insolence, but did not respond.

I'd imagine you know who we work for?

Everyone works for him.

We're like his right hand ... and his left hand, added Snake with a hint of a smile.

Mabel stared at her own hands.

Joyce thinks you're not in the right place here.

Roby hasn't complained about my work.

Don't play the innocent, that's not what I'm talking about.

Mabel was trying not to allow any of her growing unease to show through.

May I go now? she said, getting to her feet.

Double stretched out his arm and placed his hand on the young woman's shoulder, causing her to promptly sit back down.

Life could be easier for you, if you want, he said, letting his hand linger before pulling it away.

Mabel shivered with aversion.

Whore myself out, you mean, she shot back.

Right away with the nasty words. Our Lord in heaven really spoiled you, it would be a waste not to take advantage of it. What more could a girl like you hope for?

Mabel leaped to her feet, knocking over the chair, and darted off between the tables. Stunned, the two men watched her leave the bar faster than a gust of wind. Double reacted first, trying to grab her, but it was already too late.

Outside, the night was smeared with stars, and the moon, whittled down to its quarter, looked like a fat stain that some demiurge had tried to erase before being interrupted. Mabel ran madly through the streets without looking back, making sure to lose any potential pursuers. She understood that the time she had just managed to steal she'd have to pay for later, one way or another.

The old woman was kneeling on the sidewalk. Her long smock, covered in countless stains, was dragging behind her, two down-at-the-heel work boots without laces poking out from underneath. She had pulled the grille off the gutter and was repeatedly dipping a hand into the opening, pulling it back out filled with handfuls of twigs and waterlogged leaves, which she piled in a heap on the edge of the concrete. She paid no attention to the young man who had just arrived.

As he approached the boardinghouse, Mark watched the vagrant woman, busy with her task. Then he knocked at the door without taking his eyes off the woman. She broke from her work as soon as she saw him do so, and looked over, still on all fours, her head unscrewing a quarter turn on her neck in the direction of the intrusion.

What do you want there, you? she asked with a haughty tone.

Mark didn't respond.

I asked you a question!

I don't see how it's any of your business.

The woman observed him for a long while, then put the grille back in place, got up, and wiped her hands on her smock.

Nobody's going to answer that door...

Mark knocked again.

I'm the only one who's in a position to answer, seeing as it's my door you're busy hammering away at.

You...

Perhaps I don't look like you think I ought to.

Pardon me, I'm here to see my sister.

Your sister, she repeated back, giving the young man a bleak look. I will have you know in advance, my boarding-house isn't a place that tolerates any sort of hanky-panky.

Mark flushed.

My name is Mark Volny, that must be the same name my sister gave you, I'd think.

So what, it's easy to agree on a name, that doesn't prove anything.

What should I do, then?

Nothing, I'm not going to believe you either way.

The woman moved toward the entrance. Mark stepped out of her way.

Wait here, she said with a nasty expression on her face.

She opened the door, went inside, and slammed the door behind her.

A few moments later, Mabel joined her brother on the sidewalk. Her face inscrutable, she gave him a quick kiss on the cheek and then turned to look toward a window behind which a curtain was swaying.

Not very accommodating, your landlady, said Mark.

Follow me!

Mark tried to start a conversation, but his sister seemed to want to distance herself as quickly as possible from the boardinghouse, racing along with a quick step, light on her feet, wearing her black dress and little shoes without heels that he hadn't seen before. They left the town by the southern exit, heading toward the dam. As they walked past the power plant, Mabel felt a tingling at the back of her neck when she heard its characteristic humming, which for her would always be the sound of her childhood. Her face opened up little by little and she gradually slowed her pace. Soon the viaduct appeared. Mabel stopped, staring at the rope that hung down, like a tear frozen on a clown's pale cheek.

So it was true, then, she said.

You didn't believe me?

Mabel smiled at her brother.

It's not nearly worn out, either.

The young woman began to scramble up the scree at the base of the pillar. She climbed with the agility of a creature that was born to scramble across piles of rocks, a creature that would soon bring a second into the world, one that would hoist itself up below the arch by arm strength alone, then a third, conceived for waiting, patiently installed below the arch.

Once she was sitting on the ledge, Mark followed suit. They both stared down at the river. The straw-yellow maws of the buttercups dotted the banks. The small boat bumped up against the pilings like a bell without a clapper, and the birds were cheeping all around in the trees. Mabel was still looking at the river, and Mark was now watching her, trying to imagine where her thoughts were leading her.

I can't manage to remember when it was that we came here for the first time . . . or who had the idea to hang the ropes, she said at the end of a long silence.

It was your idea.

I don't remember.

Mark raised his eyes.

I've never been happier than when I was hanging up there with you all, he said.

Happy . . .

Why didn't you let us know you were okay?

Mabel turned toward her brother. Two dimples dug deeply into her cheeks.

I needed to forget for a while.

To forget about us?

Of course not, you idiot. I meant to say, to take some distance, to think.

And?

Mabel's face grew serious.

Maybe I'm going to have to go even farther away.

With a contorted gesture suffused with panic, Mark flung an arm toward the river.

What does that mean, "even farther away"?

The shifting sands hollowed out once again. Mabel caressed her brother's cheek. Mark had never felt anything so soft, yet it did nothing but accentuate the terror that had just beset him.

As she spoke of distance, Mabel thought back to what had happened at The Admiral, with Double. She couldn't stop thinking about it. She nearly told her brother about it, but promptly changed her mind: It would only have added to his anxiety. He couldn't do anything about it. She patted her hand against one of Mark's jacket pockets, finding a way to give a lighter tone to the conversation.

Still always a book in your pocket, it looks like, she said with a smile.

Always.

You should maybe take a break from your books to give the kisses of a pretty girl a try.

I haven't yet found one who looks enough like you.

She thought of Luke, who had said more or less the same words.

You should still try.

Mark took a long, deep breath.

Why was it that you wanted us to get together first, just the two of us?

Mabel let a few moments go by. She listened to the river, the murmur of which had intensified. They must have released more water from the dam.

Maybe I didn't quite feel ready yet, maybe I needed to confide in you first.

They've been dreaming of seeing you again.

Don't tell them anything for now.

If that's what you want.

You know, it's not because I left that things have changed between us all. We can still count on one another, regardless of what happens.

The intonation with which she pronounced the words was filled with determination. In truth, Mark knew that it was actually a promise she was making him, a promise to him and also to herself, and if he had been able to see his sister's eyes in that instant, he would have seen the light moving across her irises, like a horse whirling around in a miniature corral.

You'll tell me when you feel like you're ready?

A great noise rang out in the distance, lower sounding than the river, similar to the rumble of thunder, but the sky was clear.

What was that? asked Mabel.

Probably poachers fishing with explosives. Matthew's going to be in one of his rages when he finds out.

The birds had gone silent. A few droplets detached themselves from the vault of the arch, sparkling like salt crystals. After a moment, a jay cut through the silence; other birds followed.

That's strange, said Mark.

What's strange?

That we only heard it once.

Matthew first heard the far-off sound of an engine. The driver wasn't opening it up in any of his gears. At that morning hour, and on a Sunday, you didn't have to be a magician to know where he was heading.

Rifle in hand, Matthew made his way back up the river at a run, zigzagging between the trees, as nimble as a roebuck. Soon he arrived at a rocky ford where all sorts of wild animals had the habit of watering, listening to the mechanical sound typical of engine brakes. The vehicle was now descending the rugged path. Dripping with sweat, Matthew stretched out about a hundred feet from the ford, beneath a mugo pine. Stationed where he was, nothing would be able to elude him. His heart was beating at a frenetic pace. He concentrated on his breathing, chin glued to the stock of his weapon.

First off, he saw the white star with its five points painted on the hood of the Jeep. The driver maneuvered around to approach the bank in reverse. A few shadows came out to flatten themselves against the body of the Jeep before sliding to the ground. The taillights lit up a few feet away from the water, then went out at the same time as the engine. Two men got down from the Jeep and converged by the rear panel, atop of which were mounted a fuel can decorated with a skull and crossbones and a spare tire. Both of them held a bottle of beer in their hand, which they opened against the edge of the hatch. The caps clattered off the stones and came to rest like cheap party jewelry amid a drift of diamonds.

They looked at the water knowingly and complicitly as they sipped their beers. Matthew could make out their faces perfectly through the trees. He knew them. Maurice Renoir and Benji Salles both also worked at the quarry, two loudmouths that no one liked, and Matthew even less than most. Two perverse guys who made certain that they were always the ones to haze the new recruits, although management turned a blind eye to their stunts. Matthew had borne the consequences when he was hired. Mark had been spared, seeing that he worked in the offices. Their favorite gag consisted of stretching out the unfortunate victim naked on a heap of gravel and binding him to four stakes. They would then place a glass of nitroglycerin on his stomach, promising to set him free once an hour was up. Some of them had knocked over the glass, but all had ended up pissing themselves before they figured out it was nothing more than a glass of water. The ritual was well known, but because no one was sure what Renoir and Salles were capable of, people still wondered whether they might get the idea one day to put real nitroglycerin in the glass. The other workers didn't approve of their colleagues' misbehavior, but no one would have openly defied them, keeping a respectful distance, first of all because they answered to Joyce, but also so as not to miss any of the show.

The two men emptied their beers and threw the bottles on the ground. Only one of them shattered. Then Salles unlatched the hatch, and the hinges gave a rusty scream as he lowered the tailgate. Renoir pulled out a tarpaulin, unveiling a wooden crate equipped with two corded handles. They unloaded this warily and set it down next to the truck. At the sight of the engraved inscription, Matthew understood why Renoir had been driving so cautiously. Grenades dating back to the last war. Salles went back up to the front of the Jeep, opened the passenger-side door, and leaned in to grab two new beers from a cooler, throwing one to his pal, who caught it in midair. They hiked up the river a few hundred feet and stopped before a large natural basin, transparent and as smooth as glass. They continued to drink as they each smoked a cigarette, contentedly watching the abundant ripples from the feeding fish, the only thing that made evident the liquid state of the surface.

Their cigarettes finished, they tossed their butts in the water, knocked back the rest of their beers with a belch after each gulp, and then hurled the empty bottles over their shoulders in a matching gesture of nonchalance. They went back to the Jeep. Salles reached into the hold for a net with a long handle and set it down on the stones. Renoir withdrew the metal rod that was blocking the eyelet and tipped open the lid of the crate. The two men both knelt down.

Rage was roiling through Matthew's innards, a rage diffused by his blood. The river, too, was made up of blood, and if he didn't do anything, that black blood would soon emerge from the milky-white bodies of the fish that would be killed by the shock wave of the explosions. If Matthew didn't try something, that is how things would turn out, and the river would hate him, would surely even banish him for his failure. In that case, he would have to live with the stares of the dead upon him, or he would have to hide. The trees would no longer speak to him, the silence would crush him into the dirt, would forbid him forever from being one with the humus.

Sweat flowed down his forehead to his eyelids; he blinked his eyes to chase it away. The droplets slid down the bridge of his nose, reconvening between his lips in a stream of acidity, which he drank down without thinking. His blinking accelerated, and it was as if by chasing away the sweat, he was also chasing away the worst of what he had imagined, as if his rage was the only instrument that could succeed in making things right. The doubts that had been rushing around in his head gradually subsided, and everything became clear in a beam of loyalty toward the nature that had welcomed him, then communed with him.

Matthew felt a tingling sensation at the tips of his fingers, which spread through his arms and shoulders.

The anger and the rage grew no further. They transformed into a kind of foregone conclusion, a certitude. His eyelids went still, as if he was taking a photograph of what would never take place in this forest, at the banks of this river. Transformed into the savior of the entire valley, and not simply a man made of flesh and bone. He slowly shifted the lever of the Winchester's trigger guard, introduced a cartridge into the magazine, and pulled back the safety catch. Placing a finger on the trigger guard, he moved the sights from Renoir to Salles and back until he could no longer see them, only the crate. He aligned the crosshairs with the painted inscription. A pure light penetrated his mind and spread through him. In a fluid motion, his finger slid from the trigger guard to the trigger, and he squeezed without thinking of anything else. There was a terrible explosion. Matthew released the rifle and flattened his face into the moss. The echo of the blast wrapped itself around his brain. After a few seconds, he rolled onto his back, waiting for the calm to return. Never did he look in front of him, not out of cowardice but out of fear that he might recognize something human on the opposite bank.

Matthew was walking, stepping slowly the way a soldier walks as he leaves a battlefield, no longer sure of where his side is encamped. The rifle stuffed under his vest slowed his pace. The rays of the sun filtering in by way of the miniature holes that perforated his skin, and his skull having become porous to the fading explosion, which had since transformed into a stabbing rush of air. He would have liked the trees to speak to him, for them to sign off on his act, to not be confronted by reality so soon. But he was alone.

He stopped behind the curtain of poplars that was situated not far from the house. Waited. In need of some impetus from which to find his strength. Saw his mother step outside, a two-handed basket of laundry pressed against her hip. She skirted the porch, her silhouette lacerated by the leaves of the big yucca, before disappearing. Matthew took a long, deep breath, then moved off toward the house, crossing the empty porch and pushing open the door that his mother had left ajar. He walked straight ahead, not noticing Mark, who was leaning against the extinguished stove eating an apple.

Hey there! he said.

Matthew didn't respond. He reached the stairwell. Mark didn't insist, following him with his eyes, surprised that he hadn't brought back any fish that day, this boy who usually took the time to keep them up to date on the river's state; this brother who was now climbing the steps, as stiff as a monk walking through a cloister. Mark stared at the empty staircase a long while. He finished his apple and went outside to throw away the core, over the fence. He went back inside, climbed the stairs, and knocked on Matthew's door. Nobody answered. He knocked again, and then entered, despite not having been invited.

Matthew was sitting on the edge of the bed. He was cleaning his rifle with a rag coated in grease, his precise motions full of gentleness.

It seems the fish weren't biting today, said Mark in a light tone.

Matthew stopped rubbing the barrel. He fixed his brother with a cold and impenetrable look.

What?

I'm just saying that it's rare to see you come back empty-handed.

Matthew's hands began to tremble, and so he returned to rubbing his firearm with the rag.

I heard an explosion a while back, must have been poachers . . . Did you happen to run into them?

I didn't hear anything, and I didn't run into anyone.

It sure made a hell of a racket, carried all the way to the viaduct.

Matthew stopped his movements.

You were at the viaduct?

Yeah, sometimes I go down there.

Ah, sure...

You're looking pretty pale for some reason.

I must have caught a chill.

Generous sunlight lit the room. Mark stepped toward the window.

You ever get any use out of that? he asked, looking down at his mother by the washing line.

What do you mean?

Your rifle, you ever used it before? I've never seen you bring home any game.

Matthew went back to cleaning the weapon.

It isn't made for hunting, he said.

Mark turned back toward his brother.

What are you staring at me for? asked Matthew with aggression in his voice.

I can just see that something isn't right.

Matthew got up. He rolled his rifle up in a sheet and stowed it in the armoire, in behind a long winter coat that hung on a hanger.

If you haven't got anything else to say, I'd like to have a rest.

If that's what you want, Mark said after waiting a moment.

Matthew dried his hands with a clean cloth and put the cleaning materials away in a metal tin. Mark moved toward the door but stopped.

Matthew!

What is it now?

You know you can tell me anything, I'm your brother.

Go on, get out of here, and shut that goddamn door behind you, this house and its cold drafts.

Monday morning, Emily Renoir and Suzanne Salles went together to inform Lynch that their husbands had disappeared. It wasn't at all uncommon for them to go off on a bender, but up to that point they had always returned home before dawn. The law enforcement official was a man of around thirty with a polished look to him: he didn't smoke, he never touched a drop of liquor, and he wore in all situations that serious and detached air typical of people who are concerned about control and appearances. Always dressed to the nines when on duty, in his handsome beige uniform, and his hand would come to rest at regular intervals on the butt of the revolver that he wore on his belt in a custom-made leather holster, bought with his own pay. This gesture did not express any sort of edginess, it looked more like a sensual caress.

Following the visit by the two wives, Lynch drove out to the quarry in his car to interrogate Renoir and Salles's coworkers. He stopped by to inform Sokal about it, who felt the need to sit in on the interviews. Everyone was aware of the penchant the two men had for poaching and booze, but nobody knew a thing. That afternoon, Lynch went down to the dam and got the idea that he should examine the banks of the river, where the two men had the habit of hanging around. He left his car in the power station's lot and continued on foot along the water's left bank, careful not to make a mess of his lovely boots, freshly polished the night before. After he'd walked for about half an hour, a burning smell began to assail his nostrils. He slowed down, meticulously exploring the vicinity, seeking to discover the source. The first thing Lynch saw was a piece of sheet metal leaning against a boulder, kind of like a black tongue, then all sorts of debris scattered here and there; he stopped opposite a crater some dozen feet in diameter on the other bank. He began to turn around and around, feeling the excitement growing within him. He lowered his eyes to look at his boots. The water wasn't very deep near the ford, but he didn't cross there, he went back upriver to one of the basins, where there were large flat stones level with the surface. He jumped from one to the next without even getting his soles wet, then worked his way back down to the crater.

The hood of Renoir's Willys Jeep was wedged between the branches of a pine, nearly in one piece; with its white star, it hadn't flown too far. Other pieces of debris had been blown into the vegetation. Lynch reached the edge of the crater, a puddle of water stagnating at its center. All around it, the stones looked like pieces of smelting coke, and the calcified vegetation in the background looked like complex structures of dead coral. An odor became more and more pervasive, beyond that of the burnt smell, this one more overpowering, more repugnant. Lynch circled the crater. Enormous blue flies took off a few yards away from him. He stopped, and the flies landed again at the same spot. He approached the teeming heap, swung a kick through the air above the mass of flies, and they scattered with a uniform buzzing, revealing a great big piece of mangled, purplish-blue meat covered in eggs, as well as blackened fibers of flesh. A grin of disgust contorted his face. He took off his hat, positioning it in front of his face like a dust mask, then took a few steps back, the flies diving back in to continue laying their eggs on the flesh.

The lawman then moved over to the edge of the ford, placing his hat upside down on a rock, and sat on his heels, splashing his face with fresh water. Once the feeling of disgust had subsided, excitement again began to course through his veins. He put his hat back on his head, stood up straight, and wrapped his hand around the butt of his revolver. He tried to think through the scene of the accident. Renoir and Salles had hit the booze harder than they ought to have, had made their way out to the river to do some grenade fishing. They must have tempted fate and blown themselves up as well. End of story. Which was bound to happen one day, Lynch would add to anyone who felt like listening, as if he had foreseen the tragedy long before, with a tone so imbued with certitude that everyone would end up believing it, himself included. As simple as that. He would then describe the series of events in a report he would take to Joyce, before filing it away in a folder that would be clipped into the binder that sat above another that contained all the unsolved cases.

Back in town, Lynch headed to Doctor Hermann's office to share his discovery. The doc sent his patients away and followed Lynch, carrying his physician's bag. Together, they went to see the Duroc twins, who owned the only funeral business in town. Lynch gave a summary of the situation, after which the Durocs left to fill a watertight trunk with ice. The lawman took Hermann in his car and the two others followed in their hearse. Once they reached the forest, they followed the animal path down to the river, parking their vehicles a few yards away from the star-adorned hood.

Lynch pointed a finger at the spot on the other side of the passenger windshield, indicating that it was there he had found the human remains. The two men got out of their vehicle. The twins were already pulling on white overalls behind their hearse. Hermann went to inspect the site. Lynch didn't follow him. He watched the doc with a curious look while he chewed on a piece of licorice, his foot resting on the bumper. Hermann walked around the right side of the crater and leaned down at the same spot where Lynch had stopped a while earlier. Almost nonchalantly, he opened his kit bag and took out a sharp instrument similar to a knitting needle.

Once Hermann returned to the car, he told Lynch that he had confirmed the deaths of Renoir and Salles, but that he couldn't state in which order they had died.

What difference does that make? asked Lynch.

None, it's true, replied the doc, miffed that the other man hadn't caught his black humor.

Hermann had already had to treat patients who had been victims of Renoir and Salles's excesses, several of whom would suffer the consequences for the rest of their lives. He filled out two death certificates right there on the hood of the car and handed them to Lynch, who accepted them with a detached look.

Have you notified their widows? inquired the doctor.

Not yet.

I can take care of it if you would like.

No, I'll do it myself.

Hermann looked over at the crater. Lynch turned back to the twins, who were patiently waiting for the green light to proceed, each of them holding a large, black plastic bag.

You can get started! he said.

It's not going to be easy to tell one from the other, Hermann couldn't help but add.

Just make sure that there is about the same amount in each bag, said Lynch with great seriousness.

Okay! replied the Durocs in unison.

We're going to head back in, I'll come by and see you later.

The Durocs explored the site meticulously. They discovered more human remains, which they gathered up with care and without any visible emotion. From time to time they traded bags to test the weight, adding some to the one that seemed lighter so as to respect Lynch's orders. A while later, having completed combing the explosion site, they returned to the hearse, wrote "Renoir" and "Salles" on two labels, and affixed them to the bags, which they placed inside the trunk full of ice, then they set off. They reached town as quickly as possible and parked behind their shop. They unloaded the trunk and carried it into the cold room where they prepared the corpses.

Lynch informed Emily Renoir and Suzanne Salles of the news. They cried, and even as he tried his best to maintain a look of formality, he wondered what the point was in lamentations now that everything was said and done. Later that day, he accompanied them to the funeral home. The widows insisted on seeing the bodies. The Durocs looked at one another, aghast, the word "bodies" seeming so incongruous to them. Lynch hadn't told the widows everything. Without going into detail, the twins explained that given the state of the remains, it wouldn't be possible, that they were very sorry, that it would be better for them that way. Suzanne Salles wanted a further explanation. Jeff Duroc took her arm and led the haggard widow into an adjoining room where all sorts of caskets were displayed. Robert Duroc did the same with Emily Renoir. The two women selected the same model. The twins assured them that they would take care of transporting the coffins to the cemetery first thing the next morning; they would only need to wait for them there. They didn't argue. Lynch then reaccompanied them home, this time not getting out of the car.

FRANCK BOUYSSE

With Lynch and the widows gone, the twins promptly transferred the chosen caskets into the cold room. They placed a bag into each one, as well as a second bag they had filled with dirt beforehand, so that the total weight would be approximately that of a human body.

The day of the interment, the stink was already penetrating the multiple layers of plastic as well as the wood of the coffins, despite all the usual precautionary measures taken by the twins. Without waiting, they loaded the caskets into their hearse, then set off for the cemetery. The widows were waiting at the gate, dressed all in black. Emily Renoir had even painted her lips and her fingernails black. Salles's parents and Renoir's mother were also present.

Lynch and Hermann helped the twins carry the coffins, which they set on boards that had been placed across the freshly dug graves, separated by about sixty feet. The minister delivered two eulogies intended to honor the memory of the two men, adding a personal anecdote to justify his payment. Emily Renoir and Suzanne Salles sobbed through the entire ceremony. Apart from the immediate family, the few onlookers present for the burial were largely coworkers, come to make sure that it wasn't some practical joke, that Renoir and Salles were actually dead, that no one would have to endure their brutality any longer. Hermann resisted the temptation to throw in a witticism regarding the final ascension of

Renoir and Salles. Lynch, present at his side, wouldn't have understood the allusion anyway.

In the days that followed, Suzanne Salles and Emily Renoir grieved together around a table, sometimes at one home, sometimes at the other's. They had stopped crying relatively quickly, concerned above all about the loss of their status as the wives of spies in Joyce's employ. Neither had children yet. After the burial, they were never seen at the cemetery again.

The previous evening's paper was lying on the kitchen table with Renoir and Salles's faces on the front page. Their smiles didn't line up well with the headline: "Tragedy in the Black Rimstone." Mark grabbed the tabloid and left. Matthew was sitting on the front porch, busy repairing his lines. Mark took a seat next to him and set the newspaper down in plain sight between them. Matthew remained focused on his work.

You read this? asked Mark.

It's all anyone is talking about.

A stupid accident, or that's what they seem to be saying.

If that's what they're saying.

Mark leaned forward and picked up a weight, rolling it in the palm of his hand with a finger.

How about you, what do you say?

Matthew stretched a piece of fishing line, holding an end in his teeth.

You play with fire, you get burnt, he said coldly.

I'd imagine they were probably asking for it.

Matthew set to untangling a tricky knot. Mark reflected on what he was going to say next so that the conversation didn't stall out there. He knew his brother inside and out, his capacity to close up like a clamshell.

From what it sounds like, we're liable to find bits of them stuck to the viaduct, he said with a lighter tone.

I don't go to the viaduct anymore.

Maybe there will be a time again. After all, it was your idea to leave Mabel's rope suspended from it.

Matthew set the tangled line down between his legs. He stared straight out in front of himself, as if trying to disperse a vision so he could better withdraw into himself.

At the time, I thought it was a good idea, he said.

It was a good idea.

What do I know, I just don't go there anymore, that's all.

Mark placed the weight back in the box.

I've spoken to her, he said.

Matthew turned abruptly toward his brother.

To whom?

To the rope, sometimes it tells me things.

Maybe Dad isn't wrong when he says that you read too many books. It's messing with your head, said Matthew with a shrug.

I swear to you that it's true.

Mark let a moment of silence linger before he continued:

Last time, it told me that Renoir and Salles probably weren't alone when the fireworks went off.

Matthew nervously grabbed up another line to untangle.

And what else did it tell you, your fucking rope?

I figured you might be able to tell me instead.

Matthew's fingers froze. He tried to speak, but the words got caught in his throat, like iron filings on a magnet. It took him a few seconds to reverse the polarity.

What is it that you're wanting to hear, in the end?

Mark offered no reply, observing that another knot had clearly gotten snarled up in his brother's head, a knot that was a lot more difficult to undo than the ones in the fishing line.

It was an accident, he managed to say after a moment.

Mark placed a hand on his brother's shoulder.

I just wanted to throw a scare into them so that they wouldn't come back and pull their shit anymore. I don't even know what really happened, I swear.

You're sure that there was no one else there?

Matthew nodded his head. His eyes were the same uniformly pale color as dead fish.

Other than the rope, no, I don't think so, he said without the least trace of irony.

A muffled thump was heard under the flooring of the porch, a bang, and some scraping. Astounded, the two brothers saw Luke's head appear, then he slid all the way out of his hidey-hole. He got up, dusting off his clothing and looking at his brothers in turn, roguishly.

Holy mackerel, shiver me timbers, my lads, I sure would have loved to see those two jerks blown sky-high, it sure must have been something.

Shut up, for Christ's sake, said Mark, trying to stop himself from shouting.

Luke's head dipped down between his shoulders. Matthew seemed far away, as if he had nothing to do with the conversation.

I'm just saying that some men deserve to die, and who cares how it happens, added Luke, more quietly.

We mustn't talk about it anymore; it could cause really big problems for Matthew.

Okay, I won't say anything, you can count on me.

There was a long silence. A shadow came over Luke's face all at once.

Too bad Mabel's not here, he said.

Mark lowered his head at the mention of their sister. It wasn't yet the moment to bring up his reunion with her, the time would come, even if he thought that Luke was right: a secret shared by the four of them would have been less precarious.

L uke knew Renoir and Salles. One day, in search of his island, he had come across them at the river's edge. Staked out behind a thicket, he had watched them, convinced that they were up to no good. He had heard via Matthew that the two cretins often used explosives to fish. Luke wasn't buying it. He was clever enough to guess that they, too, were searching for the treasure by making holes in the river. Luke suspected that they gathered up the fish that floated to the surface, bellies up, to hoodwink everyone and make a bit of extra money to supplement their wages, but figured that the true goal of the operation was to discover the pirates' booty. According to his brother, everyone knew the sort of stuff they were into, even Lynch, who had always turned a blind eye. Who knows, maybe he was even in cahoots with them.

That time, Renoir and Salles hadn't used explosives, but an enormous car battery with two wires that had electrodes at the end which they dipped into the water. Luke didn't really understand how you could make a treasure appear with electricity, unless it was capable of things he didn't know about. He stayed long enough to make certain that the treasure didn't surge up out of the depths from a blast of the juice. Numerous fish surfaced, like air bubbles. At the least, because of the violence they had done to the river, the two morons wouldn't end up in heaven. Couldn't even just use a shovel and a pickax. The easy road had led them to go out with a big *bang*!

Luke made his way out to the viaduct that afternoon. He didn't linger there long, just cast a glance at the suspended rope. He followed the bank downstream. Insects were stridulating in the tall grasses, which were tormented by the breeze that rushed up that ceilingless corridor paved with water. Luke halted quite often, crouching down for a minute or two, his hands flattened against the tufts of green printed on the arable page of the incunabular riverside. He observed all sorts of insects coming and going, like plankton between the baleens of a placid cetacean. A worthy believer, reciting the Song of Songs in his head without having learned any of the words, simply attentive to the invisible signs that were shared by all living things. Walking, stopping, and starting again. From station to station, he advanced toward the animal ford. When he arrived, he knelt down, grating his teeth together to imitate the cricket's song. And again. Seeing as there was no response, he stood back up. Heard a door slam shut. Luke slipped away, weaving between the trees, then stretched out beneath the ancient trunk of a fallen pine. Watching in the direction from which the noise had seemed to originate.

Lynch appeared on the opposite bank. He was walking on his tiptoes, his eyes riveted to the ground, as if waiting for something to be revealed to him without knowing what it was, something specific that would be offered up to him without him even having to displace a pebble. Not a true pirate, thought Luke. Just a shady, run-of-the-mill sheriff who wanted to seem important. Luke had already remarked that a lot of people sought above all to make themselves appear to be important in the eyes of others. Ultimately, they don't really know where to set their feet, but seeing that they can't remain in the air for long, they always end up setting them down somewhere, and think that that somewhere somehow belongs to them. It was Lynch's kind of thing not to remain in the air for long. Not being a pirate didn't make him less dangerous. His obstinate way of nosing around seemed like trouble to Luke. The sheriff had the law on his side, and the power that backed that up. The boy forgot about his cricket.

Luke hated Lynch as much as Renoir and Salles. One day in town, Lynch had forced him to pick up the dirty papers that were scattered around Joyce Main, insisting that he had seen him toss one of them, even though it wasn't true, which he knew full well. Luke never discarded anything in the street, or anywhere else for that matter, other than in a garbage can. He couldn't understand why Lynch had falsely accused him, or what sort of satisfaction he could have gotten from it. He had tried to defend himself, and Lynch had simply added a further stretch of street to what he had to clean up, saying that the more he protested, the longer the list would get. Luke had looked around for allies, but the scarce few witnesses who were passing nearby had turned their backs and vanished. Lynch enjoyed humiliating the weak. His face made this clear. *It's easy to devise injustices when you're wearing a badge.* If he had been able, Luke would have ripped it off him, as he felt that Lynch didn't deserve to wear it, but everyone knows that dunces aren't nasty in the least. He had to continue to cultivate that appearance. It would eventually render him invisible, even in town, the same as it did there in the woods.

After the funerals, Lynch expedited his routine business, then went over to Samuelson's in the evening. He took a seat in a booth near the bay window that gave on to the street, as was his habit. Maguy Samuelson came to take his order of pork in gravy with fried potatoes. As she jotted this down in her notebook, Lynch remarked with distaste the traces of an ancient, chipped coat of varnish that remained on her coarse fingernails. The old woman tore the page off and went over to set it on the service counter. She ducked down, and her head disappeared through the opening. Lynch heard her say his name to her husband, who was back in the kitchen. A few minutes later, Maguy Samuelson returned with a steaming plate, which she wearily set down in front of Lynch. He tucked a corner of his napkin into the collar of his shirt, stretching it out meticulously so as not to stain his handsome uniform, and started to eat.

Two seats over, facing him, Michelle Colbert was delighting in some vanilla ice cream in a glass coupe. She was a pretty girl, barely twenty years old, and had a reputation for being up for just about anything. Once the spoon was in her mouth, she turned it upside down, then pulled it back out slowly, bringing her eyes up to rest on Lynch, who remained stone-faced. When he had swallowed his last bite, he folded his napkin into four equal sections, set it down next to the plate, which had been scraped clean, and stared insistently at Michelle Colbert until she noticed. He made a sign with his hand, smiling. The young girl feigned surprise, glanced briefly around her, as if looking around the restaurant to see if there was someone else that Lynch might be inviting to join him. He motioned again. She hesitated a moment before getting to her feet, and then went over to sit across from him, setting down one butt cheek and then the other, still wriggling once settled on the bench seat. He asked her what she would have to drink. She ordered a martini. Lynch poured himself a glass of water. He observed the young girl with curiosity. She simpered, playing at being timid, and rather badly. She drank a little gulp and mentioned the discovery of the bodies, gushing about the courage it must have taken Lynch. He accepted the flattery without really finding any pleasure in it.

The conversation stopped short. Lynch promptly regretted having invited the young girl over. She finished drinking her martini and leaned forward to ask if he felt like accompanying her home. It was late, and she was afraid to walk the dark streets at night. Just think, a defenseless young girl, who knows what could happen to her if she should happen on some wrongdoers, she added. Without knowing why, Lynch agreed to drive her home in his official vehicle. She was very excited by the idea.

Michelle Colbert still lived with her parents. She told Lynch to stop some fifty yards before the house, and he parked without turning off the engine. She remained seated there, fiddling with a tiny bag on a gold chain. The situation no longer amused Lynch in the least. He wanted her to get out of the car. He thought she was pathetic, and vulgar: in her way of moving, of speaking, even her silences were vulgar. He dryly wished her a pleasant evening once again. Michelle Colbert turned briskly away from the car door, and her elbow bumped against the instrument panel. She wriggled to avoid the gearshift and moved even closer to Lynch. Surprised by the incursion, he couldn't react and found himself pinned down by the young woman's bust. She kissed him right on the mouth, shoving a greedy tongue between his lips. He found the contact revolting, as if a slimy and panicked creature was trying to find a passage to his throat. He pushed the young woman away, stretched out an arm to open the passenger door, and ordered her to get out immediately.

Michelle Colbert clambered out of the vehicle, disconcerted. She asked Lynch what there was about her that didn't appeal to him, and he replied, "Everything," before taking off at full throttle. He saw her adjust her skirt in the rearview mirror. As he watched the trembling reflection of the girl dwindle, he told himself that he deserved much better.

Matthew had always been happy enough with his lot in life. All through the long workdays, he thought of nothing more than finding himself back by the river, amid the silence he was deprived of by all the men. The only voices he could stand were those of his brothers, his sister, and his grandfather. He didn't need much in order to live, wasn't chasing after any sort of manufactured happiness, having never experienced that word within a human community, not even his own family. He wasn't looking for anything that wasn't completely separate from these hardworking men whom he worked next to every day at the quarry, with their ludicrous aspirations, born of sterile jealousy and stunted desire for the most part. Matthew wasn't jealous of anyone. He envied the birds, capable of ascending to a considerable height, simply because of the thought of being able to see the world differently. To be able to soar high above his house, the quarry, the plant, the dam, and the town, all the structures that Matthew had for a long time relegated to the rank of evils.

No one was suspicious of him. Since the death of Renoir and Salles, tongues had loosened up some. This would only last until other spies in Joyce's employ came to take their place. Then silence would reign once more. Matthew never involved himself in the conversations. Listened to them at times. In doing so, he was quick to note that by ridding the earth of the noxious presence of the two men, he had contributed to fertilizing certain minds, to kindling some doubts. Some were speaking in terms of signs, not venturing much further. If they had known that Matthew had meted out justice in the names of all, they would probably have looked at him differently, but instead they still didn't see him at all.

Matthew regretted no part of what he had done, only that he had lied about it to his brother. He often thought of the moment he had aimed at the crate of explosives and pulled the trigger, becoming the bullet himself, the extension of his will. It had taken him nights of chaos and sweat-drenched awakenings to finally admit to himself that he had even enjoyed that instant. Judge and executioner in the same fraction of a second. He felt no guilt, and worried even less about who might judge him, about who would pronounce the sentence his mother had promised for any transgression, according to her simplistic conception of good and evil. He couldn't entertain the idea that men could judge him, and he didn't venerate the same god as his mother. He had slammed shut the door to one heaven. He preferred a different one, peopled by trees and animals and earth and rocks and water. He kept all of this to himself, hidden behind his dark scowl.

After polishing his report numerous times, Lynch went to put it in Joyce's hands personally. Joyce read it carefully in his presence, then handed it back to him without any commentary whatsoever, dismissing him with a gesture of his arm.

Every day that week, Lynch returned to the site of the explosion. The prevailing odor of rot no longer bothered him. He had discovered a hunk of flesh missed by the Durocs, a cracked bone jutting from it like a stump sticking out of festering gums. He wondered to which of them, Renoir or Salles, the fragment belonged. He refrained from speaking of it to anyone, especially to the widows, who may have argued over who should have it. As time passed, Lynch noted the evolution of the putrefaction, and found it regrettable that it changed so quickly. He had come to consider that place as the true communal grave of Renoir and Salles, an anonymous sepulchre that suited them well. When he paid the site a visit, he didn't pray for the saving of their souls, but instead thanked them for having blown themselves up to add a little spice to his life.

That Saturday evening, when the sun sat atop the crowns of the trees, its rays stabbing into the earth here and there, Lynch's eye was caught by a gleam on the opposite bank. It was probably nothing, but he wanted to be certain of it. He walked back up the river, crossed on the flat stones, and went back down the other bank to the ford. One of the Jeep's rearview mirrors had been flung there by the explosion. Lynch picked it up, noticing that the mirrored surface was no longer present. Before he left, he explored the vicinity, in case anything else might have escaped him. He thought he saw a shape disappear in the distance, between the trees. Animals were plentiful in the area. He took a couple of steps into the tree cover, clapping his hands together. No further sign of movement. He lowered his head instinctively to check the state of his boots. Hardly three feet in front of him lay a small metal object, contrasting with the moss and the twigs. He hunched down over what he identified to be a cartridge casing. He picked up a pine needle, threaded it into the hollow end, and took a long look at it, turning it around at eye level. It wasn't rusted. He stood up, took off his hat, and placed the cartridge inside. He stared across at the other side of the river, and a smile stretched across his clean-shaven face. Lynch didn't believe in chance, and even less in coincidence. The cartridge couldn't belong to a simple hunter. The scene of the accident had just been transformed into the exciting scene of a crime.

Once he had made it back to his car, Lynch took a plastic bag from the glove box, slid the cartridge into it, and stuffed both into his shirt pocket, redonning his hat. A shiver made its way up his spine. He cast a final look toward the charred memorial and drove off.

S tanding on the porch, leaned against one of the posts, Luke was staring at the open gate. He went back into the house regularly to read the time on the clock, then went straight back out. His lower lip was bleeding in several spots and he continually ran his tongue along it. Once he spotted the silhouettes of his brothers forming in the distance, he hurtled down the stairs and ran out to meet them. Without any additional commentary, he asked them to follow him. Matthew stopped him in his tracks, too tired from his day's work. Mark proposed they go talk in his room, but Luke lost his temper:

For once in my life I'm asking you to do something.

Where do you want to take us? asked Matthew in a tired voice.

You'll see, just don't argue with me!

Luke set off, followed by his brothers. They rejoined the river, avoiding the viaduct, and headed in the direction of the animal ford. As they gradually drew nearer to it, Matthew grew more and more nervous. Luke came to a stop on the bank opposite where the explosion had taken place. The blood had dried on his lips, and he turned toward his brothers with a sad look pasted across his face.

What is it that you have to tell us? asked Matthew, in a hurry to be done with it.

You wouldn't have told me anything if I hadn't over-heard you the other day, it's true, isn't it?

We just didn't want to bother you with the whole thing.

Luke bit his lip, and a drop of fresh blood started to bead up once again.

More like you don't trust me.

Of course we trust you . . .

You don't trust me because I'm a dunce.

We've never thought you were a dunce, said Mark.

I don't know if I should believe you anymore.

We won't hide anything from you again, we promise.

Is that the truth?

We're telling you . . . You didn't have to drag us all the way out here to tell us that, said Matthew.

Sure I did!

Good, well, that's settled, can we go home now?

That's just it, no, it's not quite settled.

What else?

Lynch, he comes here every day . . . This morning, I saw him bend down to pick up something . . . I was too far away to see what . . . Over there, said Luke, indicating the base of a pine.

Matthew hurried over to the tree at a run, then got down on all fours to inspect the area at the foot of the tree.

Sonofabitch, what an ass, what an ass, he repeated.

What's the matter? asked Mark.

Matthew got back up.

The cartridge, I didn't think of picking it up, that must be what Lynch found.

So what? How's he going to trace it back to you?

It's not a common caliber. When I bought the gun, it was recorded at the gunsmith's shop. And my prints will be on the cartridge.

You can't be the only person in the region to have that kind of gun.

I have no idea.

For the moment, all Lynch has is a rifle cartridge that very well could have been used hunting rabbits.

I know him, he's not going to stop there.

Don't panic, we'll get out ahead of it, now that we know, said Mark, resting a hand on Luke's shoulder.

I'll keep Lynch under surveillance, said Luke.

If you want, but be discreet so that you don't tip him off to anything.

There's no one more discreet than me.

Matthew was no longer listening to his brothers, already imagining the worst.

The next evening, Luke returned home later than his brothers. He found them inside, along with their grandfather, already seated at the table. His mother was preparing dinner. He shot a complicit look at Matthew, then at Mark, and then he walked back outside. The other two followed him. Luke led them behind the curtain of poplars that lined the path.

You have some news? shot out Matthew, impatient.

Luke waved his hands around a moment, as if trying to catch in midflight the words he needed.

I followed Lynch all day long, as planned.

He took a moment to calm down, gathering his thoughts.

This morning, he went to have a coffee at Samuelson's. He sat next to the window to read the newspaper. He kept looking at his watch, and now and then, looking outside. The news didn't really seem to be interesting him. He checked the time once more before he got up. I followed him. He went straight to the gun shop. There was a little sign on the door. He went up to read what was written on it. He tried to open the door, but it was locked. He stood there for a while looking at the street.

A guy walked by, Lynch asked him something, but the guy didn't seem to know. It was obvious that Lynch was pissed off.

Luke interrupted himself once again. A scowl contorted his face.

I don't think he likes anyone at all. You remember when mother told us that the Good Lord put everyone on earth for a specific reason. With Lynch, I don't think it was a smart idea on God's part, or maybe he's just not all that good . . .

And after that? What did he do next? asked Matthew to cut short his brother's digression.

He left. I went over to the shop door, and there was a clockface with the hands stopped at five. I followed Lynch to his office. I waited. The church bell rang noon. He came back out. He went back over to Samuelson's. He had a bite and read the paper again, or maybe he hadn't finished it earlier, I have no idea. It made me awful hungry to watch him, but I didn't want him to see me, and anyway I didn't have a cent on me. When I get too hungry, I try to think about something more important than food and it ends up going away. It wasn't all that hard this time around.

Luke let his arms drop down to his sides and his shoulders sunk as well.

Go on, said Mark.

Luke remained like that for a handful of seconds. He rubbed his cheeks, pressing hard against them, and the blood rushed in under his skin.

When Lynch was done eating, he went back over to his office. He didn't leave again until later in the afternoon. He went directly to see the gun seller. This time, the shop wasn't closed. I went and stood by the corner of the window. At first, all I could see was my own reflection, because of the sun, so I stuck my nose right up against the glass and I put my hands on either side of my eyes and it got clear inside. The first thing I saw was a whole pile of guns and knives and stuff, in the front window display. Farther in, there was Lynch, and he was showing a little clear pouch that had the cartridge inside it. The shopkeeper tried to grab it, but Lynch pulled it out from under his nose. He gave him enough time to look it over carefully. The other guy didn't try to take the pouch from him again, and then right away he went off to get his sales book. Lynch put the cartridge back in his shirt pocket. He sucked on the tip of his pencil. The shopkeeper started to flip through the pages of his book. When he stopped every now and then to point out a spot in the book with his finger, Lynch started to write stuff down. I counted the number of times with my fingers, one hand, without the pinkie. Then the shopkeeper closed his book. Lynch read over what he had written in his notebook. He kept touching the pocket where he had put the cartridge. It was weird to see him doing that. He looked really pleased with himself. He put the notebook back in his jacket. I quickly went over to stand on the other side of the street. When Lynch was back outside, he didn't leave right away, he just stayed in front of the window, with his arms folded behind his back, looking around like he was all alone in the middle of nowhere. He adjusted his hat and placed his hand on the butt of his revolver. He was obviously trying to look like a cowboy out on the middle of the Great Plains, but he didn't really look like one. I don't think he'll ever manage to look like that, even with the show he's always putting on. I might have something missing in my head, but there's definitely a name in his notebook that we don't want to be there, isn't there?

The good news is that there are three others, said Mark.

I'm not really as optimistic about it as you are, said Matthew.

You did what was needed with your rifle?

Yes, but I'm still pretty worried about it, as long as Lynch has that cartridge.

Luke stared at Matthew with intensity, as if he had just understood something, then he gathered together his ideas and went back to his story.

I'm not done, he said.

What else? asked Matthew.

I kept following Lynch, that's why I'm only getting home right now. He went back to his office. He came back out a long time later. He brushed his hand across his clothes, but it didn't look like they were dusty at all. He started walking really fast. He stopped in Joyce 8 and knocked on a door. A girl opened up. He took off his hat. She stayed there on the landing. She didn't invite him in, or he didn't ask to go in. In any case, he didn't seem to insist. It was like it was enough for him to stand there looking at the girl from the bottom of the stairs. He often looks up at people from below. The girl didn't look happy or unhappy, with this guy standing in front of her who had come to see her and who she mustn't have invited. He was talking, I could see it from his lips moving. I was too far away to hear. Her lips, they only moved at the very end, when he was putting his hat back on his head and touching a finger to its brim. And then he left. The girl watched him, making a really weird face. She didn't really look happy to see him leave, so I figured that it wasn't because he was leaving, but because he was probably going to come back. I'd bet on that. I really wanted to go tell that girl to steer clear of him, but I needed to remain invisible, and not to take my eyes off Lynch.

This girl, did you know her? asked Mark.

No, I didn't know her.

That asshole, if he didn't have his badge, he'd be nothing more than a piece of shit to avoid on the sidewalk, said Matthew.

Yeah, asshole, repeated Luke, but there's something that he doesn't know.

What is it that he doesn't know? asked Matthew.

That I can turn invisible, like Jim in the apple barrel.

Lynch turned up at the Volny place when they were having breakfast. He exchanged a few banalities with Martin and ignored Elie at the end of the table, who didn't take his eyes off him. Martha poured him a cup of coffee, and he asked for a bit of milk, "for a bit of color," he added.

We don't have any milk, replied Martha.

That's okay.

Lynch drank two or three sips as he eyeballed everyone.

You sure make for a beautiful family, the lot of you . . . Yes, a really beautiful family.

His gaze stopped on Matthew.

How're things going at the quarry?

They're fine, replied Matthew, grabbing his cup of coffee in one hand and looking inside of it.

I'd imagine that the morale must not be at its high point, after what happened. It's so tragic, Lynch said, shaking his head contritely.

I just do my work, that's all. I don't ask anyone for anything.

And damn well, too, I'm sure. Now tell me, my boy, I've heard it said that you own one of those old Winchesters, .44 caliber, unless I'm mistaken. Is that so?

You're not mistaken.

Not terribly practical for hunting, a gun of that caliber.

I don't hunt with it.

You don't hunt with it.

Lynch made is if he was thinking this over, tapping a finger rhythmically against the edge of the table.

Then why do you have a rifle, in that case?

Who doesn't, in these parts?

Now isn't that the truth, but it's not exactly commonplace "in these parts," a gun like that, you only see those in westerns these days. A real collector's piece.

I'm not a collector, Matthew said dryly.

It seems to be making you nervous for me to talk about this.

Just what is all this nonsense about, anyway? fired Elie.

You shut your mouth! volleyed Lynch without even looking at the old man.

Elie didn't pursue it. Lynch softened his tone.

Could I take a look at this rifle?

Everyone fell silent. Nobody understood what was going on, other than the brothers. Luke had his nose in his coffee mug, and Mark was bolstering his brother with his eyes. Matthew pushed back his chair, got to his feet, and went up to his room.

He returned shortly after with the rifle wrapped in a sheet.

It's not loaded, at least? asked Lynch with a smile.

Probably not, said Matthew, holding out the weapon.

Lynch gave a doubtful frown.

Take off that rag!

Go right ahead.

Hurry up, boy!

Matthew grudgingly obeyed. Lynch took a pair of leather gloves out of his jacket pocket, pulled them on, grabbed the rifle, and inspected it from every angle. Then he tried the trigger guard lever, noting the absence of any resistance. He examined the mechanism closely, pulled it back and brought it forward several times, still with no results. The aggravation was visible on his face.

It's broken, said Matthew.

Since when? asked Lynch, still looking the weapon over.

At least a year.

Why don't you get it fixed?

Ain't easy to find the original parts.

Lynch turned his eye from the stock to the barrel.

A whole year where it hasn't been of any use to you, and yet you still take good care of it, it's nicely oiled and everything.

I bought it myself, I have high hopes of repairing it one day.

So it's got some sentimental value, then.

What's got you all worked up about this rifle? demanded Martin, exasperated.

In the moment, Lynch didn't seem to even notice the question; he placed the stock cover against the floor and sniffed at the inside of the barrel. Another disappointed pout. He then turned toward Martin, as if he had just suddenly remembered the question.

I've been charged with making an inventory of the older weapons in the region . . . for an exhibition.

And how is it that you were aware of it?

Lynch offered no reply. He rubbed the tip of his nose with his middle finger, then got up. Once he was on his feet, he held the rifle out to Matthew.

One more thing, since you go fishing so often, you didn't happen to notice anything the day Renoir and Salles blew themselves up?

Notice what?

I've no idea, I'm asking you.

We were all at the viaduct, we spent the afternoon down there, interjected Mark.

I'm speaking to your brother, said Lynch, without turning his eyes away from Matthew.

It's true, that's where we were.

And you didn't hear anything?

With all the noise from the river, nothing at all.

Did they release any water that day?

Same as every Sunday.

Even so, it must have made a hell of a racket . . . And what about you, you didn't hear anything? Lynch asked, turning abruptly toward Luke.

Luke flinched and began to shake his head, still look-ing inside his mug.

If you're done, we'd very much like to finish our breakfast so that we can get off to work, said Martin.

Lynch gave him a condescending look.

I'll be the one who decides when I'm done.

A few seconds went by in silence, then Lynch turned back to Matthew.

I'll be taking the rifle with me.

Lynch moved toward the door, and turned back once he had reached the threshold.

Thank you for the coffee, ma'am, you might consider getting some milk for the next time, he added before he stepped outside.

What's this story with the rifle? asked Martin after a moment had passed.

I have no idea, replied Matthew.

Why did you say that it hasn't been working for a whole year? I saw you with it just last week.

It's true, I just find it comforting to have it with me.

Martha, whose presence everyone had forgotten, stood up. They all watched her cross the room in long strides and go up the stairs. She came back down shortly after, carrying the Old Testament. She went over to Mat-thew and placed the Good Book on the table in front of him. Then, unceremoniously, she took up her son's right hand and brought it down to rest on the cover.

Swear that you haven't done anything wrong! she said.

Matthew's hand went rigid. The extremities of the cross that poked out from under it looked like a splinter sticking out of his flesh. The tension, already palpable after Lynch's visit, rose in a crescendo. They heard a dry crack. Elie had just slammed the steel tip of a crutch down against the floor. He started in again, his face swollen with rage.

He will not swear to anything, goddammit!

Swear! repeated Martha, without paying any attention to her father's invective.

He will not swear to anything, I tell you, you crazy old witch!

Martha remained silent, now looking at her father in astonishment.

And take that blasted book back where you got it from, or else it will be me swearing that I'll make you eat it, added Elie.

Martha shot a distraught look at her husband. Stone-faced, Martin got his cigarette pack out of the central pocket of his overalls, slid one of them between his lips, lit it, got up, and left. Martha remained there petrified for a few more seconds. Luke got up next, went over to where Matthew sat, and pushed the book toward his mother, out of his brother's reach.

Crazy old witch, he said, croaking like a parrot.

Matthew maneuvered the bin full of stone so that it tipped over into the crusher's hopper, then let his gaze wander the length of the conveyor belt, which was pouring the gravel onto the top of a giant heap. A pyramid, planted in a mournful valley with no king, tirelessly pillaged down to its core by the bulldozers, and then tirelessly built back up. He thought back to Lynch's visit. On his way to the quarry, Mark had again tried his best to reassure him, insisting that there was no way a usable print could remain on the cartridge. All the same, Matthew couldn't stop himself from imagining the worst as he watched the stones from the broken rock roll down the hill like the bodies of sacrificial victims.

Hey you, over there, we don't pay you to daydream!

Matthew turned his eyes toward the source of the voice. The crew foreman was standing on an access ramp above him, leaning over the guardrail. Matthew could distinguish the sun-drenched and rocky crater that pressed down on his shadow, but the shadow did not burn, and did not fall. The man shouted an order. Matthew brought the hopper back into position, released the safety lock, and then directed the cart along the unloading rails to make room for another one. His thoughts continued to move around a closed circuit.

When it was time to clock out, Matthew went to pick Mark up at his post, and off they went. Luke was waiting for them at the entrance to the quarry.

What are you doing here? asked Mark.

Luke didn't reply. He had a feverish look to him. He held an index finger to his lips, and with a gesture of his hand, made a sign for his brothers to follow him. They walked beside the fence that ran along the earthen path with its ruts full of gravel, gashes that had the look of wounds that had been dressed in the springtime, had dried out in summer, and been reopened by the first rains of autumn. At the corner of the fence, they quit the path and pushed on into the woods, driven on by an overexcited Luke. After a few hundred yards, they were within sight of the viaduct. Luke stopped and turned toward his brothers.

Do you have something new to tell us? asked Matthew.

Luke nodded his head up and down, without unsealing his lips.

Go on, we're listening, nobody can hear us.

Luke opened his lips, letting a small, pale metal disc show between his teeth. He then cupped a hand in front of his chin, spat out the cartridge from the Winchester, and swallowed his saliva.

Holy shit, how'd you manage to pull that off? asked Matthew, rushing toward his brother to take the cartridge.

Luke was radiating happiness.

No one pays any attention to a dunce. They're terribly clumsy, dunces, they fall flat on their faces at the drop of a hat, and of course they have to find something to grab onto . . . and anyone, even a Lynch, will do the trick.

How did you know that he still had it on him?

This morning, at the house, I noticed that he was caressing his shirt pocket. I've seen him do it before. So I figured it still had to be there. So, I went into town. Lynch was at Samuelson's. I kept watch. I waited until he was leaving and then I went crashing into him. We both went down in the entrance. Once we were on the ground, I swiped the cartridge from him by grabbing onto him to pull myself up. He didn't realize a thing. They sure are clumsy, those dunces!

Matthew hugged Luke in his arms, then pushed him away and held him by the shoulders.

You're the best of us all, he said.

Shiver me timbers, I would have loved to see the look on his face when he couldn't find the cartridge, said Luke, roaring with laughter.

You should probably avoid going into town any time soon, Lynch will definitely see that something's up, said Mark.

Don't worry, I've got no reason to go there anymore.

Luke's face clouded over. He wasn't laughing anymore; he was looking at the river.

It's beautiful, huh? he said, motioning to the flowing water that wound its way around the great rocks before continuing on its way beneath the trees.

Amazing, said Matthew.

It would be even more beautiful if Mabel was here, added Luke.

Emotion brought a tremble to his voice.

I've seen her, said Mark, who couldn't keep quiet about it any longer.

Luke grabbed his brother's arm.

You saw Mabel and you didn't say anything to us?

I was going to, but so many things have been happening since . . .

Where is she?

I ran into her in town.

How is she?

Good.

You hearing this? said Luke, turning toward Matthew. But then again, you probably already knew, didn't you?

No, I didn't know anything.

What else did she tell you?

That she hasn't forgotten us and she misses us.

When is she going to come and see us?

Soon, but for the moment she's very busy with her job.

What job?

She's a waitress at The Admiral.

What if we all went there together? said Luke.

She wants to meet up with us here, like before.

When?

Soon, don't worry about it.

Luke stared off into space.

So she's not mad at me anymore?

She was never mad at you...

I hope she keeps her word.

When has Mabel ever promised us something and not followed through? said Matthew.

Luke's eyebrows joined above the bridge of his nose, then he slowly wrapped his fingers around something that didn't exist as of yet, but that he wished for with the same fervor that his brothers did. They all looked up at the rope in silence. A falcon appeared in the sky above them, swooping down on a wood pigeon. At the impact, a cloud of feathers fluttered through the air, and the bird of prey used its wings like a parachute to alight on a boulder. It set to rending with its beak the flesh grown tender in death, perpetually keeping an eye on its surroundings, like a sentinel.

It's true, you're right, she always keeps her promises, added Luke.

The blade of the knife slipped, and a red stain promptly colored the potato peel. Martha brought her injured finger to her mouth. She had always liked the taste of blood. She wondered if other people's blood tasted the same as hers did, and why the sight of it was so traumatizing for most people, whereas for her, it represented a commemoration of the suffering endured by the Son of God, as if the blood that had flowed from his own hands, from his feet and his side, were the incarnation of the boundless source of all spilled blood. And so she tried to convince herself that the taste in her mouth was the same as the blood of Christ, suffering, dead, and risen.

Martha was thinking back on the morning's conversation, which is why she had trembled and how she had cut herself. Her father had never before spoken to her like that. What right did he have? It wasn't only her that he had insulted, in reality, but also and above all else the Holy Book; and Martin, who had remained mute, who hadn't raised a finger to defend her, had even seemed to take some pleasure in her humiliation. Clearly the world was losing its religious conscience. Martha had already noticed this when she attended Mass. There were fewer and fewer people at the services. The voice of the pastor resonated in an ever-growing emptiness, and that emptiness never stopped eating away at Martha's arid belly, with its mute powerlessness. Nobody understood her, not at home any more than anywhere else. Was it in large part her own fault? Must she pay again and again for her failings? Bringing four apostles into the world was evidently not enough to sanctify her black blood, to hold at bay the diabolical presence of the spider, which never ceased expanding its kingdom, as if all the water held at check by the dam so as to bring forth an artificial light was in its very nature an inhibitor of faith. It was the spider and her succubus Joyce who were the truly guilty ones, the demons. Before, everything had been different, the hoped-for light had come from the sky, not from the water. What could Martha do against that, other than take things into her own hands when it came to her family, to reunify them around the sublime plan of the almighty Lord our Savior?

She cast a glance at the cut, already reduced to two little bloodless lips. She picked another potato out of the basket and held it in the palm of her hand. Her splayed fingers looked like strangling roots. She began to peel the tuber from top to bottom, turning it mechanically, no longer even thinking about her cut, which was now plugged with starch. Dropped the potato into a basin full of water and started on another, accelerating her rhythm as she went. The stake she had set fire to inside her head, she had set it ablaze so that it could burn away the blasphemies she had heard, as well as her shame for not having found a way to face them with dignity.

The door opened and then shut again. Martha turned her head without even raising it. Saw the big shoes draw near, the little clumps of dirt that fell from their cleats, molded in the shape of tiny bricks, dark and varied, swept along by the cuffs of the overalls as they dragged across the floor. Martin sat down at the table. He clapped his hands to his chest, then slid them inside the front section of his overalls. As if his arms had suddenly atrophied. Martha finally raised her eyes to look at him.

Why didn't you say anything this morning?

He's your father, it's your business, the both of you.

Since when, exactly, is my business not yours as well?

Martin slid his hands out of the overalls and placed them on the table, like tools taken out without a discernable goal.

Far too long for me to remember exactly when, and it seems to me you're just as responsible for that as I am.

Martha picked up another potato.

"Responsible," isn't it more guilty that you mean to say?

Guilt isn't really a luxury that people like us can afford.

And do you think Matthew's responsible for something serious?

Can you see our son shooting someone?

Martha didn't reply, holding the potato in one hand and the knife in the other, frozen.

It's been a while since we stopped talking to each other, added Martin.

Martha doubted that the remark was destined for her son.

You should try to talk to him about it, she said.

What would that change?

It's our job to keep watch over what goes on in this family.

Martin brought his fists together, pushing one against the other.

This family, don't you see what's happened to it?

You've always been as close to your sons as the sun is to the moon.

And your daughter, why don't you ever talk about her?

No reason to anymore.

I'm sorry I wasn't there the day you threw her out.

And just what would you have done?

Martin looked at his wife the same way he would have looked into the water from the riverbank, trying to see all the way to the bottom, but not being able to make out a thing. He took out his cigarette pack, still observing Martha, who had gone back to peeling the potato. He knew that she didn't like him to smoke in the house. He took out a cigarette, lit it, inhaled deeply, and then blew a thick curl of smoke in her direction. With the hand that held the knife, she fanned at the smoke, her lips pursed in disgust.

You know what, Martha, I think your father's right.

Martin let his words hang there. He got up, walked toward the door with a heavy step, and hesitated briefly before he passed outside.

Martha served them each a fried egg and some navy beans. She poured coffee into their cups, and then into her own. Sat down at the table, set a sugar cube onto a teaspoon, dipped it in, half submerging it in the coffee, watching it melt and take on the brownness. She mixed it in, scraping her spoon across the inside edge, and once she had finished, raised her eyes to look at the men busy eating in silence, using large hunks of bread to mop up the yolk that colored their lips. Her gaze stopped on Martin. She could make out his eyes, two failing sparks behind the steam that rose from his cup. He got up from his chair first, going over to Matthew.

You mind walking a ways with me? he said.

Matthew looked at his father with an incredulous look.

I'm going with Mark.

You could make an exception, just this once.

You don't really go the same way as me.

That's alright.

Matthew cast a glance at Mark.

Okay! he said.

Martha watched father and son leave in that precise order, and that order suited her just fine.

A short while later, they were walking side by side along the edge of the road, carrying their tin lunch pails, their shadows jostling together in the distance.

We don't talk much anymore, you and me, said Martin.

Matthew stopped and stepped to the side, his shadow tearing itself away from his father's.

What's come over you?

Martin shot a quick look behind him. There was no one there and they could no longer make out the house.

The rifle, he said.

What about the rifle?

I could try to help you fix it when Lynch brings it back.

Didn't you hear me when I said I didn't have the part I needed?

We can probably figure something out.

Martin stuffed a hand into his pocket and brought out a curved piece of metal with a small spring attached to it.

With this, he added.

Matthew took a step back.

What the hell, now you're going through my room.

I did it for your own good.

My own good, since when has that interested you?

You ought to be more cautious with Lynch.

Matthew lowered his eyes.

What happened to Renoir and Salles?

I didn't shoot at them, if that's what you want to know.

Martin was fiddling with the piece from the rifle.

You don't believe me?

I don't really give a damn about those two morons.

What, then?

I'm worried about you.

Matthew couldn't hold in his nervous laughter.

Good God, I ought to have that engraved on something.

You don't want to tell me any more about it?

There's nothing more to tell. I don't understand why you're showing so much concern for me, after all it's definitely not what you usually do.

I admit that I've made some mistakes in the past.

Holy God in heaven, "some mistakes"...You want me to show them to you, all of the mistakes that you made all over my back when I was a boy?

There was a silence, and then the sky quivered with the passage of a flock of starlings.

I realize that I never knew what to do with you...

It isn't because of the marks that I'm going to hold on to all the anger I feel about you. If I have any real hate for you, it's because if I were ever to have kids, I don't know if I would take the belt to them to teach them how to live or not...I'm not sure I'd know any other way, because of you. The rage that builds up inside of us, it has to come back out some day.

An oily cloud masked the sun for a handful of seconds. The shadows of father and son both disappeared, then appeared again, unchanged, still separate from one another. Martin held out the rifle piece to Matthew.

Stash this somewhere better.

Without even looking at his father, Matthew jammed the piece into his pocket. They remained there a long, silent moment, then Martin got out his cigarettes and held the pack out nervously toward his son. Matthew shooed them away with a gesture of his hand.

It's all good, I've got my own. I'm going to go if you've nothing else to say to me.

Wait!

What now?

I want to try to be better.

Matthew shot a cold look at his father.

What's the point? You don't need me to tell you that you can't train the same animal twice.

Martin watched his son move off into the distance, his arm still outstretched, his hand clutching the pack of cigarettes.

Three

It arrived from the south, once night had fallen, and came charging into the valley, mouth agape, spitting out its sandy breath, odorless and tasteless. It had been born God knows where and God knows how, in a land full of dunes and upheavals. Pushing its way up the river like it was the neck of a bottle, bowing, decapitating, uprooting, with greater or lesser ease depending on the age and species of the trees, all of it raising a terrible clamor. An army of giants advancing straight ahead without the slightest concern as to where they placed their feet, what was trampled underfoot and what was spared, the lights noticeably extinguished as they passed, like candles blown out by some enormous maw. Humans and animals alike hid themselves, in the depths of their dens, among the brambles, behind their walls, all of them driven to earth by the same fear. Subjected to its rage, hoping to escape from punishment.

For two full hours, the storm stretched out its body with powerful gusts that devastated, jostled, or hammered against obstacles. Everyone did what they could to suppress its assault, hustling around attics to seal the breaches in the roof. They waited for it to weaken, to push on into the moonless and starless night, to continue on its way, to move on and sound its roar elsewhere. Where and how, that didn't matter, as long as it was far away. Next, torrents of water pelted down. The rain sometimes came rushing in through the roofs, despite the townspeople's efforts. When the rain finally stopped, they waited for day, without finding sleep.

Once dawn broke, the doors opened to haggard faces, pallid complexions. The damage was assessed. All through town, the streets were littered with broken slate tiles, as if the scales of a giant fish had been peeled off and hurled all about. The church's stripped bell tower revealed its bell between the remaining beams of its framework. And even before seven o'clock, the bell tipped to one side in silence, then to the other, and began to ring, the way a heart resumes its duties after a cardiac arrest.

It wasn't the first time they had had to rebuild, and it wouldn't be the last. *Catastrophes force humanity to grow,* the man in the starched robes decorated with their sword-shaped cross was delighted to say.

Light returned to the homes over the course of the next few days, a wait that took longer depending on their distance from the plant. Each family then returned the gas lamps to their cupboards and the candles to their drawers. The residents gradually erased the remaining traces of the storm, but would always wear the scars of it on their flesh; as for the forest, it would get by. It paid no attention to time or disorder. It paid no attention to man; it paid no mind at all.

A thick litter of leaves covered the ground; the river also swept along its share. Such bareness gave the forest the appearance of a ceremonial robe made of some well-worn noble cloth, lacerated in spots, with holes showing, through which fear could still be seen meandering about.

Before returning to his duties at the plant, Martin went out to inspect the house. A gutter had come unsoldered, but the roof had held fast, that was the most important. The curtain of poplars that had been planted in front of the house had perfectly played the role of windbreak. During the day, Martha and Luke would take on the task of gathering the branches littered everywhere and the few objects or debris that had come loose, or what part of it they managed to find. Martin would repair the gutter later that evening.

Mark and Matthew left for work, as per usual. Even when there were electricity outages, powerful generators kept the crushers and conveyers humming. The trucks would continue to leave the quarry with their bins full of gravel, once the roads had been cleared by squads of woodcutters. Luke accompanied his brothers as far as the gate, and asked them to meet him at the viaduct as soon as they got off work. He had something important to tell them.

The two brothers left the quarry and set off into the forest, noticing along their way the great carnage of trees fallen to the ground or entangled in one another. When they reached the viaduct, Luke was already there waiting for them. They didn't have time to ask him anything. Their brother began to speak without interruption, sharing with them the idea he had been thinking about for several days. Matthew raised his eyes to the sky; Mark kept his poker face. On the spot, neither of them knew how to react once Luke had finished.

You've nothing to say?

Matthew looked at Mark, visibly worn out.

Well, are you going to help me, or not?

Why would you want to do this? asked Matthew.

This, as you put it, this is called a stockade, and a stockade is made to protect you...

To protect you from what, Luke?

From pirates, by the powers! You seem to have a short memory, don't you remember Renoir and Salles?

Mark raised a hand to prevent Matthew from speaking.

These pirates, we'd see them coming just as easily from up on the viaduct, wouldn't you think?

See them coming, maybe, but to defend yourself, you need a barricade, that's what Captain Smollett did.

Captain Smollett, right, of course, repeated Mark.

Mark had read *Treasure Island*, had opened with pleasure the doors of that book. But Luke had entered into the story without ever really coming back out. Mark was well aware that the idea of building a fort was absurd, but at the sight of his brother's enthusiasm, he told himself that he had no right to shatter his dreams so quickly. He even found the idea of gathering around such a project to be rather charming. All that remained was to make sure that Matthew got on board.

Where were you thinking we should build it, this stockade? he asked, firing a wink at Matthew.

Luke clapped his hands together, and a great child-like smile stretched across his face. Matthew raised his eyes skyward once more.

Shiver me timbers, I knew I could count on you, my lads! We're going to build it just upstream from where the pirates got blown up, so that we can see our enemies coming from a distance.

You've thought of everything, it seems . . .

We'll work on it in the evenings, after dinner, or at least while the days are long, and especially on Sundays, added Luke.

Okay, but we'll only use the trees that were uprooted by the storm, interjected Matthew, rallying behind the cause at last.

You can be the one to choose them, said Luke, his eyes flooded with joy.

Have you thought about giving a name to this fort of yours? asked Mark, with great seriousness.

No, you're right, I hadn't thought of that.

What do you think of this? Fort Jim.

Luke considered it a moment.

I don't really know.

It doesn't suit you?

It's not that, but I think I'd prefer to call it Fort Mabel, if you don't see any reason against it, said Luke, a bit sad to contradict his brother.

Good idea...

That way, maybe it would make her come back faster. She could even live in it, if she wants.

Good, if we're all in agreement, we should probably head back home now, said Mark.

Hold on, I've got something to tell you both too. Dad knows that I tampered with the rifle, said Matthew.

Were you the one who told him? asked Mark.

No, he found the piece hidden under my mattress. That was the reason he insisted we leave together for work the other day.

I suppose he got all hot under the collar about it.

No, he kept calm. He just told me to be wary of Lynch.

That doesn't sound like him.

There was something even more surprising than that... he admitted to me that maybe he had made some mistakes with us.

What sort of mistakes?

He didn't really go into detail, he just added that he wants to try to be better.

Wild, and how did you react to that?

I took the opportunity to get some things off my chest. He took it without protesting...

Maybe he was being sincere, said Mark, pensive.

If you ask me, it was nothing more than empty words, and in any case, it's too late.

He's never said one nice thing to me, said Luke.

He never treated us any better than you, you know. We've all got the same marks of paternal charity, said Matthew.

What does that mean, charity?

Lashes on the back with the belt.

Oh, okay!

Luke thought for a moment, then added:

Lynch is the one I'd like to give some charity to, if I could.

Julie White worked at the quarry as a secretary. Her parents had died two years earlier, poisoned one winter's night by the emissions from an old coal stove. They fell asleep in their bed in the fetal position, and never woke back up. A week before that, their only daughter was still living with them. Seeing their serene faces when she discovered them, she thought they had finally decided that they were both done with living, choosing to take their love with them so that fate couldn't take one away before the other. In that moment, Julie White had understood that even a slave can decide to break free of his chains, that there is always a way to achieve this, and that the power of the master resides in making the slaves believe he is offering them a fate that is preferable to the endless corridor of death.

Julie White's parents had left a letter addressed to her lying on one of the bedside tables. She kept it in a box; she had never opened it, not out of a fear of discovering some sort of judgment inside, but to leave her parents the ability to freely visit her in her dreams, and to be open to letting them speak to her. In this way, when she thought of them, she could do so without influence and almost without pain.

Julie White had endured a variety of difficult experiences during her adolescence, of which she recalled no more than a series of long periods of unpleasantness followed by brief periods of isolation. Since the passing of her parents, she no longer socialized with anyone. People talked about it, thinking at first that their death was responsible for her detachment, then soon they just found her haughty. That worked just fine for the young woman, as it kept everyone at arm's length. She learned to enjoy solitude, and loved returning home to the closed space of her apartment. After having experienced the outside world, she withdrew into herself. The day would come for her to return to the world, and this time without artifice.

She read books that she borrowed from the library, and there she had crossed paths with a young man who had recently been hired at the quarry as a load inspector. A boy who was serious about his work, timid and reserved, and who spoke to no one. As she watched him progress, she often wondered what sort of books he read. He reminded her of Bartleby the Scrivener, someone who was voluntarily absent from the present, when boys of his age are usually busy spending their energy on taking everything they can from the moment. At the quarry, his name was inscribed within each of the logbooks that he turned in. Mark Volny intrigued her without really attracting her in any way other than by the silence that surrounded him. She had grown wary of the sort of attractions she had had before, where the sheets had started out on fire only to end up ice cold.

Julie White had already noticed the young man's gaze sliding over her, and had done nothing to encourage it, but nothing to discourage it either. She quite liked his eyes, and yet she wouldn't have been able to say what color they were. She liked that gaze, which he let wander over everything. Where others might have seen sadness, she recognized a perimeter of dreaminess within which he confined himself, recognized some part of herself, a mistrustful spark that wouldn't let itself be extinguished.

Mark ran into Julie White in the big administration office at least twice a day, in the morning to retrieve the lading logbook and again in the evening to return it to its spot in the file rack suspended in the cupboard. The young woman was four years older than him. They were both always the first to arrive at work, greeting one another with a reflexive hello before they each headed off to their posts.

Mark never took his lunch break with the other administrative employees in the common room that had been put at their disposal, and neither did Julie White, although most likely not for the same reasons. She ate dried fruit and some cheese wrapped in cellophane without leaving the office. As for Mark, he went off to find Matthew so that the two of them could empty their lunch boxes of their contents together, most often the leftovers from the previous night's meal, which they ate outside and in silence, the other's presence precious and reassuring. Ever since the deaths of Renoir and Salles, the ambiance had changed at the quarry; it had become more serene. No one ever brought them up. Once they had finished their meals, the two brothers returned to their respective work, waiting to meet up once again when it was time to clock out and return home together.

Mark sometimes saw Julie White a third time, when he would return from lunch to find her standing under the awning of the administration office, smoking a cigarette with a detached look, her arms crossed, with just enough freedom of movement to reach the hand that held her cigarette.

That morning, when Mark entered the office, the young woman was already at work, bent over a number-covered page that he had filled in himself. A curtain of hair masked the larger part of her eyes. Mark greeted her, and she replied without looking up. He grabbed the week's logbook from behind her. As he turned back around, Julie White's rear end and hips caught his eye, looking like a swollen heart, delicately placed atop the wooden seat of her metal-legged stool. She maybe wasn't quite as pretty as Mabel, but she also wasn't his sister.

Why was he looking at her more insistently than usual?

Why did he notice the spit curl that hugged her earlobe so perfectly?

Why didn't he return to his office immediately, taking the logbook with him?

What was in the air that day?

Was it because of the words Mabel had spoken to him, which came rushing back into his memory? *You should maybe take a break from your books to give the kisses of a pretty girl a try.*

Feeling watched, Julie White threw her head back, revealing a look of surprise on her pretty face. She was smiling without appearing to be uncomfortable to find that he was still planted behind her.

Is there something I can do for you?

You...are you making out okay with my notes? he asked, without recognizing the sound of his own voice.

Yes, they're quite clear; if that wasn't the case I would have already brought it to your attention.

Very well, then, very well.

As Mark still hadn't moved along, Julie White set her pencil down on one of the logs.

Was there something else you wanted to ask me?

No, pardon me, I didn't mean to interrupt you.

The young woman took up her pencil and continued to move its point along above one of the columns, as if she was alone once more. Mark pulled the logbook to his chest and moved toward the door, which was still open. He was about to step through it.

Mark Volny!

He turned around, disconcerted to hear the young woman use his name like that for the first time. She was staring at him, and there was nothing haughty about her gaze. She looked like someone who was hesitating between silence and speech, but it was just a ploy.

Yes, what is it?

I would like to know, is this your awkward way of telling me that you fancy me?

Mark was knocked off balance by the question. He attempted to mumble out some words, but they remained stuck to his palate, like sleeping bats suspended from the roof of his mouth. He would have had to let a stream of air in to wake them up, but he was unable to do so.

The others will be here soon. Would you like to walk me home this evening?

Yesthatwouldbegreat, he managed to say in a single breath.

Alright, then, see you this evening.

Julie White promptly dove back into her accounting, and Mark left the office, reeling like a drunkard.

At noon, Mark told Matthew not to wait for him before going home, saying that he would be working late. At the end of the workday, he went to return the log to the cupboard. Julie White had already left, the other employees as well. He lingered for an instant in the room, looking at the pencil that the young woman had been using, as well as her stool, tucked in under the surface of her desk. Then he left. Once he was outside, he looked for her. Not seeing her anywhere, Mark thought that he must have gotten the wrong idea, that she had simply been amused by his awkwardness, or that he had misunderstood what she had said. He walked around the building toward the gate and found her sitting on one of the tree stumps that marked the parking spots in the lot. She turned her head to watch him walk toward her, elbows resting on her thighs, face resting on her hands. A cigarette was burning away between her fingers.

I was waiting for you, she said.

She ground the cigarette against the stump, stood up, and stretched out her arms like a ballet dancer.

How do I look?

The bats flew off immediately.

Very pretty.

That's a good start, she said seriously.

He tried to add something else, but the bats had already returned to their roosts.

That's all? You sure are a bit of a bumbler, Mark Volny. Hopefully your legs work better than your tongue.

Mark smiled timidly. They crossed the parking lot. The guard watched them pass through the gate with a spiteful glare. After a few dozen steps, Julie White stopped. She looked Mark up and down, as if trying to raise him into the air with her eyes, to take possession of his inconsequential form, like a ventriloquist about to bring his creature to life.

Maybe this wasn't a good idea after all, she said.

How do you mean?

You're not saying anything, you don't really want to walk me home.

Mark met her gaze.

Just because I'm not saying anything doesn't mean I don't want to talk.

A pair of dimples took shape on the young woman's cheeks.

There's the first sensible thing to come out of your mouth, Mark Volny.

Reassured by those words, Mark concentrated on trying to seem as if he was composed.

You've never gone out with a girl before, have you?

Mark hesitated before answering.

Not really.

Well then, most importantly, don't try to imagine what it is I want to hear.

I'm not imagining anything. I'm just surprised that someone like you would want to be with someone like me, right now, I mean.

What you are doesn't bother me at all.

And yet, it bothers lots of people.

Not me . . . How about we walk a bit?

Sure.

Mark had already started out, but the young woman remained standing where she was.

You're not interested in holding my hand, Mark Volny?

He turned back, flabbergasted by the proposition. He cast an eye into the distance, still able to see the guard's little shack.

Here?

It seems you still have a lot to learn about women.

Mark smiled.

Everything, I'm pretty sure, he said.

He moved shyly toward the young woman, held out his arm, and she hooked her fingers around his hand. The contact seemed strangely cold to him at first. As they walked, she raised one of her fingers from time to time, and when it

returned to its original position, it was as if it were inject-
ing inexpressible happiness into the young man's skin. By
the time they reached town, the cold feeling had completely
vanished. Julie White led Mark to the apartment building
on Joyce 8 where she rented a room on the ground floor.
She let her hand linger when it was time to let go of Mark's.

You're an odd boy, Mark Volny, she said with a hint of
solemnity to her voice.

Odd in what way?

Usually, a boy's in a rush to kiss a girl he fancies.

Mark didn't move, not knowing if this was an invitation, a promise, or a regret.

Do you still fancy me, Mark Volny?

Of course.

Julie White spun on her heels and slid the key into
the lock, pushed the door open, and turned back around,
still with that serious look that hadn't left her.

You're definitely special, and I'm really not sure if
that's a good thing.

She didn't leave Mark enough time to reply, entering
and closing the door behind her. He stared a long moment at the entrance, as if he had the power to make the
young woman reappear to offer him the kiss. His mind
returned to the words of Victor Hugo, which he had read
in one of the books from the library, words that had
stuck with him even though he hadn't understood what
they meant: "All the suppleness of water, woman has it."
And he knew what it was the author meant.

Julie White placed a hand against the door, bending one knee after the other to pull off her shoes. Holding them by the straps, she crossed the main room of the small apartment, which connected to a bedroom and a bathroom, and carefully returned them to the shelf with the others. She poured herself a glass of water from the faucet, then went off to the bathroom, taking her glass with her. She plugged the drain of the tub, sat down on its edge, and turned the two taps, finding the right combination of hot and cold by testing the temperature with a fingertip. She remained there a long moment, lost in thought. Now and then she took a small sip, lulled by the muffled sound of the water as it fell upon more water, the steam slowly transforming her silhouette into a rough sketch. This Mark Volny definitely wasn't like the other boys she had known.

She didn't hear the first knocks at the door because of the burbling of the water and her daydreaming. It wasn't until they resumed, insistent, that the thumping reached her. She turned off the taps with a smile. It hadn't taken the young man long to come back, perhaps he hadn't even left, maybe he had remained standing there on the doorstep, waiting the necessary time to get up the nerve to finally kiss her. She stood up, in no hurry, set her empty glass down on the sink. Facing the mirror, she traveled her tongue across her lips, bringing a shine to them, gleaming with a touch of saliva. She thought about putting her shoes back on, but let them be. Walked over to the door. She had painted her nails red that very morning. She was impatient to see how he was going to go about this newly revealed intimacy, what he would do next, if he would only stand there looking at her. She turned the key in the lock. The knocking stopped. She grasped the doorknob, holding back the smile that had crept up on her, and she opened the door.

Good evening!

The young woman stood there, petrified. Lynch faced her with a cheerful look.

No response? You're not happy to see me?

Good evening, she said with a glacial tone.

She cast an anxious look down the street in either direction.

You looking for someone?

No, I'm just surprised, that's all . . .

It looks like maybe you were expecting someone else.

Lynch tugged his hat farther up on his forehead and turned back toward the empty street.

It wasn't one of the Volny boys that I just ran into a moment ago?

Possibly.

I thought he might be coming from your place.

It's possible.

It's possible or it was?

We work together, he walked me home after work.

Lynch put on a chagrined look, as if he was sympathizing with some unfortunate news.

And has he been walking you home for long?

It was the first time.

I'd imagine the two of you mustn't have gone unnoticed.

You find him too young for me, she said with a sarcastic tone.

Lynch's face changed immediately, as if he had just used a magic slate.

Don't pretend you don't understand, my dear.

Understand what?

A boy who walks a girl home always has an idea in the back of his mind, and the girl who agrees to it cannot ignore that, that's what there is to be understood, seeing as you need me to spell it out for you.

And this is subject to which law, in your opinion?

Don't play with me.

I'm not playing at anything.

So then you will understand easily enough that the boy in question, he's not suitable company for the girl in question. You deserve better than a hick from the valley.

I'm old enough to decide who I keep company with.

Infuriated by Lynch's insinuations, Julie White wanted to close the door, but he moved a foot forward to block it.

I don't think you've quite understood me . . . Perhaps I need to refresh your memory?

Julie White knew exactly what it was Lynch was alluding to, the night she was caught in the older Dubois boy's car smoking marijuana, many years earlier.

That's ancient history, she said.

It's up to me to decide how long stories last, I've kept the statement you signed safe and sound.

Lynch slapped his forehead with the palm of his hand.

Darn it, I think I might have forgotten to write the date on it, he said.

We weren't doing anything wrong . . .

If this ever made its way to Joyce's ears, you could say goodbye to your job.

You wouldn't dare.

That depends on you.

Julie White felt Lynch's eyes roaming all over her.

You can go now, please, I'm tired, I've had a hard day.

Precisely, so have I, I've had a hard day. A bit of relaxation would do us both some good.

Lynch's foot was still blocking the door.

Go on, get your shoes, I'm waiting for you.

Another time, if you don't mind.

Lynch violently threw the door open.

Go put your goddamn shoes on!

Julie White thought about the now-cold water in her bathtub, about the bath that she wouldn't end up taking, about the evening that Lynch had just ruined, and night fell like a heavy metal curtain in front of a shop full of promises to be forgotten. Lynch was parading her around on his arm, greeting everyone whose path they crossed by grazing the brim of his hat with a finger. She avoided their eyes, embarrassed to be out walking with the guy.

After several pointless detours, they arrived in front of Samuelson's. Lynch invited Julie to go in for a bite. She wasn't hungry. He said that that wasn't a problem, that appetite often picks up when you eat. She didn't bother arguing for long. He entered first and went to sit at his usual spot, pointing out that the imitation leather was the same color as her nails, and she imagined planting them in his throat. He placed his hat upside down on the bench next to him. She took a seat opposite him, praying that the farce would end as soon as possible, cursing herself for those few puffs of marijuana that could cost her her job and what little liberty she had as a woman. Lynch was the representative of the laws enacted by Joyce, and the use of drugs was one of the offenses for which there was the least leniency. Everyone knew what kind of solution remained when it came to the survival of a girl with no employment.

Now isn't this lovely?

Lynch pulled a menu out of the wooden stand and began to read it to her.

You haven't got anything to say, he added without raising his eyes.

I'm tired.

You want me to order for you? I know what's good.

Do whatever you want.

Maguy Samuelson came over with her order book and a pencil. Her face showed how uncomfortable she was. Lynch ordered two plates of fried chicken and some water. Maguy noted it down and immediately left. Lynch stretched his arms out along the top of the backrest, surveying the room with a satisfied look.

I've never seen you here before.

Julie White gave him a hard look.

I don't make enough to afford eating in restaurants.

Me neither, said Lynch quietly, shooting the young woman a wink.

Shortly thereafter, Maguy brought their meals. Lynch immediately began to eat with gusto. After a moment, he lifted his head to look at Julie White, who hadn't yet touched anything.

You not eating? he asked with his mouth full.

I'm not hungry.

Lynch held an arm out above the table. His hand indicated the young woman's bust, as if he were conjuring with a crystal ball.

You should eat, if you want to maintain your lovely curves.

Julie White pulled back abruptly, her back glued to the vinyl of the booth to distance herself from the poisonous hand. Lynch stopped chewing and put on a look of fake outrage. And yet the young woman's attitude wasn't actually displeasing to him. Truth be told, he found it amusing to have to break this wild creature, to have to win her over, with the risk that she might not interest him after it was done. In any case, it would last longer than with that little slut Michelle Colbert. He stared at the chest, molded in its brassiere. What he knew about women he had learned by reading dirty magazines, show-and-tell lessons where the object didn't need to say a word, just arouse desire with a big, toothy smile. Being desired was obviously a pleasure in its own right for all girls. What he hadn't needed to learn from them he could find in his own blood, the blood of a man, but up until the present, the fulfillment of his own desire had always taken the form of a simple eruption without much genuine interest. He focused on Julie White's chest, which expanded and contracted to the rhythm of her breathing, revealing two points that darkened the fabric slightly, then he finished his meal in silence. Once he was done eating,

he sucked on his gleaming fingers and wiped his mouth
with a barely creased napkin, which he then folded into
four equal parts. He drank, placed his hands flat on the
tabletop as if he was about to get up, and said:

Good thing I don't have to pay, you didn't eat a thing.
I'll ask for a doggie bag.

It's not worth bothering.

I don't like to waste.

Can we go now?

Lynch grabbed Julie White by the wrist.

I don't ever want to see you consorting with a Volny
again, is that understood?

You can let go of me.

I end up knowing everything in this town.

Lynch released the young woman and looked at his
watch.

I don't have time to take you back home, duty calls.

He put his hat back on and got up, smiling.

I've enjoyed your company, let's do this again soon.

He instinctively tapped his palm against his shirt
pocket. His hand remained glued to his chest, like a pa-
triot during the national anthem, and his smile instantly
disappeared.

The full sun of the afternoon looked like the lens of a projector busy unfurling its reel across the screen of the valley, a film made of a multitude of scenes played by actors who were improvising their roles as the day progressed.

Despite Mark's recommendations, Luke had gone to hang around in town, not being able to resist his desire to see his sister before she decided she was ready. Sitting at the fountain's edge, he stared at a precise spot in the sky. A cloud that looked like the head of a fox. The animal had returned to his thoughts, now that he knew he would soon see Mabel again. Occupied by the vision, he didn't hear the man approaching without the slightest discretion. His heart stopped beating when he felt a hand grip him by the collar, and all the daydreams that had been dancing in his head melted away instantly. He threw up his hands to protect himself, catching a glimpse of Lynch's scarlet face and the whites of his eyes, streaked with blood.

Dirty little shit, I know it was you who stole the cartridge from me in front of Samuelson's.

I didn't steal anything, I didn't steal anything...

You thought you'd get away with it that easily.

I didn't steal anything...

Give it to me or I'll lock you up.

The fox's head flew apart in downy tatters.

I don't want to go to prison.

And yet that's what is going to happen to you if you don't admit what you did.

I didn't do anything, I swear to you.

Stop lying... Was it your brother who asked you to get it back?

Luke thought of what would happen to Matthew if he fessed up, but he didn't want to go to prison either. He didn't know what to say or what to do, other than bury his head entirely in his hands.

Leave him be!

Luke lowered his arms and turned toward the voice. The gigantic silhouette of Long John Silver, solidly planted atop his crutches, had stepped between Lynch and the sun.

You stay out of this, old man, this business is between me and him.

What do you want with him?

He stole something that belongs to me and he's going to return it, if not I'll arrest him.

Do you have any proof of what you're claiming?

Lynch hesitated, then gave Luke another contemptuous shove.

I swear to you he won't get away with it so easily.

If word ever got out that a representative of the law had had something important stolen from him by a child like this one, I don't know how Joyce would take the news.

Are you threatening me?

I'd never do anything of the sort, replied Elie.

Lynch flew into a tirade.

Waiting won't make it any easier on him, believe you me. His looking like a dumbass won't save him forever. Your family's nothing but a band of thieves and criminals.

Elie stopped himself from responding to the provocation. Lynch walked off, cursing. Luke began to cry, fixing his grandfather with his big, misty eyes. There were plenty of words jumbled up in his mouth, like when you need to puke but you can't, and others were forming in his head, turning around and bumping into one another as they sought a way out. The idea of going to prison hadn't left him. He struck a fist against his head, trying to knock away the bad thoughts, seeing as he couldn't chase them away.

I don't want to go to prison.

The old man leaned down, a crutch fell to the ground, and he grabbed Luke by the forearm to prevent him from hitting himself, then he sat down next to him and rested a hand on his shoulder.

It's all over now, you've nothing to worry about... What's this stealing business he was going on about?

I have no idea, he must have made a mistake, said Luke, sobbing even harder.

It's okay, we don't need to discuss it any further.

Little by little, the tears stopped. Luke could feel the general's shadow weighing down on him, and Grandpa Silver seemed as if he were a part of that shadow, as if this fortuitous ally was himself a benevolent shadow, and had always been one. Luke realized that the shadows of things weren't any different from those of living beings, that they could mix and blend and that that was something to keep in mind. He moved even closer to the old man and allowed the general's shadow to envelop him, too, entirely, three overlapping shadows, adjusted so they made only one, like a thick puddle of oil. He told himself that in the future, he would seek out the biggest shadows to hide himself in, so he could protect himself from bad people. Even more than his grandfather's lifesaving intervention, it was the shadows that finally calmed him down.

You want to go home? said Elie.

My legs still feel like they're made of jelly.

As long as they're not made of wood, said Elie with a smile.

Still focused on the shadows, Luke didn't catch the old man's joke. He waited until the general's shadow grew shorter. That was a whole new mystery, the fact that a shadow isn't the exact replica of what makes it, that it is always changing, that it brings to life that which is not alive, and does this a bit less to that which already is. From that moment on, Luke would be able to see shadows for what they really were; even when there wasn't any sunshine, he would still really see them, convinced that a shadow isn't just a bag with holes in it so you can breathe, and even less a coffin.

Elie stuffed his pipe and lit it. He took a series of pulls off the stem and said:

You feeling better now, my lad?

I think so.

You still thinking about Lynch?

He has a star.

It's just a badge, all sheriffs have badges, and regardless, they're far from being as solid as a good crutch, you'd better believe it.

Luke wiped his nose a few times with the back of his thumb, then placed a hand in front of his mouth before he began speaking:

I know who you really are.

I sure hope so...

You're Long John Silver, the pirate.

Ah!

And me, you know who I really am?

Tell me!

Jim Hockens.

Elie furrowed his brow.

How is that possible?

Our mom says that people live more than one life, that we're just forms that the Savior stuffs full of what he hasn't finished shaping yet, that he'll put the final touches on it on the day of reckoning, that's what she says.

Your mother is crazy.

Me, I'd like to look like something more than a dunce in another life.

You are not a dunce, said Elie, pointing at Luke with his pipe.

But there are things missing in my head. They didn't want me at school anymore.

Well I didn't go to school either.

Is that true?

I'm telling you it is.

Luke turned his eyes to his grandfather's stump.

Maybe there wasn't even school yet, back in your day.

Sure, school existed.

Why didn't you go there, then?

Got to believe that it wasn't my place.

Luke thought in silence for a moment.

Like me, he said.

Elie looked around, then he leaned toward Luke, like a co-conspirator.

And what is it that we should do with our secret now?

Maybe we can come to some sort of deal.

Go on, I'm listening.

You tell me where the treasure is, and I'll do the digging for you, seeing that you're no longer in any shape to do it yourself, and then we'll split it afterward.

Elie made as if he was considering this.

That seems like a pretty fair deal to me. There's just one problem, though, I don't remember where it is anymore. Blasted memory, he said, pushing a finger against his forehead.

But the map, surely you've got a map that shows where it is?

The old man took on a vexed look.

The map, I lost it... at sea.

Luke looked his grandfather over with suspicion.

You're not lying to me, I hope.

And why would I do that? Like you say, I'd be incapable of digging even the smallest hole.

Maybe it will come back to you.

We old people forget more than we remember, you know.

Is that why you're always looking for your parrot, then, so he can help you remember?

My parrot!

It's him that you shout at, sometimes, isn't it? I've seen you do it.

Elie immediately understood what Luke was alluding to.

Ah yes, that cursed creature, he never listened to me very well...

You've got to continue, I'm sure that he'll come back.

Agreed.

Good, does that mean you accept my proposition?

I accept.

Luke held out his hand. Elie shook it.

From now on, you can call me Jim, and I'll call you Silver.

That might not be a good idea, it could raise suspicions.

You're right, I hadn't thought of that, it has to be our secret.

Exactly, our secret, my lad. Come on, let's get going!

Do you think I'll scare your parrot away, if it should happen to show up while we're on our way home?

I wouldn't worry about it, he's got a foul temperament, but he's rather social.

People often ask themselves, after the fact, at what moment life turned into uncontrollable destiny, when exactly it was that the machine took control, whether a chain of past events presides over that change or whether the change itself is written in the future.

Usually, at mealtime, Martha would sit down after she served everyone their helping. That evening, she was already seated when everyone took their place, observing her with curious eyes. She didn't get up. The stew was simmering away in a pot on the stove. She continued to wait, joining her hands together above her plate.

What's going on, are you ill? asked Martin.

Martha took a good look at each member of the family, then, with a solemn tone, she said:

It's time we became a real family again.

A long silence hung in the air after her words. Martin could perceive an echo of the conversation they'd had a few days earlier. A crutch scraped across the parquet floor.

What is it that you see around this table? asked Elie, raising his voice.

I'm hungry, said Luke.

Martha let a cold stare linger on her father.

I see a bunch of strangers who have lost the faith that they ought to have in each other.

And whose fault is that?

I'll admit to my share of it, but for the moment, it isn't a question of deciding who is to blame. We've got to look at things straight on. Lynch coming around with his accusations, and after, the storm that came blowing in, no one knows where it's all going to end, said Martha, shifting her gaze over to rest on Matthew.

The storm isn't going to come blowing back in tomorrow, said Martin.

And we've nothing to worry about with Lynch, added Matthew, looking defiantly at his mother.

That's not what he seemed to think.

I'm hungry, repeated Luke.

I'm not stopping anyone from serving themselves.

What is it that you're waiting for, in the end? asked Martin.

Hungry, I'm hungry, blared Luke again.

The grandfather slammed down the steel tip of his crutch several times on the parquet, as if he were a judge demanding silence in the room.

This farce has gone on long enough... How much longer are you going to go on with this show of integrity, you sanctimonious zealot? he said, pointing a finger at his daughter.

Whatever are you talking about?

Don't tell me you don't understand the words . . . And you, you're no better than she is, he continued, turning toward his son-in-law.

What exactly is it that you're accusing us of? asked Martha.

You say that we need to become a family again, so why don't you show your son some trust?

I'm not asking for anything more.

But you surely understand that you've got no right to ask this.

That's enough, you've gone too far.

Elie put his weight on his crutches and got up with a grimace. His livid face showed the many scars of time.

No, that's not enough, while we're at it. I don't know how much longer I've got to live, but before I go, I want to see that beautiful girl back here at this table, so the both of you need to stop pretending she never existed and stop thinking that you can never be wrong.

Martin lowered his head. Martha tried to brave her father's attacks.

And our family's reputation, what would you do about that? she said.

What reputation are you talking about? The one that consists of us living like slaves with our heads bowed, like your husband right now? Christ almighty, Martha, I lost one of my legs and my dignity along with it and you talk to me about reputation! What is it that you do about it, this reputation of yours?

Surely you've noticed all the efforts I'm making right now to glue this family back together.

You poor thing, that glue will never hold if Mabel doesn't come back, and the worst thing is, you know it.

That's not her name.

It's about time that you did something about that once and for all.

The grandfather turned toward Martin and brought his crutch down on the ground once more.

And you, you've got nothing to say anymore? Might be the time to start acting like a man.

Martin slowly brought his eyes up to look at the old man, and thought he looked quite impressive.

Well? insisted Elie.

I'll try.

It's most likely your last chance, the last chance for either one of you.

Martha shot a lost look at Martin.

A long silence followed, then Elie sat heavily back down on his chair.

I'm hungry too, he said.

Luke gazed lovingly at his grandfather. He hadn't grasped all of the content during the conversation, most notably what his mother had been trying to get across with her bit about real family. There would always be time later on to ask his brothers to explain it to him. One word, and one word alone was burning in his mind, and he let it burst forth from his mouth with all of its light:

Mabel!

Nobody had anything at all to add to that. Martha got up laboriously, as if she was obeying an order, and went over to get the pot. Luke held out his plate, and she mechanically served him first, then the rest of them. They began to eat in silence, each of them thinking in their own way about the one thing missing from the table. Hanging on the wall, the clock divided time to the furious pace of its two hands, tick-tock, tick-tock, tick-tock, Ma-bel, Ma-bel, Ma-bel, two syllables chanted by a mechanism, two syllables as gentle as a kiss upon closed lips.

Julie White didn't come to work. This had never happened since Mark had been hired. He tried to find out a reason for the young woman's absence, but he was told abruptly that it didn't concern him. He figured that she must be unwell, and the time until evening filed by like a heavy train full of merchandise.

He didn't have time to go into town. He and Mabel had planned to meet their brothers at the viaduct. Matthew had already left to join Luke.

On his way there, Mark couldn't stop thinking about Julie White. She would be back the next day and would explain everything to him. He would be reassured. He would walk her home again. They would laugh together over his anxiety. She would be touched by it, perhaps even filled with emotion. Once they arrived in front of her place, they would put aside their joking. She would invite him in so that there was no one watching them. He would follow her inside, closing the door behind him. She wouldn't go far. She would turn around. He would carry out the necessary first step. She wouldn't back away. He would lean toward her. She would move her mouth forward, with her lovely face around it, which he would already not be able to make out, because he would have already closed his eyes to better taste her lips, like people do to better enjoy the fragrance of a fruit. He would become a little more to her than the other boys she had kissed before. They would send the ordinary off into limbo to focus on the unique. The promises of the flesh. And so it would be. The rest would be a story of suns scattered through the night. The rest would be their story. The following day would be as well.

The boys were the first to arrive at the viaduct. They stood below the arch, their eyes all cast in the same direction, east to where the sun rises, like diurnal animals waiting for a sign of the first rays of day, mute, filled with anxiety at the thought that their dearest wish might not come true, that of being reunited once again, that their triangle would stretch out and retake the shape of a perfect square. A shiver went through the tops of the trees.

You sure she's gonna come? asked Luke.

She shouldn't be long now, replied Mark.

It's taking so long.

We've only been here for ten minutes.

I've been waiting way longer than that...

There, said Matthew, stretching out an arm.

Mabel appeared in the distance, coming along the path that was still strewn with tattered leaves. She was walking right in the middle, where there were fewer stones. They watched her draw near and then scamper up the rocks. Once she had arrived below the arch, she wiped her hands on her jean jacket, then filled the vacant space that her brothers had reserved for her. Nobody dared speak, and they all stared at the river. Tiny little hearts danced around all over under their skin, like a fear-stricken herd galloping in every direction, drunk on a delicious panic, and one same smile lit their faces.

I've missed you all, she said after a moment.

Not being able to hold back any longer, Luke launched himself into her arms. Mark and Matthew eyeballed one another, as if seeking permission from the other to join the communion. Neither of them moved. It was Mabel who, after having liberated herself from Luke's embrace, hugged and kissed them both in turn.

Once he had at least partially gained control over his emotions, Luke pointed a finger at the rope that still hung above.

Did you see? he said to his sister.

I see.

How about we go back up there, like before?

I can't stay long today.

Luke couldn't conceal his disappointment.

Why not?

I've got to work.

Working is more important than the four of us going up to hang from the viaduct?

No, but I can't be late, or I could lose my job. Next time I'll stay as long as you want.

When?

Soon.

Luke lowered his eyes.

You're not angry at me anymore, then?

I wasn't ever angry at you about anything.

But I thought that . . .

Let's not talk about it anymore, it's forgotten, I swear.

Mabel turned toward the others.

How's it going at the house?

Mom is really strange right now, she wants us to become a real family again, that's what she said, replied Mark.

She must have heard a voice coming from the sky.

How come we're not telling her? interrupted Luke.

Telling me what? asked Mabel.

Matthew blasted Luke with a stare.

No point in glaring at me, she's our sister, there's no reason to hide that Lynch came to the house.

Lynch, what did that guy want?

It's been dealt with, cut in Matthew.

That doesn't answer my question.

He wanted to see my rifle; he's taking inventory of the old guns in the region.

Any reason I should be worried about this? asked Mabel, looking from one brother to the other.

Luke tried to jump back in, but Matthew beat him to it:

No, like I told you, it's been dealt with.

Okay, well, then why do I get the feeling you're not telling me the whole truth? Is this why Mom isn't acting in her normal way?

There was the storm, too, and then Grandpa, who's really been on her case...

He called her a crazy old witch, said Luke.

Holy moly, and how did she react?

She didn't really have time to defend herself. He said that there was no point in talking about family, so long as you weren't back yet, replied Matthew.

Well, that's not going to happen anytime soon, said Mabel, clenching her fists.

He also took a run at Dad...I swear, they weren't having a very good time of it, neither one of them.

Mabel unclenched her fists. She remained pensive a moment.

He comes to The Admiral every night, he ignores me on purpose, I can tell that he's ashamed of me.

He said that he would speak to you.

Well, I won't be listening to him anytime soon, either.

Everyone fell silent, then Luke started to clap his hands cheerfully.

We're going to build a stockade in the woods, so we can give charity to the pirates, he said.

Mark winked discreetly at Mabel.

Fort Mabel is what we decided to call it, added Luke.

I'm flattered.

Flattered, what does flattered mean?

She fixed a tender look on her brother.

It means that I'm proud to be your sister.

So then it works both ways.

A sad smile crept across Mabel's face.

What if we just sat for a moment and looked at the river, before I have to go? she said.

They all sat beneath the great brickwork eyelid, squeezed one against the next, the four of them making up the iris of a cyclops's eye traced in the milky pupil of the sky, still in their kingdom, and thus escaping a destiny that had been mapped out for them long before by the adults. They breathed deep and drank in the wind that flooded up the valley, spitting it back out like gusts from the storm that swirled inside their young heads.

The silhouette materialized slowly in front of the mist-enshrouded plant, while the building faded away in the background. The collar of his jacket up, his hands in the pockets of his overalls, the handle of his empty lunch pail imprisoned in the crook of his elbow slapping against the top of Martin's thigh with each step he took. All day long, he had been wondering whether Martha was sincere in her stated desire to put the family first, before her faith. Deep down, he didn't believe her enough to even ask himself such a question. He had made do up until that point, before Martha's confession and what Elie had said. Should he trust his wife and listen to his father-in-law? Was there still room left somewhere for him in all this, a gap into which he could slide what remained of his attempt at fatherhood? This man who had always believed that silence and blows were the best cement to assure the cohesion of his world, realizing as he walked that silence was nothing more than the emptiness that each person strives to fill in their own way, and blows, just another more physical form of silence; these dissimilar ways of asserting oneself by force could never allow a structure to remain standing very long. The only thing that could was language. The words that we say, and those that we hear. That after, and only after, gestures can express.

Over the course of their conversations at The Admiral, Gobbo had made him understand that silence is a vast prison in which we lock away our fears. Martin wasn't easily duped, he was pretty sure that the sailor had recognized where exactly it was that the demons had holed up inside him, and that those demons had been familiar to him, or maybe they were to all men. That evening, like a lieutenant taking counsel with a general before going into battle against himself, he felt like asking Gobbo from which flank he should first attack that *himself*, which wound he should inflict upon himself first to bring surging forth a Martin who would finally speak, who might even love.

A few drops of rain crossed the sky to flatten themselves against the path, thick drops that looked like mercury. Martin counted seventeen impacts before one of them collided with his forehead, then felt it slide down the bridge of his nose before it fell to the ground, with less of a smack than the others. Eighteen . . . The rhythm accelerated and he quickly lost count. The crust of the earth, the stones, the grass, the leaves from the trees scattered along the path all gave rise to different notes, which clumped together, compressed into a single echo, like a swarm buzzing around a queen.

In the distance, Martin could make out the dam through the curtain of rain that was tilted by the west wind. You would have thought that the structure was attracted by the river through some sort of supernatural tropism, pulling it away from the town as if it might collapse at any moment, like the walls of a ruin that had seen its day. To him, its upper section had the look of a parapet. He imagined armed guards keeping watch over his arrival, without being able to make out a single figure. He thought back to the men at the fortress that had fallen in the middle of the desert. Maybe it was time to switch sides, to trade this forced march for a simpler wait. To retrace his steps, to trust in the rain that was showing him the best direction to go. Everything in its own time. He would talk to Gobbo later.

Martin kicked the tips of his shoes against one of the risers of the stairs to knock loose the dirt caught in their grips. He crossed the porch and entered the house. Sitting at the table, Martha stared at his clean shoes with a surprised look while she finished trussing up a cabbage leaf filled with stuffing. Martin set his lunch pail down in the sink, unfastened the cover, and started pouring water into it, then he washed his hands and shook them dry. He pulled off his jacket and hung it from a coat peg, and walked over to the table to stand next to his wife. Large, unfolded leaves like small bowls, lined with ribs, were stacked next to a glazed earthenware platter, a pan full of stuffing, and a roll of cooking twine.

I spoke to Matthew, he said.

Ah!

He's angry with me.

Martha dove her hand into the pan, and took out a fistful of stuffing, which she set to kneading, then placed the compact ball delicately on one of the cabbage leaves.

He's angry with all of us, she said.

Martin pulled out a chair and sat down. He grabbed a leaf. Drops of water slid along the leaf blade like tiny steel ball bearings, falling to splatter on the tabletop.

What you were saying about our family, the other night, do you really believe that?

I never say what I don't believe, you should know that.

Maybe it's too late for us to do what you're saying.

Something is coming, it's now or never.

And what is it that's coming, in your opinion?

I don't really know, but I know that it's serious, and that we have to prepare for it together. It's one thing to turn your attention away from God, it's surely another when it comes to signs he sends us from heaven.

Martin set down the leaf and clasped his hands together. He looked vulnerable, pitiful even, in the unconscious way he stapled his palms together. He inhaled long and deep before speaking:

You know, when I came back from the war, I felt like I was stomping around in the cold, jumping from one foot to the other to try to get myself warm. Even if I wasn't expecting anything . . . when we met, I felt like I was putting both feet down on the ground at the same time, that I wasn't as cold. I thought that time would erase what I had lived through, that a family would help with that, that it was an acceptable kind of balance, a wife and kids, even if I didn't really want to have either. I went along with it all, Martha, because you were locking a horizon of memories away behind me by offering me a new one, in front of me, totally unknown, with that certainty, that facility that you have, all of you women, when it comes to convincing us men that we can become heroes without any effort.

Martin observed his wife, still focused on her task.

Nothing to say? he asked.

I did what I could, she replied with a weary look.

No, you didn't do what you could, you did what you wanted.

Martha's hands froze, and she raised her eyes to meet Martin's.

And it was evil, in your opinion?

I never said that.

And yet you seem to think so.

Evil, no, that isn't evil . . . I've seen evil up close, a long time ago, and you never really recover from it. No, what I want you to understand is that I have decided to help you.

To help me, repeated Martha.

With her free hand, she drew a cross, moving her thumbnail to her forehead, her chin, her cheeks, first left and then right.

Martin grabbed the stuffed leaf that Martha was holding. She let him take it without resisting. He took the twine, then started tying off the leaf, cutting the string with his teeth. Martha watched him do this, something he had never done before. A great wave of emotion flooded through her hands, and she quickly busied them fashioning another small planet of ground meat so as not to allow herself to drop her guard too quickly.

Are you going to talk to her as well?

To Mabel? he said without provocation.

You said that you would try.

I said I would.

It would be good for you to do that.

Martin set down the tied-off ball and waved a fly away from the pan.

You really think we can still sort this out? he asked.

It wasn't me who was talking about being a hero.

Mabel seemed to dance between the tables. Her tray in her hand, she served, reserved, came and went as if she was declining invitations to dance, leaving to float behind her notes of lemon, jasmine, and cedar. Over the course of the many evenings, she had ended up bewitching the customers, all of them, without exception. Those who had resisted could no longer remain unmoved by her savage beauty; none among them could ignore her. Her way of moving set the space alight and singed people's gazes. She avoided her father's eyes, which she felt weighing more heavily on her every night.

Mabel was embodied desire. She did nothing to appear provocative. Her body simply needed to exult, to experience pleasure. The carpenter's apprentice had gotten engaged to another, someone more respectable. She missed the gentleness of his hands. When she happened to cross his path in town, he acted as if he didn't know who she was, and it upset her the first time. Beyond that, she continued to choose whom she would undress for, never a customer from the bar. She didn't want to find herself in a sordid room upstairs one night, never again able to get back down. She had promised herself. The river was now too far away for her to experience her pleasure there. It was understood that it always had to happen at his place. She would enter secretly, and be gone before dawn so as not to be seen.

Roby had circled back to the argument many times, explaining that she could make much more money and tire herself out less than in the bar, she only had to go upstairs with the other girls, it was a waste not to use all of what the Good Lord had given her, *a sacrilege, even*, he had added with far too much seriousness to be taken for genuine. *A girl like you, more than anyone could ever hope for.* A girl like her. A great lot that meant coming from Roby's mouth.

The Good Lord doesn't give away anything, and plus, I get vertigo as soon as I go up even three steps, so, a whole floor up . . . is what she had replied.

That's not what people say.

What people say only matters to those who do the saying and those who listen to them.

You should at least take the time to discuss it with the other girls.

I already did discuss it with them, but it seems we're not all saying the same things.

Roby was caught unprepared by Mabel's obstinacy.

Think it over carefully, before other people make the decision for you, and it won't be anything like a fairy tale, you can be sure of that.

No one, at any point, has ever told me a fairy tale.

———————

For the past several days, the customers had been avoiding Mabel's gaze, no longer brushing up against her or making their lewd jokes, no longer suggesting that she conclude the night with them, in a bed. A predator had marked his territory, and was watching her. Everyone knew what Double had in mind.

That evening, Snake had already gone upstairs with his big redhead. Mabel knew Lila pretty well. They often chatted before opening time, smoking a cigarette. With her coarse talk, Lila had told her about the difficulty the dwarf had getting erections, the never-ending protocol that had to be respected right up until he "shot his sauce all over my belly. I figure it must be so he can remind himself what a miracle it actually is each time he manages," she had said one day with a giggle. And added: "His prick isn't all that big, and he doesn't have much venom for a snake. At least he pays, and he doesn't get violent." With those words, Lila's face had clouded over, then she had held her cigarette out in the empty space that separated them. "If you can swing it, never end up up there!" Lila had then taken a nervous drag off her butt, blowing the smoke up toward the ceiling, and fell quiet.

The giant was sitting alone at his table. He watched every little move that Mabel made. He raised his arm once again, passing his tongue across his lips. He insisted that only she bring him his beers. She returned a moment later and set one down on the table, with a contemptuous look. Double's eyes, resting on her, looked like two cankers on the trunks of dead trees, and what came from them burned the young girl like it was acid.

Have a seat for a minute, he said with a somewhat shaky voice, as he pulled out the empty chair next to him.

I've got work to do.

Sit down, I'm telling you, Roby won't say a thing.

Mabel sought out her father with her eyes for the first time. He wasn't there. Only the guy he usually drank with sat there, watching her insistently.

What for? Why should I sit down?

I was hoping that we could really get to know each other.

I've got a pretty decent guess what sort of ideas you've got in your head.

Double moved his torso closer to Mabel. He tried to give her a wink, but both of his eyes closed at the same time.

And not just in my head, he said.

Mabel took a deep breath. She leaned toward Double, pressing the top of her thighs against the edge of the table, and the fabric of her dress pulled taut. Double didn't know where to look anymore.

I'm out of your price range, and I will always be out of your price range, she said in a voice that sounded like it was coming from the bottom of a well.

Double was still wedged against the back of his chair. No one had ever dared provoke him in such a way, and it was a woman who had just done so. Mabel backed up. The fabric of her dress relaxed, and she drifted back over to the counter before the giant's astounded stare.

She cleared the empty glasses from her tray and set them on the counter. Roby was busy pouring a beer, his eyes moving continuously between Double and Mabel, then they stopped on the young woman.

What did you say to him, he looks like somebody just socked him a good one.

The truth.

And what is this truth that has left him in such a state?

That I won't open my legs for him.

You didn't actually say that to him?

What do you think?

He's not just anybody, you know.

I'm not just anybody either...

You could let him stew for a while, buy yourself some time.

It wouldn't change anything, he'll never get what he's been imagining.

For goodness' sake, have you never asked yourself why you have such power over men?

We've already had this conversation, and I never asked for anything, not for any kind of power.

But you're certainly clever enough to realize that not everyone is so fortunate.

Mabel turned her head, raising her eyes toward the upper floor.

As fortunate as all of them?

They all say that you get used to it quickly.

I'm not interested in getting used to it.

Roby cast an eye over toward Double.

You should at least go apologize.

Out of the question!

Roby picked up the beer he had just poured and set it on Mabel's tray.

Take him this beer and apologize, or else you're fired.

Seething with rage, Double stared at Mabel. She looked among the customers for her father one more time. She didn't find him there, and a cold winter's rain streamed across her skin.

Gobbo wondered where Martin was, why he hadn't yet come to meet him at The Admiral. He didn't take his eyes off the giant's table, making certain not to miss a thing. The chair next to him remained empty all evening.

He had seen Snake head up the stairs, his back knotted up by scoliosis, and his head looking like it had been screwed on directly between his shoulders.

Then he had seen the dwarf walk along next to the railing, his profile cut in pieces by the slats as he continued along, like a series of Muybridge photographs.

He had seen Snake turn and go into one of the rooms. Hadn't seen him since.

He saw Double at his table, his vicious stare winding around Mabel like a creeping vine.

Saw him putting back beers at a frantic pace, and guessed at the obscene thoughts that were running through his twisted brain.

Saw the giant's eyes grow narrower, a bit at a time, his hand hesitating from the effects of the alcohol as he went for his glass. Saw his face twist up after the girl had said what he obviously hadn't expected her to say, or perhaps his face had simply twisted up because of her beauty, her sensuality, because of the pain brought on by that beauty and sensuality, because that is often what is felt when one is confronted with such beauty. The same way it twisted up Gobbo's insides, the way it jostled around in his head, the way it made light shine in, but also night.

Saw Double looking punch-drunk.

Saw Roby speak to the young woman. Saw her go back to put another beer down on the table.

Saw the eyes of the giant riveted on the affront that needed to be erased, the woman who needed to be debased, to be defiled. To be destroyed.

Sensed the invisible demon bargaining with him, explaining that to the east, the west, and the south there were hells that had already been explored, that the north was a new hell that could be discovered with that girl. That girl. For Gobbo, a shooting star to rescue.

Saw the first customers leave and the chairs flipped over onto the tables, their feet like the frail paws of dead animals floating in water with no current.

Saw the washed glasses returned to the shelves behind the bar.

Saw the smoke from the cigarettes fade away, the entrance door open, close, open, and close again, the final customers gone.

Saw Double get to his feet with a stagger, approach the counter, speak to the young woman, and his words also seemed to stagger out of his mouth, heavy like sheets left out beneath the rains.

Saw fear take shape in the young woman's eyes.

Saw it again, and decided not to watch it anymore.

Gobbo hurriedly counted out a few coins onto the table, got up, walked to the door, and left without closing it behind him.

Tucked away in the shadows on the other side of the street, a few yards down from The Admiral, Gobbo lit a cigarette. Soon enough, Double appeared. He was alone. He didn't notice the sailor's presence. Walked shakily into the middle of the street, turned back around, his arms hanging like mast rigging, then threw his head back. It was as if the blade of a sword had almost completely decapitated him. He gathered his strength, cleared his throat, and spit in the direction of the bar, only managing to reach the sidewalk.

Gobbo moved over toward a streetlamp and positioned himself at the center of its cone of light, like an actor making his way onstage. With a flick, he launched the butt of his cigarette toward the giant, who didn't notice.

Hey! shouted Gobbo.

The giant's head swayed to one side, almost causing him to lose his balance. Gobbo greeted his audience.

Who's there? asked Double, seemingly dazed.

Doesn't matter who I am.

What do you want, then?

Gobbo took a deep breath.

By God's sonties, 'twill be a hard way to hit, he said emphatically.

Double pivoted in place, first in one direction, then the other, looking to see if there was someone else in the street.

Are you talking to me?

This father, though I say it, is an honest exceeding poor man and, God be thanked, well to live... and even to defend himself.

The giant was fuming. He walked toward Gobbo, zigzagging his way, and the silhouette danced before him, like a reflection endlessly tossed around by the current.

The sailor moved away and stationed himself under a different streetlight. Double followed him with difficulty.

Stop moving so much, you coward, you... You know who you're dealing with?

Alack, sir, I am sand-blind; I know you not.

I'm gonna make you dance once I catch up to you.

Marry, Godforbid! Never would I provoke someone who has *got more hair on his chin than Dobbin my fill-horse has on his tail.*

Double swung a fist in front of him and Gobbo nimbly stepped aside, like a toreador. The giant almost fell over backward, then straightened himself out, after a fashion, trying to find the stability that his legs were contesting.

What in the hell are you playing at? C'mon and fight, if you're a man.

Are you afraid of dying? asked Gobbo.

You're the one who should be afraid of death right about now.

You're mistaken, it isn't death that should be feared, but rather the dying.

What is it that you actually want, if you don't want to fight?

Gobbo gestured down the road with his chin, toward where The Admiral stood.

The girl, you're going to leave her be.

The giant slapped his hands against his thighs.

You mean that little waitress? That's why you're putting on all of this theater?

Her name is Mabel, *indeed, the flesh and blood of my friend.*

My next afternoon snack, if you really want to know, said Double with a chuckle.

Afternoon snack? But it's only midnight, I fear that you've maybe decided too early, you're going to have to cancel those plans.

Double stopped chuckling.

And what do you think you can do to stop me?

Gobbo stepped back into the light, still standing outside of the giant's reach.

If I have to sacrifice you to save the girl's honor, know that I'm capable of measuring up to the task, and that your master's protection won't be enough for you.

Double was no longer reeling. He stared at the sailor, without paying any mind to his last words.

I recognize you now. They say you used to be a sailor.

If that's what they say.

We're not on the sea right here, as far as I know.

We're all tossed along by the swells, no matter where we find ourselves. I've harpooned many a whale in my day, but also a few sharks that got in my path on solid ground.

Solid ground, you better believe that that's where I'm going to put you!

Double threw himself forward in an attempt to reach his prey. Carried along by his weight, he fell heavily to the ground and found himself on all fours, tangled up in a body that refused to obey him, like a big animal trapped in the mud. Gobbo pulled a knife out of the sheath he wore on his belt, stepped around Double, straddled him, and brought the Damascus blade up to his throat.

Now cool it! I know how to make use of this sort of harpoon too.

Put that down and I promise you this will all be forgotten! said the giant, almost without opening his lips.

What makes you think I want any of this to be forgotten?

At least let me get up.

Alright, but don't you try a thing or I'll cut your throat.

Gobbo swung a leg over Double and helped him struggle to his feet, then dragged him a ways farther into the shadows. He was thinking of Snake, who wouldn't be long in leaving The Admiral.

Now what do we do? asked Double.

Are you going to do what I told you?

Double relaxed somewhat, he no longer felt the blade against his neck, as if the alcohol had ended up dissolving it.

I don't really understand why you're going to all this trouble for that girl...unless...

The giant stopped short. A smile spread across his face, and he never smiled for anyone.

...unless you're hoping to fuck her yourself.

Gobbo firmed up his grip.

Shut your mouth! he said.

If that's all it is, we can work something out...I promise I won't wreck her so badly that she can't still be enjoyed.

There was a brief moment of silence. And that silence stretched out into a definitive gesture, as lively and as discreet as a kestrel skimming the ground at full velocity, a gesture provoked by age-old words come out of a throat that was now open from one side to the other and spraying blood like a hose with a hole in it. Double felt no pain whatsoever. By reflex alone, he brought a hand up to his wound, took it away to look at it, dumbfounded to discover the additional quantity of darkness that it was holding, which at first he took for a sticky shadow cast aside by the night. His vision grew cloudy. The alcohol had nothing to do with it. He attempted to speak, but nothing intelligible managed to come out of his mouth. The night was drawing closer, and it wasn't unfathomable, not even an abyss, contrary to what Double had always believed. This night was like a solid wall you could lean up against, quite simply, in the middle of a liberating calm. He went without resisting, without thinking about what had just taken place, or of how the events might have turned out differently. Only one thing was on his mind: From where, exactly, was death going to appear? Because he wasn't afraid of death, which was still no more than a hypothetical territory to be trampled. And then he finally got the answer to the question that all men ask themselves as they die, and he took it with him.

Gobbo let go and bent his legs to accompany the giant to the ground. Crouched down like that, an agent of the night, he probed with his eyes into the two sides of the deserted street and set his knife down on the sidewalk. Then he dragged the body by the feet to rest under a porch. Before leaving the body where it lay, he picked up his knife and whispered a few words for the dead's ears alone, a few phrases that he imagined might weigh down the soul of the deceased so as to take some of the weight off his own. Then he ran off, the slender blade stabbing into the darkness. He understood at that moment that no man can believe in his own lies for long.

Snake came down the stairs with the kind of mollified look that only comes from being liberated from desire, that moment devoid of animal needs, that pure moment of short-lived self-satisfaction. He looked around the empty bar, surprised not to see Double there. He asked Roby where his companion had gotten to, and the barkeep replied that he had seen him leave a little before midnight, drunk and ill-tempered, the new waitress having refused his advances. The girl had left by the rear exit. Roby didn't know what had happened after that.

Snake left The Admiral. Roby promptly lowered the curtain behind him. The dwarf scanned the deserted street, which was demarcated by the cones of light cast by the streetlamps. It wasn't like Double to leave without waiting for him. He went up the street. His eyes gradually grew accustomed to the darkness that was interrupted by the splashes of light. Soon, he noticed a shape poking out onto the sidewalk. Walked over to it, more curious than suspicious. Straightaway he recognized the shoes from their outlandish size. Snake took out his lighter, turned the thumbwheel, and a long, rippling flame lit a circle of almost three feet in diameter, his hand at its center.

He stepped forward, discovering the shapeless mass sprawled in its entirety under a porch. Double. The giant was asleep, not quite sitting down, his legs stretched out on the ground, chin resting on his chest.

Oh, Double!

As his partner didn't reply, and didn't even move, he tried again:

It's me, Snake . . . Get up, let's get going.

He swung a kick at the side of one of the shoes, and it made the same movement as the second hand on a watch that wants to move on, but then returns to its initial position, refusing to consent to the forward movement of time.

Don't count on me to help you get up if you're still too drunk.

Snake released the button on the lighter, bent his knees and crouched down. Concern had supplanted curiosity before the complete lack of reaction from the giant.

You hear what I'm saying?

Snake sat back on his heels. He looked like a bird reaching up uncomfortably on its small feet. He shook Double again, told him to get up once more, told him to stop it with his *bullshit*, that it wasn't funny anymore, and then surveyed the surrounding buildings, but none of the windows let through the slightest glimmer of light.

That's enough now! he said with a slight tremble to his voice.

With his left hand, he pushed against the giant's shoulder. As it moved, the head flopped to the side and came to rest in an improbable position. Snake relit the lighter, quickly pulling away the hand that had touched Double, and held it under the flame as if it were an oracle capable of revealing to him some inconceivable truth. Then he let the lighter fall, and it bounced in a pool of blood.

Shit, this isn't goddamn possible.

Snake rubbed the palm of his hand that wasn't bloody against his mouth, the other floating in midair, a few inches above the ground. He recovered his lighter and started to mull over, as coldly as possible, a situation he had never expected. He couldn't just leave the body there in the street. What explanation could he give to Joyce if it was found there the following morning? They were a team. If he caught wind of the fact that Double had been killed in the territory they had been tasked with keeping an eye on, he would make him pay dearly, he would be banished, perhaps even worse. He had to act quickly. No one was likely to have witnessed the scene, other than the murderer. There would be time to figure out his identity later on. Nothing to lose on that front by waiting a bit. What was urgent was to transport the body outside the city limits.

Despite his size, Snake had been able to carry a bag weighing two hundred pounds on his shoulders since the age of sixteen. It was a question of technique, of distribution of weight more than of physical strength. He knelt down next to Double, throwing the limp arms over his shoulders, no longer concerning himself with the blood. Rage engulfed him, and that rage wasn't directed toward

the nameless murderer, it came from the hatred he har-
bored for the giant, who hadn't known how to defend
himself and whom he was going to have to carry on his
back, or rather, whom he would never cease carrying on
his back, because he knew full well that even once he had
put him down somewhere, his death would still weigh
heavily upon his shoulders, one way or another. And so
Snake made use of the rage and the hatred, lifted the body
halfway off the ground and started out, skirting the walls
so as to remain in the shadows, thinking that at least if
someone happened to look out one of the windows, all he
would see would be a drunkard being carried back home,
or some misshapen beast shrunk down by the night.

After a moment, Snake could no longer feel his own
muscles, which were paralyzed by the effort. Behind him,
the last houses of the town receded little by little into the
imperfect night, and then they vanished. He reached the
path that led to the river, knelt down for an instant to
rest himself, no longer at risk of being seen. Then he set
out again, with the sensation that Double's body was no
longer an independent weight to be carried, but instead
a kind of carapace fused with his own back, the feeling
that he was one single penitent animal for which dissim-
ulation is the only form of salvation.

The sound of the current intensified, causing the
darkness to swell. The moon was like a giant eyetooth
set in the lattice of the undergrowth. Soon the river appeared. A few rays of light glued to the surface of the

water were driving the current wild. Snake let his burden fall on the bank, leaning its back against a large rock. The head, thrown backward, looked like the hood of a heavy winter coat. He caught his breath and began speaking clearly to this man who was no longer a man, nothing more than a corpse held up by the shadows of the night. Freed of his hatred, he let all his anger flood out, directing it at the inert mass now responsible for its own fate. He knew that the words were all lies, but he uttered them all the same, without belief or conviction. Then the anger subsided, and the tone of his voice took on the same tones as the water. The dead rush into everything more quickly than the living, he thought. It would be the water that had the final word: he had decided that it must be so.

Snake tried to speak again, but his tongue rubbed against his lips, and nothing further came out of his mouth. Several boulders took shape in the moonlight; they had the look of Buddhas of various sizes, chanting in unison, the voice of the dead on the road to oblivion. The corpse by this point looked like a blotter full of the ink of the night. Snake groped around in front of himself, found the dead man's feet, slid his hands up to their calves, grabbed hold, and dragged the body toward the river. He entered the water, and once it was deep enough, that which had previously been a man began to float. Snake had water up to his neck. He pivoted the body around, so that the head would join with the weak current like the figurehead of a ship, then he gave the body a shove and watched as it moved off slowly, escorted by liquid twinkles like embers that burned out as it passed. Snake still wasn't feeling any pain, and no longer felt any hatred, not even any anger. He watched Double disappear in the distance in one final chaotic ripple, and when there was nothing left to see but the never-ending repetition of the swells, he backed up and sat cross-legged on the bank.

Coming out of the river itself, the giant's voice circumvented the darkness to reach Snake:

You know what your problem is, Snake?

The current returned to murmuring for a few seconds:

The blood that flows through your veins is frozen, that's what your problem is.

For the first time, an uncontrollable fear overcame Snake. He so would have wished that Double was right, for him not to feel anything inside, not to feel anything more at all. He so would have wished not to have to ask himself by what miracle life continued to flow through his own veins, or rather at what point that miracle would cease. Would he even know? By what portentous sign would the process be set in motion? Was there some kind of advanced warning? Would he be able to make out the final words of his story? When the moment came, would someone lean over him, glue an attentive ear to his chest, listen, and not hear anything at all? Would he feel himself dead, he who had always fed off the fear of others to make himself believe that he was alive? This was the reason he had never liked going to sleep at night, that exact moment when he became vulnerable, when he had to listen as his body grew weaker and rid itself little by little of the protective trappings of the day, when there was nothing left but his own body to listen to. Would he be alone at the end? Are we always alone when we reach that moment where we fall asleep forever?

Snake had never considered Double to be a friend, he had never had any real ones, wasn't even sure exactly what it meant, other than a vague trust to be placed in someone that had been selected to carry out a shared mission. He didn't hate him anymore. How can you hate a corpse? He was only angry at him for having such an incredible weight in death, and for turning the order of things upside down, for leaving him alone at the edge of the river. He couldn't yet resign himself to the fact that he was gone for good, to act as if he had never existed. Because he didn't hate him. Would never again be able to hate him.

Snake opened his mouth. His tongue swirled around, oiling itself with saliva, then the words came tumbling out, like iridescent moths, in response to this man who had offered him a truth that he didn't want to hear.

My blood isn't frozen, it's just cold, that's why they call me Snake, he said.

And his lips trembled a little less after he uttered these words.

Four

We kiss, we adapt, we go stark raving mad, we patch things up, we make the best of things, we bargain, we take, we rebuff, we lie, we do what we're able, and we end up believing that we can. Men are supposed to believe that time flows from one point to another, from birth to death. That isn't true. Time is a whirlpool we enter without ever really moving away from the heart of it, which is childhood, and when our illusions disappear, when the muscles begin to grow weak, when the bones become fragile, there is no longer any reason not to let ourselves be carried away to that place, where our memories appear like the shadows projected by a vanishing reality, because only those shadows can guide us on this earth.

Mark reached under his pillow and grabbed *The Odyssey*. He slid the paperback into the inside pocket of his jacket and left. He heard the sound of dishes coming from downstairs. Everyone was already eating breakfast. He stopped before the door of his parents' bedroom, which had been left ajar, and slid his head through the opening. Nobody there. Mark went in, deadening his steps on the floor as best he could. He couldn't remember the first and last time he had been in this room, the day of his birth. He let his gaze wander at eye level, without even being able to imagine that anything living had been intertwined among the furnishings just a few minutes earlier. He lowered his eyes. A Bible rested on the bedside table, framed by two dried boxwood branches. Mark looked at the Holy Book, threadbare and worn, its spine thorny with a multitude of wisps of straw, and its cover indented in the middle like a clay tile deprived of water for too long. He considered this book an enemy; he, who loved books so much, hated the use that his mother made of this one. For the time being, she was letting the family alone as far as her Holy Scriptures were concerned. The presence of the Bible always within hand's reach proved that she hadn't set the Good Lord aside, but at least she was going to speak to him alone in her bedroom when she felt the need, and during her nights as well, most probably. Mark noticed a piece of straw that stuck out farther than the others. He turned back toward the door, listening for any sign of noise, then hurriedly grabbed the Bible and opened it to the indicated page. A psalm, its opening line underlined in pencil: "Blessed is he whose transgressions are forgiven."

> When I kept silent, my bones wasted away through
>   my groaning all day long.
> For day and night your hand was heavy on me; my
>   strength was sapped as in the heat of summer.
> Then I acknowledged my sin to you and did not
>   cover up my iniquity. I said, "I will confess my

transgressions to the Lord." And you forgave the
guilt of my sin.
Therefore let all the faithful pray to you while you
may be found; surely the rising of the mighty
waters will not reach them.
You are my hiding place; you will protect me
from trouble and surround me with songs of
deliverance.

Mark read the psalm again, then closed the Bible and put
it back on the table between the boxwood branches. He
stood there lost in thought, looking for the meaning of
the words in the way his mother would have interpreted
them. Every time a situation arose, she drew on the Bible
for an answer that fit the circumstances. This time, she
had chosen the words of a penitent, and the words may
have led her to her own disavowal: "For day and night
your hand was heavy on me." She who had herself taken
on the role of "hiding place" to "protect" them "from
trouble," had she finally understood that words alone
could do nothing, thousands of years old though they
might be, that beyond their beauty, they can also trail a
quantity of treachery in their wake? Had she voluntarily
broken the silence with the goal of finally considering
her children to be innocents? Mark wanted to believe in
the miracle. He backed his way to the door and pulled
himself away from the soft light that was lapping at the
surfaces of the furniture.

Gobbo was sitting in an armchair parked at the center of a circular rug. After a moment, he began to make it slowly turn clockwise. The sailor had taken up this ritual every evening upon his return from The Admiral, a prayer offered to each one of the divinities that appeared one after the other in his line of sight, held aloft by a piece of furniture, a cord, or a simple length of fishing line. He recalled the place, the circumstances, and the reason he had been given each item as a gift, the location he had bought them, found them, and on occasion stolen them. He took the time to listen to those objects that were talkative about their history, a way for him to resist the effacement of his own memory, to prove to himself that there had been a time when he had traveled the world without any apparent goal, to forget the moment when appearances had been brutally turned into purpose. And finally, that object. A stone, which never failed to make him slow down, lowering the temperature of his body below zero. This stone in the shape of a fish, picked up on a beach, reminded him of a woman, all women contained in a single woman; it reminded him of love, of a time when he didn't yet know that love was nothing more than a hoped-for woman, one whom he never should have even met. A single woman, and yet he had somehow met her. Who had held hope out to him at the tip of her copper fingers. Who had a name with a savage ring to it, sensual, sexual. Gobbo's memory never stopped painting her face, around which flowed her long, black hair, and that body he would have loved to caress with upstrokes and down, eternally.

That evening, Gobbo sacrificed the memory born of that stone, and continued to turn his chair. He attempted to anchor himself in the bay of another memory, to continue on his route, so as to no longer be at the mercy of a single one. Inventing a fate for himself hadn't been enough for him for a long time, ever since he had come to understand that telling stories to others is first of all telling them to yourself. Ever since, he had considered hopes to be like walls constructed by men, and dreams to be of negligible quantity, digits after the decimal point that fade into obscurity. All the same, that boundless quantity of dreams was all he would have a right to in this lifetime.

When he had finished making a complete turn, he asked himself if he hadn't invented it all. An imposter who knew his imposture. And yet there were these objects, which bore witness. The sole expression of his freedom that culminated in irrevocable pain. He no longer wished to know which parts of it were invention and which the truth, to untangle the real from the false. All of it would come to a conclusion. That moment would come soon, when the armchair would no longer turn, his legs having grown too feeble.

Motionless on that motionless chair, Gobbo found himself back in the world of the real, the world where he had abandoned Double in the street after having slit his throat. The act hadn't cost him a thing. He asked himself if he hadn't committed it with the goal of paying for all of his mistakes with a single crime, and he contemplated the nature of those mistakes. He came to the conclusion that heroism is a way to pay a debt that one hasn't incurred oneself. And what a terrible hypocrisy to believe that in saving someone you might save yourself. He wasn't a hero. He didn't like heroes. By protecting Mabel, he had simply wiped clean someone else's debt. He knew it, and still regretted nothing.

Gobbo relived the scene once again. As he had returned home through the darkness of night, he had cleaned the blood off the knife, and then he had set it down on the pedestal table where it remained. He locked his eyes on the blade, which looked like the hand on a watch, not made to measure hours or minutes, but more precisely to prevent them from continuing on, a monstrous hand that represented the true form of time, which doesn't measure itself, which cannot be measured, not even in reverse, like learned men and old men do so well. Gobbo wasn't either of those things. And so, he hoped that they would come. That they would finally come for him. They, who sometimes appeared at the edge of a shadow, but who had as of yet not carried him away, had never dared to pursue him. The ghosts.

M ark clocked in first. Other employees were already getting to work by the time Julie White arrived. She had tied her hair back with a black satin ribbon and wore a dress of the same color. Mark crossed the office to join her, and greeted her. She didn't offer a reply. He insisted. Since she continued to ignore him, he recovered the logbook and returned to his office without understanding what had earned him such a brusque dismissal.

Throughout the rest of the day, the young woman acted as if Mark did not exist, even avoiding him, making sure to never end up alone with him. Not knowing anything about women, he wondered what he could possibly have done to deserve this contemptuous attitude. He wondered if she might be toying with him to test the strength of his feelings, or maybe she had simply been playing during their walk together, and she was no longer playing anymore, and he had been nothing more than a fleeting amusement. He tried to rationalize it, telling himself that something promising, as understated as it was, could be forgotten, that this would be a lesson to remember in the future, that it wasn't so bad for it to remain at the level of possibility, that not having tasted

Julie White's lips, not having caressed her skin, all of this would help to keep him distanced from the pains of love that he had only come close to in books up to that point. He closed the door so he wouldn't have to see her anymore and concentrated on his work. Or he tried.

When the afternoon came to an end, Mark went to return the logbook to its spot, and the explanations he had dreamed up to rationalize everything to himself flew to pieces. Julie White got up to leave for the day. He tried to speak to her once more and she moved away without a word, without even a look. Then she left. He began to follow her from a distance, his head again full of questions. What could he have done or not done, said or not said, to merit being rejected in such a way? What was it that he had stolen from her, to make her think him capable of taking it from her again? The answer was perhaps to be found in the final words spoken by the young woman at her doorstep: *You're special, Mark Volny, and I'm not sure if that's a good thing.* That door that he had seen open for him, and then close again, and that was doing so once more inside his head, a door whose existence and function he had never before suspected, which had dismissed him and erased him in an irrevocable gesture. Trapped in her perfumed wake, he tried to find another explanation among the many kinds of defects that were concentrated into one single flaw, the social status that was marked on his skin, with which no girl from town like Julie White could ever be comfortable. That had to be it, that was the only thing it could be, that could earn him such contempt. So she had pretended to be indifferent to that difference, and she hadn't managed to do so for more than one day. Julie White ought to tell him that to his face, at the very least. He slowed his pace and let her put a bit of distance between them. She passed through the gate. The guard waved to her and turned around to watch her as she left. Mark waited until she reached the road before catching up to her, once they were out of range of indiscreet eyes.

We need to talk, he said.

She continued on her way without paying any attention to his words, or even to his presence. He drew up alongside her and grabbed her arm to stop her.

You can't treat me this way.

The young woman's eyes were filled with amazement, but Mark couldn't detect an ounce of contempt. He was still holding her arm.

What do you want? she said.

I'm Mark Volny, do you remember me?

Obviously!

Why are you acting like I don't even exist today?

What was it that you thought?

We said things to each other, don't you remember?

Things...

I should have kissed you, is that why I don't interest you anymore?

Certainly not.

So then it's what I am that bothers you today...

That has nothing to do with it, I changed my mind, that's all.

What happened to make you change your mind? I need to know.

Mark was still holding Julie White's arm. He relaxed his grip a bit, she didn't take advantage of this to try to free herself.

Tell me I was mistaken, and after that I promise I'll leave.

Mistaken about what?

That's for you to tell me.

Julie White looked at Mark's hand wrapped around her arm as if it were a piece of jewelry he had given her that she didn't know how to refuse. There was no awkwardness whatsoever in the look, it was more like resignation, waiting for the moment that he was going to free her of this grip that she had wanted before, but that she did not fight. Her lips stammered silence, deliberately holding back words so as to force others to appear, colored by lies, words that, by their nature, contradicted the urges of her body.

There's someone else, she said.

Mark let go of the young woman's arm.

I don't believe you.

I thought I'd be able to forget about him.

I don't believe you.

I'm sorry...

Who is it? Mark asked dryly.

It doesn't make any difference...

Someone who you can walk with in the street without feeling ashamed, I guess.

You're talking nonsense.

I hope at least that you had yourself some fun.

I was never playing with you, I swear to you.

Mark implored the space that separated them, but the space was empty, and Julie White was too far away. Her eyes were riveted to the ground. Mark saw her lightly painted eyelids, like the wings of a moth as it travels through the night.

Look at me, in that case, and tell me you don't feel anything for me.

Julie White still wasn't looking at him. Not thinking anymore, he took a step forward, leaned in, and placed a clumsy kiss on her lips. Surprised, the young woman didn't shy away. After receiving the kiss, she rested her forehead on the young man's chest, her arms dangling the length of her body. He delicately took her by the shoulders and pushed her back softly, so that she might finally take in what was there to see.

Look at me! he repeated.

Julie White raised her eyes.

What if we go back to the moment when we went our separate ways in front of your place?

It's too late, we can't go back anymore.

Of course we can, tomorrow is Sunday, we could meet up, wherever you choose, and start again from zero.

No, it wouldn't do any good.

That's not what your lips were saying a second ago.

The young woman's features hardened.

You can lie with your lips, she said.

You can say anything you want, but I don't believe that kiss was lying.

Julie White let a moment go by. Her gaze grew softer.

You sure believe a lot of things, Mark Volny.

And would I be wrong to believe them?

She took a step back. Mark didn't try to stop her.

You're definitely special.

You already told me that . . .

Exactly, and I know now that it isn't a good thing.

Mark witnessed what took place next as a simple spectator, the moment during which one silhouette swung away from another in a wavy, indistinct future, a distance that it was impossible to bridge in steps. This woman he hardly knew was leaving, a woman to whom Mark no longer dared even raise his eyes, not to avoid the discomfort of a hypothetical hope, but to prevent himself from having to fight off his own desire. He stood there like that, frozen in a moment where nothing was possible anymore, where nothing had ever truly been possible, immobile on the dusty path, as if he were some sort of dust himself.

The next day, the three brothers quit working at midday. They ate buckwheat crepes and cheese. They had already sawed up a dozen young trees that had been uprooted by the storm. Mark hadn't spoken a single word all morning.

Is something the matter? Matthew asked him.

No, nothing.

Doesn't look that way, you seem like you're elsewhere.

It's true that you haven't been talking, added Luke with his mouth full.

Just tired, I guess.

Is something bugging you? insisted Matthew.

I'm okay, I promise.

If you say so, but just remember, what affects you affects me too.

Mark caught the reference, the day when he had told Matthew that there shouldn't be any secrets between them, but he had no desire whatsoever to talk about Julie White. They continued to eat in silence, each of them focused on their own interior voice, more or less benevolent.

Oh, by the way, I forgot to tell you! said Luke.

He stopped speaking, licked the cheese stuck to the blade of his knife and wiped the blade on the moss that covered the bottom of the tree trunk he was sitting against. Then he folded his knife and stuffed it into his pants pocket, looking for a reaction from his brothers. Only Matthew seemed to be paying attention.

What is it that you didn't tell us? he asked.

Lynch tried to make me talk the other day, at the fountain.

What do you mean? I thought you weren't going into town anymore.

He scared the piss out of me, telling me that he was going to put me in jail if I didn't confess I had stolen the cartridge.

The scumbag...

Don't worry, I didn't say a thing...

You stood up to him?

Grandpa helped me a bit, to be honest.

Grandpa was there?

Yeah, he told Lynch that if he didn't have any proof, he had to leave me alone.

And Lynch backed down?

He just cussed us out two or three times and then he left.

Matthew relaxed. He turned toward Mark.

You hearing this?

Mark didn't react.

You have to stop going into town and hanging around, okay? said Matthew, turning back to Luke.

I won't go anymore . . . There's another thing I didn't tell you about Lynch . . . He's found himself a new hobby.

Luke cleared his throat and spat straight out in front of himself.

You remember when I saw him in front of that girl's place the other day, well, he went back to pick her up, and they went to Samuelson's together.

Luke took a crumpled piece of paper out of one of his pockets. He flattened it against his thigh and smoothed it a few times with the flat of his hand.

I can't read, but I copied as well as I could what was marked on her mailbox.

Luke held the page out to Matthew.

Look at this, Mark, you likely know her, this girl works in the offices, at the quarry.

Mark raised his eyes. He read the letters that were clumsily traced and connected together with dashes, then, as if awakening abruptly, he tore the sheet out of Luke's hands.

Good God, what's going on with you? asked Matthew.

Mark offered no response, his gaze fixed on the written name. Julie White had not entirely lied to him when she told him she was seeing *someone else*. She must not have had a choice, judging by what Luke had told them. He needed to go see her right away, to let her know that he knew everything.

Go on without me, he said, getting to his feet.

Goddammit, it's time you tell us what is going on! protested Matthew.

We agreed we'd work on the fort all day long, added Luke peevishly.

Do you see any pirates anywhere? Mark shouted, getting carried away.

Luke's head ducked down between his shoulders.

You don't have to bawl him out, said Matthew.

I'm sorry, Luke, this isn't about you, I promise that I'll explain everything to you later.

Mark grabbed his jacket and flew down the hill to the path, his brothers watching him go with astonishment.

Julie White wasn't home. Mark sat down on the steps. On occasion, people walked past on the sidewalk, pretending they didn't notice him. As for him, he didn't even see them. He rested his head against the wall and closed his eyes, repeating to himself what he planned to say. He dozed off a while later. A repeated clicking woke him up. At first he thought he was dreaming. The sound grew louder. Mark didn't know how long he had been asleep. He rubbed his eyes with his closed fists like a little kid. Julie White and Lynch were walking toward him. He was holding her by the waist, and the studded soles of his boots were clattering against the sidewalk. Mark didn't move, no longer knowing what he was going to say, or reply, whether he should speak first, if he should even speak at all or just close his eyes again to erase what he was seeing.

Well look at that, it seems as if you've got a visitor, said Lynch, tightening his grip on Julie White's waist.

Go away! the young woman said firmly to Mark.

Mark's head tipped to one side, as if he was trying to see a bit of blue sky.

Are you deaf? The lady told you to get lost.

Mark felt as if he was underwater, as if Lynch's voice was coming out of an eddy at the surface, right above him. He couldn't see anything clearly anymore, he was too busy struggling not to float to the surface and make a spectacle of himself, waiting for a lifesaving current to carry away the hated body and the voice that came from that hated body, but the whirlpool grew even larger, twisting the voice further down like a screw until it could reach him and torture him.

Please, go away right now, repeated the young woman, her voice less firm.

Lynch was jubilant.

You can't win 'em all, he said.

Incapable of speaking, Mark implored Julie White with his eyes. Lynch took his arm away from the young woman's waist and placed his hand on the butt of his revolver.

Clear out, right now, before I lose my patience.

Do what he asks you, please.

Mark came brutally back up to the surface. There was no longer any whirlpool. He struggled to his feet. His eyes pierced through the man with all his hatred, sparing the young woman. His gaze then shifted toward the twisted street littered with purple maple and sweetgum leaves, which looked like wavy dagger blades spotted with blood. People moved along in slow motion on the opposite bank, little silhouettes flattened by the light of a weekend afternoon. There were also a few insects flying about, darting through the same raking light. Then there was nothing at all, and Mark turned back into the darkness.

It smelled of sweat, rancidness, piss, and cheap fortified wine, and miniature meteorites traversed the dark space. Mark struggled to open his eyelids. The meteorites continued to trace their routes for another few moments. At first he didn't even try to move his head, his cheek glued to a wooden plank that was smooth and gleaming with grime. A partition and an open door, both of them made up of metal grilles, entered his field of vision, and beyond that, a narrow corridor. He had no idea where this place he found himself was, whether it was only a dream, or if he had just awoken. Once he had at least somewhat gathered his wits about him, he slid his hands under his thighs, heaved his chest up, and recovered his balance to take a seated position. The soles of his boots scuffed against the floor. The sound they produced smashed against his skull, then was snuffed out, like a fire covered with wet sheets. He soon recognized the sound of more boots, as well as another, undefinable, intolerable. Lynch appeared in the corridor, dragging a chair by its backrest, and its metal feet scraped along the concrete with the long, agonizing scream of a dying animal. He entered, placed the chair across from Mark, and

sat down, resting his elbows on his thighs and his fists
under his chin. Mark immediately knew where he was
and that he was not dreaming.

You're finally awake, and none too soon!

What am I doing here?

Lynch played up his annoyance.

You see, I would have wagered that it would have
been one of your brothers that I would have brought to
this cell for a visit first... How wrong we are, sometimes.

Why have you locked me up?

You're not locked up, the door was open.

Are you going to tell me what I'm doing here or not?

It's not just a put-on, then, you really don't remember
anything at all?

Mark shook his head. Lynch leaned forward, and
the sweet scent of his cheap aftershave mingled with the
other smells.

You just packed it in on the sidewalk, without any
warning. The doc says that it's some sort of illness, that it
isn't serious, that we only had to wait for you to recover,
and seeing that I'm not a bad guy, I politely suggested
that I might take care of you here.

You could have taken me home.

Lynch shifted backward on his chair. The annoyance
had disappeared from his face.

I wanted to have you handy when you woke up to
make sure that you got the message...

Which message?

Julie White, you were in front of her place when you bowed out.

Mark could remember Lynch holding the young woman by her waist, but what happened next had been sucked into a black hole.

I was in the middle of explaining to you that there was no point in your seeing her anymore.

The black hole spat out the scene in its entirety. Lynch tilted his head in an attempt to appear compassionate, taking great delight in Mark's reactions.

You see, a wheel doesn't only spin in one direction.

Mark kept his lips sealed; he felt sick to the stomach.

Nothing to say?

Lynch waited another few seconds, then got up, stepped around the chair, and placed his hands atop its back.

I take it we understand one another.

Lynch made as if to leave, but then turned back. A move he had copied from a movie, that he had practiced in front of the mirror countless times.

I'm positive that you know what happened the day Renoir and Salles were killed, that you and your family are covering it up for your brother. If you're half as clever as you look, you ought to tell me the truth, before I end up putting you all away as accomplices. It's now or never.

We've told you the truth.

You're very clearly all the same, Lynch spat back at him.

Mark blasted him with a stare.

Now there's nothing left for you to do but dream of Julie White's cute little ass, because it will never be for you, said Lynch, miming the young woman's shapely hips and rear end with the palms of his hands.

Lynch left the cell, abandoning the chair. Once he had disappeared, his voice floated back down the corridor.

It's in your best interest to have cleared out of there before I'm done in the shitter.

Lynch had taken on the role of master of the forces governing the attraction between bodies. A new cosmogony established itself in Mark's mind. A few of the meteorites reappeared. Some passed through space without leaving a trace, others converged in one spot and clustered together, blending their light to form a star that he was being ordered to watch move off into the distance without looking away.

Snake went back to question Roby, to find out whether anything unusual had taken place while he was upstairs that night. Other than the fact that Mabel had stood up to Double and he had then begun to drink more than usual, Roby had nothing more to add. Snake asked whether the girl's father had been by that evening. Roby replied that he hadn't, that he was certain he hadn't seen him. Before he left the bar, the dwarf took down the waitress's address and then set off with his gnomish gait.

The Widow Brock greeted him with a dubious look and told him he was to wait at the entrance, the same as all visitors. A few minutes later, Mabel joined the dwarf on the sidewalk. She said she'd refused Double's advances, then left by the back way to avoid him and return home as quickly as she could. She hadn't seen the giant since. Snake watched her reactions, looking for anything that could betray her being nervous. Nothing telling. She looked sincere, and her version of the story differed in no way from Roby's. He allowed her to go back into the boardinghouse, and remained for a long moment in front of the closed door. The dwarf's instincts, keen in normal times, were of no use to him in his attempts to figure out what had happened the night of the murder. He waited a long time, dawdling in the streets, before he went to fill Joyce in on what had happened.

Joyce was sitting in an armchair behind a coffee table on which had been placed an eggcup, a place setting, and an immaculate white napkin. Snake wanted to speak. Joyce raised an arm in the air to signify that he should remain quiet, picked up his knife, and tapped meticulously on the side of the shell with the sharp side of the blade. He looked like a surgeon executing a trepanation according to the rules of that art, operating expertly and with the utmost attention. Joyce pulled off the top of the eggshell and set it down on the lip of his plate. Then he plunged two fingers into the opening and extricated, by its neck, an embryo with bulging, blind eyes, covered with a coarse down slicked with mucus, kind of like a bundle of thin tapeworms. Its heart, still filled with blood, painfully raised up the deformed little body. Joyce tore off the yolk sac, across which spread a complex tree of blood vessels, and the two little feet went slack. He held the little creature suspended before his eyes a moment, moved his head under it, and then let the chick fall into his open mouth, as if it had taken him all that time to convince the expressionless uniformity that made up his face to obey him. He began to chew slowly, and the cracking of the tender bones between his teeth could faintly be heard. When he had finished, he wiped his mouth with the napkin, then looked at Snake, who got the feeling that he was the same sort of creature in Joyce's hands.

You're alone, said Joyce.

Snake repeated what he had been planning to say:

Double has disappeared. We parted ways last night, as usual, after The Admiral, and when I went by to pick him up this morning, he wasn't home.

I'd imagine he sleeps elsewhere from time to time.

Of course, but he always goes back home, and never leaves me without any news for such a long time.

Do you think something has happened to him?

I have no idea...

If you didn't, you wouldn't be here, isn't that so?

Joyce backed up in his chair.

I placed all my trust in you two, he added.

I'm sorry.

I don't give a damn if you're sorry. Do you have anything else to tell me?

No.

Then why don't you go look for him, instead of wasting your time here.

Snake hesitated an instant.

And what if I can't find him? he said, as if he was talking to himself.

Nobody is to disappear in this valley unless I decide they should, do you hear me? And especially not one of my men.

Very well, sir! Should I go and talk to Lynch about this?

Not for the moment . . . and it isn't worth your coming back here without him.

Alright.

Snake felt even smaller than usual, insignificant in the face of this man who gave him his orders. He wondered for a second if Joyce ever had to take orders from someone else. Not finding an answer to his own question, he moved toward the door and stepped into the hallway, without bothering to ignite his lighter. It was as if he had been gulped down by the dark.

Seated atop a boulder, Gobbo was watching the power plant. The building looked like a trompe l'oeil painted on the front of the dam, and a fine mist erased some of the rough patches here and there. Soon, the frozen image began to thaw as the first workers began to exit, one after another, by way of the little door cut into the stationary larger one with its suspended track, which was only opened to take in large equipment. Once outside, the workers gathered into little clusters of varying sizes, like drops of water sliding down a windowpane. Some of them spotted Gobbo on his boulder, and a few of them went over to see him. They asked him what it was he was waiting for. He told them that it was none of their business, and they went on their way without further discussion. Martin was one of the last to leave the plant, by himself. Gobbo got down from his rock, and Martin went over to him with a surprised look.

What are you doing here?

Waiting for you.

Waiting for me?

I need to talk to you, he said in a serious tone.

We could have met up at The Admiral, like usual.

I didn't know if you'd be coming.

I had some things to do yesterday.

Follow me!

Martin didn't remember ever seeing Gobbo so ill-tempered. He fell into step behind him. Normally, the sailor's gait was limber, but in that moment, it was heavy, because a great part of his energy was taken up by a machinery other than his muscles, far more deeply anchored. They reached town. As they passed before The Admiral, Gobbo didn't slow his pace.

Where are we going?

Don't need any witnesses.

They continued on.

What's the big idea with all this mysteriousness, anyway? asked Martin after a while.

Never you mind, we're almost there.

Martin couldn't remember the first time he had followed this path. It had been Gobbo who had guided them that night, him and his snootful of booze. The seaman's house was at the opposite end of town. A small cabin made with spruce logs. Once they arrived, they climbed a flight of stairs and Gobbo took a key from his pocket, opened the door, and went in.

Close it tightly behind you! he said without turning around.

Martin slammed the door shut and followed Gobbo into the room where he had slept and awoken a few days earlier.

The sailor pointed at the sofa.

Sit!

Martin sat down without even removing his jacket. Gobbo dropped into the armchair. He put his forearms down on the armrests, and his hands dangled in the void. A silence set in, a silence inside which the objects seemed to take over so they could help the two men in what was to follow. Martin waited, letting his gaze wander across the statuettes, the masks, and the suspended rostrum, while the sailor gathered his thoughts.

I'm going to tell you a story that I have never told anyone before, he finally said, with great and urgent seriousness.

The sailor took some more time, then thrust his chest forward and placed one of his fingers on a pockmarked cheek. Martin had always taken these blemishes for the remnants of badly healed acne scars.

You see these scars here, I made them with the point of a knife, for a girl... one of her country's traditions. I met this girl on an island in the Pacific. In all the time I had sailed the seas, I had never felt any desire to quit my traveling. Women, I had known many, some of whom likely wanted to hold on to me. But she was the one who caught me, without any warning. From the moment I saw her, the seas and the oceans all seemed too small. I didn't even have to think it over. The boat on which I had arrived set sail without me, and it did nothing to me to see it disappear on the horizon. I was relieved to finally stop

somewhere, for someone. I stayed six months on that island, afloat in the gentle waters of happiness. Our plan
was to build a hut and to fill it with a flock of little ones,
to make ourselves a family. Her father didn't look on this
with a favorable eye, but we thought he'd come around
if we gave it some time, that what united the two of us
would be enough to overcome his reticence, that's how
obvious it was. I had decided to put away my rucksack for
good. Before I did, I just needed to settle up with my past
so that I didn't have any regrets. I told the girl I needed
to go back to my own country to say goodbye to my parents, so they could see their son one last time, and that I
would come straight back. She didn't try to stop me, she
understood. It was important to me.

Gobbo inhaled long and deep.

I boarded the first boat that made a stopover and I
ended up finding my way back home. When I got there,
my father was already dead and buried.

The sailor raised his eyes to rest on the dusty books
lined up on a shelf.

As an inheritance, he left me a pile of books, and he
left my mother the arrears on his resentment toward me,
which she seemed ready to make me pay in full if I stuck
around too long. I went to say two or three words over my
father's grave, but all I found was a stone, gray and cold.
When I returned to the house, I got the feeling that I was
entering his real tomb, one dug by my mother, in such a
way that everything evoked her husband. I was no longer

welcome; I had been gone too long. Every look from her reminded me that I had abandoned them both, that I would always be considered a deserter, and never again a son. And so I didn't disappoint her. I turned around and left. I would have bet that my mother would soon follow after my father, but I wasn't going to still be there when it happened. I didn't want to see what she was going to become, didn't even want to know. I didn't owe her anything. The only thing that counted was to get back to the girl I loved, so that I could stop thinking about anything that wasn't us. So back to sea I went.

The sailor went quiet. He was no longer looking at the books. His lids fell in front of his eyes, like the curtain being lowered for a set change between acts.

I was gone for three months. Three short months. Upon my return, I no longer needed to build a cabin... there was no longer anything to fill it with. During my absence, the girl's father had taken advantage of the opportunity to marry her to a man in their tribe. She hadn't had a say in it. I saw her again in secret. She still loved me. I tried to get her back by every means possible. Her husband and his brothers made me understand that my place was no longer there, but since I didn't want to hear it, they gave me a beating and left me for dead on the beach. Death wanted no part of me. As soon as I was more or less recovered, I returned to the village, where I was welcomed with a hail of stones. I tried at night, but I was fought off again. I thought she would find a way to come back to me, that something was going to happen, that it wasn't possible for it to end that way. They were holding her prisoner. I never saw her again. For weeks, maybe months, I stayed on the beach, living off shell-fish, entirely by survival reflex, despite the fact that I no longer wanted to live. All of my dreams had died. One day, a ship came ashore. I boarded it. From the deck, I watched the island dwindle and disappear. Apparently I eventually fainted, and they carried me to a bunk where I slept for days on end. The memory of that girl has never left me.

Gobbo's fingers gripped the armrests.

It took me a long time to recover, physically. After that, I sailed the seas for years more. Solid ground scared me. You can capsize more easily on land than on any ocean, believe you me. Time was not a problem, right up until the day I felt too old to continue. It was chance that led me here, as well as the river. Here or elsewhere, it didn't matter. Nobody knew me. I could tell people stories of lives, pile up my souvenirs in this cabin, I could lie all I wanted, navigating in other ways, lying to all of these gullible men, in whose eyes I pass for an adventurer, even a hero . . . Lying to others is easy; to yourself, it's impossible. There is always that girl, like a star in the sky, whom I will never reach, the one who was supposed to guide me, and who got me lost . . . and whom I lost.

Gobbo stopped speaking once more. He was looking for the stone in the middle of the shamble of objects, the stone in the shape of a fish, the light of which had been burning in his brain for years now, and which he had tried in vain to extinguish.

Why are you telling me all of this today? asked Martin after a long silence.

Gobbo didn't hear the question.

And you know what drives me mad the most after all these years, it's that I can no longer bring myself to say her name. Sometimes I feel it get as far as my lips, but it never tips toward the correct side. I can remember the beautiful lines on her face when she laughed, and the way she walked, all of the ways she had of moving without concerning herself with the havoc she was creating, but I cannot say her name to find some relief. There was no one freer than her, and they stole that freedom from her, that freedom into which I wanted to slip without shaking up anything around her, without damaging any of her beauty... there is nothing more beautiful, in my mind, than to want that for someone, and for me, well, it wouldn't have cost me anything.

Gobbo emphasized the "anything." After a few seconds, he raised his head. The rings around his eyes looked like ancient bark.

Your daughter is that kind of person, he added.

A handful of seconds went by. Martin felt a fire growing in his insides.

Why are you talking to me about my daughter? he asked dryly.

Last night...

The seaman stopped short. A nervous smile cut across his face, making the rings around his eyes vanish, then the smile faded away.

Don't worry yourself; I did what needed to be done.

What did you do last night, and what does my daughter have to do with it, for the love of God?

Double, he wanted to defile her... She doesn't have anything to worry about anymore.

What do you mean, anymore?

Gobbo nodded to the knife on the pedestal table.

I don't believe you.

The sailor didn't respond. His smile reappeared for a fleeting moment, like a ripple formed by a gust of wind on the surface of a pond.

If you were telling the truth, they'd be talking of nothing but this in town.

Exactly, they'd have already found his body.

So you see that you've invented the whole thing, because of all the booze you drank last night, I suppose.

The filament of the light bulb began to buzz up near the ceiling. Martin saw shadows flitting across Gobbo's face, like little mirages. The sailor's eyes would no longer let go.

Promise me that you'll take care of your daughter from now on.

That's my business.

Gobbo leaped to his feet, grabbed the knife, and moved toward Martin.

You see this knife, neither it nor I can go back anymore. And so you're going to do what I tell you, assuming I haven't misjudged you.

Martin stared at the blade, peppered with dark stains.

Swear to me!

Martin looked up. There was no defiance at all in his expression.

Alright, he said, and that word was like a door that someone had opened to him.

Gobbo set the knife back on the table and fell back heavily into his armchair.

Now leave me, he said, pointing a finger in front of him, without ungluing his arms from the armrests.

Matthew was kneeling on the riverbank. It had been a long time since he had dropped his lines into the river. He spat into the water and his phlegm danced nervously in the current, like a frightened jellyfish. He wiped his lips with the back of his sleeve. Had the feeling that something was out of place, a dissonance, similar to a wrong note during a symphony. He instinctively turned upstream, and he saw a strange-looking piece of timber wedged between two rocks. He stood back up to better make out what it was. A series of creases stretched out across his forehead, and his fingers clenched around the lines he had brought with him. Matthew spit again, then turned back once more, hypnotized by the vision as it was bombarded by glints of light vomited up by the river, incapable of focusing on his target, which wasn't a large branch, or even a tree trunk, but a human body. At one point, under the effects of the current, the corpse's pale face pivoted in his direction, and two eyes filled with astonishment looked straight at him. The wide-open mouth appeared to be screaming at the delicate natural background made up by the shadows of the ash, the willows, and the false acacias. The corpse seemed to be animated by invisible forces, almost dancing in place.

The dead have the power to seek vengeance, thought Mark. He saw the faces of Renoir and Salles, one after another, and he begged the waves to cover over the corpse, to nourish themselves with it over the course of the liquid centuries; he begged them, not knowing whether he was being punished by the wandering souls of the dead or betrayed by the river itself. He, its tireless servant. As if his prayer had been answered, the corpse shifted slightly and its head flopped over to the other side. A mop of black hair floated behind its skull. The cold found its way under Matthew's skin, rejoining the feverish fire burning in his heart, but neither the cold nor the burning were able to blend together in the pale westward light that bathed the river, which, at that moment, had the look of an empty table in a morgue.

Nobody remembers who it was that gathered most of the men of the town together at the river's edge. The news spread as if by a powerful wind. They were assembled on both banks, well downstream from the Black Rimstone, their gazes fixed on one specific spot, where the rocks seemed to come flying apart under the impact of the current, where a body that was as tall as two bodies, but had been controlled by only one person, was impaled on a slender branch wedged between two boulders. You would have thought it was a ship torn apart by the storm. The pitiably writhing arms sought in vain for something sturdy to grab onto, and the legs, stuck together, snaked back and forth behind it, like two amorous eels. Now and again, under the blows of stronger swells, the branch lifted up an inch or two, the corpse followed, apathetic, and the pale eyes on that pale face swept intermittently across both banks of the river, questioning, like an accused man watching his jurors.

Snake was standing at the water's edge. He was muttering a vengeance-filled prayer. Lynch was nearby, his face hidden in the shadow cast by his hat, one hand on the butt of his weapon, ready to draw if an evil spirit were to come climbing out of the river.

A cry cut through the forest and lingered in the putrid air. A few seconds later, a fish hawk emerged from the curtain of trees on the shore, its wings beating like percussion caps being struck repeatedly by a hammer. The bird landed on a branch, right next to the corpse's head. It continued to beat its wings a moment as it sought its balance, then folded them back, defying the spectators with its cruel, black gaze. It planted its beak in one of the corpse's eye sockets and emptied it of its contents.

Snake crouched down, picked up a stone, and threw it in the bird's direction, without managing to hit it. He had to try again several times before the bird flew heavily off to regain the forest, having already devoured the second eye.

Two bloody streams marked Double's cheeks, painting him with the look of a clown in makeup. Lynch barked out an order on the spot, that someone go and fetch the body. The men lowered their heads, then one of them broke ranks and walked away, the others following him without paying any attention to the lawman's words.

It is said that later, after the last man left, Snake dismissed Lynch, saying that he would take care of everything, and that the other man had not argued. It is said that once he was alone, the dwarf stepped into the river, walking cautiously, his hands at surface level as if he were pushing down on the water so he wouldn't fall. It is said that he freed the corpse and that, not being able to take it to solid ground because of its weight and the current, and not even trying, he hung on to it and let himself be pulled along with it for a long while, until he reached the calm of a deep basin. It is said that the scene had the appearance of a baptism. It is also said that the bird came back to whirl around above the two men with their one life, not as if it wanted to make off with any additional organs, but instead wishing, by way of its shadow, to soften the traces of death in the arms of that man who asked for nothing. It is said that night had fallen by the time Snake finally brought the corpse up onto the bank, and that once the night was over, day arrived to find him still sitting there, his back resting against a grave covered in stones, and that he was throwing little pebbles into the distance while he spoke to the river.

The boys didn't give a damn about the giant that had been found dead three days before. They went back to work building their stockade. Mark thought nonstop about Julie White. Despite Lynch's warning, he hadn't given up, looking for any means to free the young woman from the lawman's clutches. No solution had come to him yet that wouldn't have been dangerous not only to her, but also to Matthew and the rest of his family.

At Luke's request, Elie had accompanied his grandsons. Seated on a stump, the old man observed with an expert eye the progress of their construction, sometimes offering his advice. It had been a long time since he had seemed so lighthearted, almost joyful. At one point, he got up, his back to the building site, and rested there on his crutches, like a fantastical animal sporting a fossilized exoskeleton, his disheveled hair looking like a crown of thorns.

Pirates, he squawked, imitating the sound of a parrot.

Luke ran over to him.

Did you hear him too? asked Luke, all excited.

I heard him, replied Elie, scanning the sky with a serious look.

Can you see him?

Elie looked at the eternal child, shaking his head with a miffed look, but with glints of amusement in the veiny irises of his eyes.

I don't see him, said Luke.

And yet the cretin's around here somewhere, that's for certain.

Luke was turning in place. The old man made as if he was looking as well, then he lowered his head, bothered by the light.

Hot damn, what on earth is that? he said after a moment, his gaze fixed on a shape farther downriver.

You see it? Where is it? said Luke, his nose still raised to the sky.

Over there! added the old man, stretching out an arm, talking loud enough that the others could hear him.

Matthew and Mark had continued working up until that point, following their grandfather's little game with a distracted eye. They went over to join the other two, discovering for themselves the strange scene unfolding near the river. Snake was following the ash trees that bordered the water. He was on all fours, completely naked. Sometimes, shadows clung to his body, like little traces of leprosy healed the next instant by the light. He made his way over to the water, waded in, cupped his hands together, and slaked his thirst, looking around with a detached air. Then he retreated, climbing back up on the bank, at the exact spot where all the men had stood a few days earlier, silently, religiously, with that particular look that the incarnation of death paints on the faces of the living.

Next, Snake squatted down, his arms dangling like stays on a ship, fixating on an image that no longer existed other than in his memory, the image of a corpse wedged between two rocks, like growths on a monstrous spinal column. Indifferent to the sun, to the muck, to the ticks clinging to his flesh, to the cuts on the bottom of his feet, to the underhanded beauty of a world with a thousand dangers; indifferent to life, because he found himself beyond all sensation, entirely given over to an unchanging emotion for which he had never prepared himself, which he had never even imagined, and yet which confronted him from the depths of loss and absence. His torso began to move forward and back to the rhythm of an internal prayer that he recited each morning, and had for three days now, facing a liquid pathway that separated him from the grave built by his own hands, a grave of monumental proportions that bore no cross. His prayer told of the end of all things and the impossibility of overcoming the pain engendered by a promise that had never been made. In this way, Snake bared himself, robbed of everything, suddenly anonymous, voluntarily exiled from the rest of the townsfolk, out of obligation and by choice; reduced to a skeleton with flesh and deprived of a soul to be saved, a madness set down on the polished stones by the passage of the waters, dead and bleached by the sun.

This is what had become of this man who no longer wanted to be one. And if it had been possible for him to bury himself in a grave, he likely would have done so, just opposite the other one. After a while, feeling that he was being watched, he raised his head, discovering the four silhouettes on the other side of the river, a little farther upstream. He didn't appear surprised or concerned, looking at them as if they were part of the hillside. He leveled at them his impenetrable stare, thrown away from him, abandoned, disconnected from his own mind.

Go away, you rotten pirate! Luke began to shout, his hands cupped around his mouth.

Snake could hear the cries clearly, but he didn't move, curious. The shadows were now dancing around him, without touching him. Luke reached down, picked up a rock, and threw it as hard as he could. The projectile landed far from its target. Snake took a couple of steps toward its landing spot, stopped, and reached down, selecting a stone at random, but with infinite care. He held it for a long moment between his fingers, as if it were an egg ready to hatch, then he turned away from the river, set off half-heartedly, and disappeared into the forest.

That was Snake! said Matthew.

If we didn't all just dream it, that was him, said Mark.

He's clearly not in his usual state of mind.

Maybe we should bring weapons the next time we come here, said Luke.

I don't think it's worth bothering, he doesn't really seem to be very dangerous, added Elie.

How would you know? I think we ought to be cautious of him. He could maybe come back with more pirates.

The only pirate he ever teamed up with is dead.

Luke nervously rubbed his hands together, and the ocher tinge of the earth that covered his hands contrasted with his skin.

And what if he finds the treasure before we do?

That would surprise me, and anyway, he wouldn't do anything with it, replied Elie.

Why not?

He's already dead, if you want my opinion, and even if he were to find the treasure, he wouldn't be able to pick it up, because the gold would pass right through his hands.

Luke considered his grandfather's words for an instant.

Like a ghost, you mean?

That's right, like a ghost.

At The Admiral, everyone had seen Mabel's exchange with Double at his table the night he disappeared. No one had heard what they had said to one another, but having seen the scowl on the giant's face after their conversation, it was obvious that she had resisted him. They whispered and cast furtive glances her way. Despite the fact that the path was now clear, not one salacious remark was thrown her way. The men at The Admiral looked at her differently, some of them even suspecting her of having dark powers. Others imagined a guardian angel tasked with protecting her, because their minds could not conceive of a human capable of killing such a giant. Mabel's presence aroused suspicion, curiosity, and even fascination. They waited until she was out of hearing range to speak of all the signs that were piling up. Double's murder, in echo of the deaths of Renoir and Salles, all men in Joyce's pay. And now, Snake hadn't given any signs of life since the discovery of his companion's body. All this upheaval in such a short time. They didn't go any further. Not yet. Lynch, in charge of the investigation, had taken up quarters at The Admiral, always the last to leave.

The bar had emptied out. Gobbo remained seated as Martin rose to his feet. He went resolutely over toward his daughter, who was putting glasses away on a serving tray that sat on the bar. Roby had already started to step around the counter, but Mabel signaled for him not to intervene. Martin stood before her like a great wading bird awkwardly resting on a tree branch.

I was wondering if we could talk, he said.

She shot him a hard look.

Talk?

Yes, if you're willing.

Mabel moved the glasses closer together on the tray.

I've got work to do, she said.

After?

After, I've got things to do then too.

Tomorrow, then?

Not tomorrow either.

Okay, well, you tell me when.

Mabel stretched her arm out across the counter, her palm facing up. Martin began to move, thinking it an invitation, but she slid the tray onto her hand to carry it away.

That's right, I'll tell you when, she said, before walking away.

Martin left the bar. Gobbo later told him that after he had gone, his daughter had looked at the closed door for a long time.

———

After closing, Roby asked Mabel to stay a bit longer.

It's maybe not sensible for me to talk to you like this, he said.

How do you mean?

People tend to disappear afterward.

I don't understand.

All of these coincidences... Double, found with his throat cut, and now Snake, who has gone off into the wild... From what I hear, he went to pay you a visit at the boardinghouse you're staying at?

So what?

So, it's strange.

There are plenty of people who have talked to me today, maybe you should go and check that they're all still alive and kicking, said Mabel.

Which reminds me, what did your father want, earlier tonight?

I have no idea, I didn't listen to him, I'd have hated to endanger him as well.

Quit taking me for a fool!

My father couldn't care less about me and my life.

That's not the impression I got. He even seemed to be in a pretty good mood, unlike that other time.

What are you trying to say?

I'm wondering what might have led him to change his tune.

And what business would that be of yours?

Don't raise your voice to me, little lady! Everything that goes on in my bar is my business.

You don't actually believe he's capable of committing a murder?

I don't know your father.

You saw Double's size, compared to his!

People aren't nearly as strong when they're drunk.

Everyone hated Double.

Roby looked around the empty room.

That may be so, but I can't imagine any of them taking the risk.

I don't understand why this is getting you so worked up.

Attacking Double and Snake is also provoking Joyce, and that's just not good for business.

I didn't notice there being any fewer people tonight.

It's hard to say how things will go, and what's more, I don't like it when things change.

Is that all you wanted to talk to me about?

Roby let a moment go by, giving Mabel a harsh stare.

Yes, that's all . . . for the moment.

381

In the days that followed, the entire town began to murmur. What people thought in the comfort of their own home they began to share with others, at first in muted tones, deep in the forest, in alcoves, in attics, where they held secret meetings. The giant, whom they had believed invincible, had been vanquished by an anonymous vigilante, an unimaginable, evidently superhuman, being, who had pitted himself against Joyce. The sight of the corpse floating in the river had chipped away at all the forms of servitude that had been accepted until then. Bit by bit, the townspeople grew aware of what had been lying dormant, a form of revolt inexpressible prior to the murder, anchored deep in the past, one that predated their parents, their ancestors. They rose up timidly, comforting each other, getting a feel for their dignity, like a nestling tries out its brand-new wings.

The community grew larger, began to organize. Resentment evolved into discreet rage, climbing into throats and stirring up bodies that were ready to fight to assert their rights. They eventually became conscious that revolt was the only way that they wouldn't begin dying the moment they were born. No one made any mention of the lessons of history, which taught that it is pointless to burn one idol only to install a replica in its place, that all idols are loathsome, that victims are easily transformed into executioners without the slightest hesitation. They did not want to go back. Their only concern was that the present instant be stretched out into a future victory. They made use of big words: *struggle* and *resistance*, words that they had had in their mouths since the last war. The more they talked, the more self-assurance they found, but still they remained hidden, their doubts walled in behind their faces like a mask, and fear floated everywhere, like a unique and heady body odor. Ideas were thrown out in no logical order, after which they took stock of what they had, began to give them some shape, and eventually began to translate them into a manifesto. A number of demands were fleshed out from this, as well as the means necessary to see them adopted. They laid the foundations of a union. The community of dissenters continued to swell. They continued to conspire in secret, but they began to feel stronger and stronger. Their fear receded from one great speech to the next. They forgot all about Lynch and his authority. No point in focusing on the wrong adversary. They believed that the battle could be won if they could remain united and in sufficiently great numbers. Soon, that number was reached, and once they asked themselves if they had the momentum and the courage necessary to bring their revolution out into the open, it became clear to them that they needed a leader, a charismatic head that the herd could follow. They observed one another carefully, seeking their chosen representative, but they did not recognize anyone of that caliber among them. They began to muse aloud. One name was spoken a first time, then repeated, and that name established itself as the only choice. It became a forgone conclusion for all of them, and yet the man who answered to that name was not among them.

There were at least a hundred of them when they crossed the square. Many carried musical instruments, strings or wind instruments. Silent musicians now composing a great orchestra, who had up until that point rehearsed alone or in limited formations. They advanced with solemnity, not parading, walking in one same rhythm, similar to armed troops making their way to the front line, without knowing what they would find there, or even what a front line actually was. These men who had always been satisfied with the *here* were making their way *there*, toward some ideal that had until then been inconceivable; these men who had always walked in small groups now advanced in tight ranks. A geometry of combatants. They advanced resolutely, each one upheld by the others, with the courage of a herd, their number bringing with it the belief that there was always someone they could count on, without suspecting for a single instant that that someone was simply themselves.

Women watched them pass from the windows, from main floors and upstairs rooms. Carnival heroes even before their first engagement, caught up in a war that had been declared so many years ago and for which they had never even contemplated taking up the gauntlet. Feeling themselves watched, they did not turn away from the nascent glory they were being pushed toward. Nor did they look at the statue of the general, no longer concerned with that age-old glory, his shoulders covered by a wide-brimmed hat of dried bird shit, an antiquated warrior in his rags, fixed in place by four rusted sets of nuts and bolts, whose sword, thrust out in front of him, pointed in a direction opposite their own. They were heading off to meet their leader, and they knew where to find him. By mutual agreement, they had designated him the man who would aid them to become heroes by association, the one who would turn this herd into a veritable army.

They slowed down at the instigation of the man with the clarinet, who let ring the first note, and then a recognizable melody, one of those that dress up wars with the sounds of the fifes. Everyone tuned up. The group soon left the square. As they passed through the streets, other men, drawn in by the music, came to further enlarge the horde. They added words to the music, which blended together into a chant taken up by all in the streets. They sang to convince themselves of their own strength, to free themselves of their stupor.

They arrived in front of The Admiral. The voices went silent, and the musical notes slowly died out, like tiny flames gradually running out of oxygen. The clarinetist, whom everyone called Laz, went in first, to the speechless look of the few occupants. He sat down at a table, on which he set his instrument, which looked like the neck of a cormorant emerging from dark waters, its slender beak thrust up into the cigarette smoke. The rest of the men followed. A few sat with Laz, the others at the neighboring tables. They ordered beers, and each of them was served. There was no boasting, just talk in low voices, assent, and glances toward the back of the room that were hardly discreet. Lynch was seated at the first table, right up against the great bay window that gave on to the street. After a moment, no one paid any attention to his presence, or to his hand under the table, clutching the butt of his weapon.

Laz finished drinking his beer, then got to his feet; those who were sitting at his table got up in turn. He directed himself slowly toward the back of the room. Men stood as he passed, like nails planted in reverse, coming up through the flooring, and it was beautiful to see, this agreement; even Lynch stood up out of pure reflex, and then promptly sat back down. A great emotion accompanied Laz's walk. Once he stood before Gobbo, he swept his gaze across the tavern, seeking from each of his companions a bit of additional determination and courage. To carry him to the end of this mission that had been assigned to him, to be the messenger who would most certainly be remembered. No one lowered their eyes. A few of them held their glasses in both hands, as if brandishing an altar candle. The scene had the look of the end of a procession, where the relic to be honored was a man in whom they were ready to place all their trust, without even knowing yet whether he would agree to receive it, and even less whether they themselves were deserving of it. An unusual calm reigned within the bar, occasionally interrupted by the click of a lighter. The girls on the landing all stood along the railing, as if they were watching a performance from up in heaven, excluded from the scene and protected from the actors. Laz sat down nervously between Gobbo and Martin. Silence took hold.

You want something? asked Gobbo after a moment, without looking up from his empty glass.

Laz cleared his throat and began to speak softly so as to not be heard by Lynch.

We've decided to ask Joyce for better working conditions.

I don't see what concern that is of mine, and speak up, replied Gobbo loudly.

We want you to help us.

Why? These are your demands, not mine.

Gobbo raised his eyes and stared at the men crowded around the table, stopping again at Laz.

To me, you look like you're perfectly capable of helping yourselves, he added.

We know that you wouldn't waver facing Joyce.

How do you know I wouldn't waver?

After all that you've lived through, all of the stories you've told us, I would be very surprised ... whereas us, we've never been outside of this hole.

Gobbo looked at Martin.

Were you aware of this?

Martin shook his head no.

How's it possible that he doesn't know about this?

He does now, replied Laz.

Gobbo gave him a curious look.

So then do you accept? asked Laz.

Order us two beers first.

The man signaled to Roby. Soon after, Mabel brought the beers and put them down on the table. She was about to return to the bar when Gobbo asked her if she wouldn't mind staying. Surprised, she looked at the sailor, hesitating a moment. Some of the men squeezed closer together to make room for her, opposite her father, and she slipped into the opening. Gobbo clinked his glass against Martin's, and a bit of the head went flying, like sea-foam above a jetty.

What do you think of all this?

Martin hesitated, troubled by his daughter's presence in his field of vision.

Nobody's asking my opinion.

Me, I'm asking for it.

Martin took a swallow.

It's true that you're likely the only one who can stand up to him, he said with a touch of irony in his voice.

And you'd be prepared to accompany me . . . to stand up to him?

We don't need him, Laz cut in.

I'm not talking to you, and if it bothers you, I'm not keeping you here!

Laz scowled. Gobbo didn't take his eyes off Martin.

What do you say?

I say that someone else would likely fit the bill better.

It isn't someone else that I'm asking.

I need to think about it . . .

Either way, it's that or it's nothing, said Gobbo, raising his voice.

Martin felt everyone's eyes weighing on him.

Well, have you had enough time to think?

I'm not sure that everyone is in agreement.

To the contrary, of course everyone agrees, isn't that so, you lot? fired Gobbo at the room.

Nobody responded.

We'll do as you say, said Laz after a moment.

Good, then it's understood, and you, you'll come too, said the sailor, motioning to Laz with his glass.

The other man acquiesced. Gobbo finished his beer, then stood up. He crossed the room, and the men moved aside, like cardboard cutout people hit by a shot in a carnival shooting gallery. At Lynch's table, he planted himself before him with an arrogant look.

You won't forget any of this, he said.

Forget what?

When you go to parrot to Joyce what you have heard here, you won't forget a thing, and especially not that a general strike has been declared.

A shiver ran through the bar.

Who do you take me for? asked Lynch.

That's what you were going to do anyway, after all.

Nobody gives me orders.

It wasn't an order, just a simple clarification.

Lynch remained pensive, casting a suspicious look around the room. The workers stared back at him, reassured by the sailor's words and his self-assurance.

If I were you, I'd consider the fact that the tide can turn pretty quickly, added Gobbo with a smile.

Lynch offered no reply. He promptly left the bar with long strides.

Gobbo returned to his seat.

Is it totally necessary for us to strike? Maybe it doesn't have to go that far, asked Laz.

The seaman shot an amused look at the man sitting next to him.

You were planning on going whaling with a toothpick, perhaps, he said.

Lynch immediately went to provide Joyce with his report, without of course specifying that Gobbo had asked him to do so. At the mention of the strike, Joyce gripped the armrests tightly, trying to better control his rage. Lynch assured him that no one at The Admiral had paid any attention to his presence, and that he had the situation well in hand. Joyce knew the man well enough to know that he never went unremarked, that he was above all an opportunist, a conniver without any great intelligence. Whatever took place next, Lynch would try to run with the hares and hunt with the hounds, thinking that both the hares and the hounds would be taken in by his little game. Joyce did not keep him for long, sending him to take his reply to The Admiral: he would agree to listen to the workers in the near future, but only if they were all at work the next day.

Back at The Admiral, Lynch delivered the message, then went over to the counter to order a drink.

We need to discuss among ourselves, said Gobbo from the back of the room.

Go right ahead, I'm not stopping you, replied Lynch, turning around.

Actually you are, we'd like you to leave.

I have every right to be here.

It's true that you have the right, but it would really be too bad for you to choose your side before you even know where the sides stand, don't you think?

Lynch didn't reply. He reflected for a moment, staring defiantly at the sailor. The others all smiled when he left the bar, and they would have happily thrown out a few contemptuous jeers if they hadn't all agreed ahead of time not to do so.

The discussion was initiated by Gobbo, who then turned it over to Laz. The debate didn't last long. The sailor didn't need to intervene; everyone was in agreement that Joyce's proposition was unacceptable.

The next day, no trucks left the quarry. A skeleton crew was set up at the plant, to make certain that it spat out just enough megawattage to keep the town's lights on.

Quite a few years earlier, once he had established himself, Joyce had given work to a few, and then, over time, directly or indirectly, to everyone. The man whom they had at the time considered to be some sort of messiah had become an exploiter and a tyrant. So moves history. Were his days finally numbered? Did this revolutionary movement signal his downfall? He had read books about the building of empires, about their collapse. He knew that the weak always win in the end, not by an accumulation of their strengths, but by the subtraction of those of the powerful, and he understood that nothing can be durably achieved against the contagion of a multitude devoid of reason or fear. He knew that whatever one builds already prefigures its own ruin from the very first stone. That the builders and the stones eventually disappear, and that only ideas cross the ages, on occasion, surviving the disasters even as they upset the balance, the best and the worst of them. Joyce had built so many walls that he had forgotten about the power of ideas, their power to nourish old beliefs and give birth to new ones.

He had been dreading this moment since that first day, when he had rented his hotel room. Sitting in the

armchair in room thirty-two, in the dark, he reached
for a satchel, opened it, and slid in the one thing he had
hoped he would never have to use, then set it back on the
floor. He got to his feet and left the room. Before exiting
the building, he verified by way of a dormer window that
his sentries were still at their posts, and congratulated
himself for paying them handsomely. He wondered how
long they would remain faithful to him if things evolved
in the wrong direction.

Once he was outside, his men saluted him. Three of
them came over to escort him. They all crossed the street,
but Joyce alone went into the building where his wife and
son lived. It was a Tuesday.

Joyce recognized Isobel's voice on the other side of
the door to the dining room. He lingered a moment, listening to what she was reading to Helio:

> I stand in the dark with drooping eyes by the worst-
>   suffering and the most restless,
> I pass my hands soothingly to and fro a few inches
>   from them,
> The restless sink in their beds, they fitfully sleep.
> Now I pierce the darkness, new beings appear,
> The earth recedes from me into the night,
> I saw that it was beautiful, and I see that what is not
>   the earth is beautiful.
> I go from bedside to bedside, I sleep close with the
>   other sleepers each in turn,

I dream in my dream all the dreams of the other
  dreamers,
And I become the other dreamers...

Isobel went silent at the first knock on the door. Joyce entered to find Helio standing next to his mother, both of them anxious to see him there on a weekday. She placed her arm around her son's shoulders, and slid a finger in between the pages of the book, marking the spot where she had been interrupted. Joyce could read the title and the author's name on the cover: *Leaves of Grass*. Walt Whitman. Without waiting any longer, he explained the situation. From her husband's shaky delivery, Isobel remarked his uncustomary nervousness, and her anxiety gave way to surprise. There wasn't a minute to lose, he added, ordering his wife to pack her bags so that he could get them away as soon as possible, until things settled down. Just a question of a few days. Their departure was already prepared for the following night. Isobel asked what it was that was forcing them to leave. Joyce didn't wish to get into the details. She didn't want to leave town without letting her parents know. He replied that it wasn't a good idea, that it risked putting them all in danger, but he promised to have them evacuated as well if things should ever go downhill. At no point in the conversation did he become antagonistic or cynical, despite having shown a tendency for both. Isobel thought that the sincerity her husband was demonstrating spoke to the gravity of the situation. She was still clutching Helio. The child was staring at his father, his eyes wide, the book pressed against his heart. Before he left, Joyce gave a sympathetic look to his wife and his child, as if noticing for the first time that they seemed more important to him than his ambitions.

He returned to his building and went back up to room thirty-two, so that he could think about the chronology of the events to come. Buy some time. Regain the upper hand. He would agree to receive the strike's delegation the next morning at the plant.

With half of his rear end parked on the fountain's edge, Elie was securely under the general's protection. With the steel tip of a crutch, he was writing diligently on the water, tracing tortured letters, his head leaned forward, and his still-thick gray hair, which he only cut once a year, hung down over his cheeks in such a way that, of his profile, it was only possible to make out the hooked nose, like a cliff looming free of the tides. Exposed to the direct sunlight, he wasn't bothered by the rays beating down upon his back, the nape of his neck, and his head. For several days now, a stabbing pain had been making its way up his hip, gnawing away at the bottom of his stomach. He hadn't spoken to anyone about it, and didn't let it show, withdrawing when the pain became too intense. He had sworn to himself that he would never again allow a doctor to lay hands on him.

Clenching his teeth, he stuffed a pipe full of tobacco mixed with some herbs that helped take the edge off his suffering as much as anything did. He struck a match, set the tobacco ablaze, took a long draw. After a few minutes, his mind wandered far beyond the lost bones, flesh, and muscles. An image materialized on the water's surface, a face saved from aging within a transparent oval affixed to the headstone of a grave. The face of his wife Lina, at the base of which began to grow an entire body, that body he had so desired, so often embraced with his own ardent mass, so long ago. He threw his head back, begging the sun to make the apparition disappear.

Am I disturbing you?

Elie's lips barely quivered out an inaudible *thank you*, and the lines of a childlike smile appeared in the gaps of his beard.

That'll be the day, he said, casting a tender glance at his granddaughter.

I'm sorry it has taken me so long to come and see you.

What's important is that you're here.

How are you doing?

Better.

Mabel placed one hand on the old man's emaciated forearm.

What would you say to us taking a walk? she asked.

A great idea, it's almost time to eat, you'll be my guest.

Where?

At the house, by Jove!

There was a long silence. Mabel withdrew her hand. Towering above the fountain, the general was still not finished confronting the enemy.

That's not a good idea, she said after a while.

Personally, I think it's the best idea I've ever had.

Mabel sat down next to her grandfather.

I don't really want to go back there, and also, I don't expect I'll be welcomed with open arms.

Your mother is still ill-advised, but she has come a long way since you left. As for your father, it's different... You know, men often say what is in their heart far too late, or they never say it at all, and sometimes they don't even understand that that's where those things are, in their hearts. Your father doesn't know how to go about it... no more than anyone else.

Mabel looked up at the sky wearily.

I'm not sure I want to forgive them.

Who's talking about forgiving them, and what's more, think of your brothers, they'd be over the moon to see you.

Mabel imagined Luke's smile, but then her face clouded over again just as quickly.

Do you really think they can change?

Of course not.

So what's the point, then?

They don't have to change, because they both know that they made a mistake... They simply need to find the words to admit it, and without you, that won't be possible.

What you're trying to say is that I don't really have a choice.

You do, I'm just saying that this would be better for all involved.

A group of a dozen men crossed the square, all greeting them as they passed. They wore flannel pants and clean shirts, and their unwrinkled shadows followed them indolently. Elie watched them pass, incredulous, and waited until they were gone.

How strange, they don't ordinarily say hello to me... And what's more, this is neither the day nor the time to be walking around all decked out like that.

You haven't heard the news?

The news about what?

The workers have voted to strike.

Elie slapped the water's surface with the flat of his hand.

Great Scott! A strike, no less!

It was decided last night at The Admiral. Dad didn't say anything when he got home?

No.

And yet he was there, he's even one of the leaders, with Gobbo, this old sailor, and a fellow called Laz...

Your father's one of the leaders? How's that even possible?

It's that sailor he's always hanging around with, he dragged him into it.

And the others didn't say anything?

The sailor didn't give them a choice, they all lap up everything he says.

Elie shot a glance toward the northeast corner of the empty square, in the direction the men had disappeared.

I think I understand why they said hello to me now.

He put his weight on his crutches and got up.

You can tell me all the details on the way, you know what a stickler your mother is for mealtimes.

After the heavy rain, the path's surface looked like sunburned skin that had begun to peel. The old man concentrated on the effort required to walk. The effects of the herbs mixed into his tobacco were starting to fade. The tip of one of his crutches kept getting caught in the ruts, and he would lean more heavily on the other with a grimace, struggling not to fall and to better absorb the jolts that reverberated within his stump. Mabel remained close by, just in case he was to stumble. She told him everything she knew. Elie didn't ask any questions. Then, as they drew nearer to the house, Mabel began to imagine the worst forms the reunion could take. Soon, she slowed to let her grandfather take the lead. Once they reached the gate, he stopped to catch his breath, waiting for her to join him.

You go on ahead! he said, nodding toward the front of the house.

I'd rather you go first.

No, my dear, the present won't be as nice.

Not sure that it will be a present for everyone, and what am I supposed to say to them, anyway?

Hello.

Mabel forced a smile. It was too late to turn back. She pushed open the gate, crossed the space between it and the porch, and climbed the steps. She hesitated a moment in front of the door, then raised her hand to knock.

People don't knock on the door to their own houses, as far as I know, said Elie, who was right behind her.

Mabel gently turned the knob, pushed open the door, and stepped inside. A long time afterward, she tried to piece together the scene in its entirety, to put back in order all the fragments she had seen in one glance. After the moment of astonishment brought about by the appearance of her daughter, Martha had nodded her head, then went over to the sideboard, as if she had just remembered something essential. She opened it, pulled out a plate, cutlery, and a glass, and then set them down between Luke and Mark, who both moved over a bit. The three brothers were walking on air, it could be seen on their faces, but only Luke couldn't manage to control his emotions. He fetched a chair, which he put next to his own. Elie took his place at the end of the table, relieved to finally sit down. Martin watched him, and he kept staring at him as Mabel sat down between her brothers.

Well, what, I still have the right to bring a guest home now and then, said the old man, addressing his son-in-law.

Martin turned toward his wife.

I've nothing against it, he said.

Martha nodded in agreement.

Good, well then let's eat.

I'm hungry, said Luke, grabbing the pitcher.

He poured some water into his sister's glass.

Martha spooned a portion of jugged hare and another of potatoes onto each plate, and everyone began to eat. At one point, Elie used his fork to pick a strand of stringy flesh from between his teeth, then he said:

So then, it seems there's to be a strike.

Martin didn't react.

There was a barricade in front of the quarry, nobody was able to work today, said Mark.

And at the plant?

Martin remained stone-faced. He finished chewing before he replied:

We're assuring basic services.

The old man slammed his fork down on the table.

You ask me, that's idiotic, he said.

The strike?

No, I mean your basic services. It would do everyone some good to spend a little time in the dark.

It's not my place to make the decision.

And yet it seems that you're not exactly watching this from the sidelines, said Elie with a sly look.

Martin raised his eyes and glanced over at his daughter, but there wasn't the least bit of reproach in his gaze.

Elie moved another piece of rabbit to his mouth and began to chew slowly as he spoke:

There was a day when, if I had heard this, I wouldn't have believed it. And you have asked to speak to Joyce?

We're waiting for his reply.

This had better not go on too long, we all need your paychecks, interjected Martha.

It won't drag out, Joyce has nothing to gain by letting the situation deteriorate, said Elie.

I hope that's true.

And this Gobbo, does he seem reliable to you?

Martin cast another glance at Mabel.

He's on our side, he said.

There was a day when, if I had heard this . . . , repeated Elie while he mopped his plate with a hunk of bread, then he nodded his head in his daughter's direction. I'll have another tater with some juice on it.

Martha rose to serve her father. The old man thanked her with another nod. The others looked at him, this man who usually ate like a bird.

Am I the only one who thinks this is really good, he said, immediately mashing up his potato in the juice from the stew.

I'd like a little bit more too, said Luke.

That's good, my hearty, you have to keep your strength up.

They exchanged a wink, then the old man clicked his tongue and straightened up.

It sure is nice for us all to be back together again . . . Wasn't this what you wanted? he added, addressing his daughter.

Martha served Luke, then hovered next to Mabel.

Can I serve you a little more while I'm here? Doesn't look like you've put on any weight.

I'd like that.

Shiver my timbers, it sure is nice indeed, said Luke.

Joyce had wanted to meet with the strikers at the plant so that he could find out more about their demands. He was already waiting inside when the delegation entered the hall, standing on the walkway in the company of his armed men. At the sight of the new arrivals, the watchdogs, tied to the guardrail, slid their big heads between the bars and growled, showing their teeth through the leather straps of their muzzles. One of the guards, who had remained in the hall, pushed the heavy door along its track to shut it behind them, locked it, and rejoined his comrades on the walkway. Wire-covered portholes above gave off an evanescent glow, which sliced up the silhouettes as if they had been eviscerated.

Fear was visible on Laz's face. Martin appeared indifferent to the situation, letting his gaze wander from one end of the gangway to the other. Since he had walked in, Gobbo had been staring at Joyce like a gladiator waiting for his opportunity to tear someone apart. All that could be heard were the dogs whining as slobber flowed from their muzzled jaws, dripping to the ground in little puddles spaced out by three or four yards each. A light bulb began to hum, then the filament broke with a dry pop, and one of the guards was thrown into the shadows along with his dog. An object clinked against the metal guardrail.

I want this strike ended immediately, said Joyce with a peremptory tone, and his voice continued to resonate throughout the building's interior.

It was understood that Gobbo would speak first. He waited for the silence to return.

That all depends on you, he replied, without sounding impressed.

I'd imagine this is a question of money.

The sailor looked at each of his companions, then back at Joyce.

Of working conditions, and of dignity, as well.

Joyce made the shape of a gun with his hand, and aimed it at each of the three emissaries in turn.

I could just have you all gunned down where you stand, if I wanted, and that would be the last we'd hear about any of this.

Laz was growing more and more nervous.

As a matter of fact, if you want to turn a strike into a war, that's exactly what you should do. History is full of examples like that.

Joyce lowered his hand and grabbed firmly onto the railing, like a big-shot attorney.

First, you will give me the name of Double's murderer.

What's the point in that?

Take it or leave it.

Gobbo stretched out his arms. Joyce's men raised their weapons.

The guilty party stands before you, he said solemnly.

I don't believe you.

Martin placed a hand on Gobbo's arm to pull it down.

I was the one who killed him! he said.

You're bullshitting me!

Gobbo smiled.

And I suppose you're guilty of it as well, barked Joyce at Laz, who was completely falling apart.

And outside, you likely couldn't even count them all, cut in Gobbo so as to not leave Laz the time to respond.

Joyce signaled his men to lower their weapons.

It would seem that we have reached an impasse, he said.

You're the only one who knows the way out.

I'll need to think on that some more.

Good, but while we wait, no one will be returning to work.

Laz turned on his heels. He moved toward the door, like a sinner released from the confessional, then he lifted the metal bar and started to open the door. Gobbo and Martin followed him, taking their time.

You, you can stay a minute, I would speak with you, announced Joyce.

Gobbo turned around.

Me?

You.

I have nothing to hide from them.

What's the risk...unless maybe you're afraid?

Laz had already exited the plant. A rectangle of light was cast on the ground, like a carpet woven of golden thread.

Go on, said Gobbo to Martin.

Are you sure?

Yes, I won't be long.

Martin complied.

Close the door behind you! said Joyce.

Gobbo pushed the panel of the door back into place. He turned back to face Joyce.

So, you're the famous mariner!

Say what you need to say so that we can get this over with.

What are you doing with all these rats, when you don't even work for me?

That is none of your concern.

And what if I were to offer you enough money to last you the rest of your days.

The rest of my days! And how much would that add up to, in your opinion?

We can discuss it.

Gobbo made as if he was thinking.

I don't think you have enough to cover the price of my betrayal.

Every man has his price, and I do have a lot of money.

What would I do with your money? I have nothing to buy.

Joyce began to walk the length of the railing. His men wanted to escort him, but he instructed them to remain where they were. He descended the stairs and went over to meet Gobbo. The two men stood face-to-face, only a few feet apart, staring each other down.

You know what I think? said Joyce. I think you're too intelligent to waste your time defending them.

If I'm following you correctly, then I would be an idiot if I were to abandon them.

The lines of Joyce's face melted away to nothing.

What is it you're looking for, if it isn't money... Are you after my head as well?

I don't give a shit about your head, and they don't really care either, it's what you represent that they can no longer stand.

Joyce furiously extended an arm toward the door and let his hand hang there like some ridiculous artifact.

Not one of you can ever lay claim to what I've obtained, not one of you will ever want it as badly as I wanted it. They'd rather destroy me, because what I represent forces them to face up to their own incapacity to surpass themselves. But even if I gave in to their wishes, their lives wouldn't be any better... and you know it.

What I also know is that their cause is just, that's the reason I agreed to be their spokesperson.

Don't tell me that you believe in their cause. They have only found common cause so they can hide the sum of their individual failures, their lack of ambition and courage.

Perhaps not everyone thinks the same way you do . . .

Unless you're just hiding your own ambitions, and you're only using them.

Gobbo turned his hands around, showing his empty palms.

You see any ambition here?

As he was unable to make Gobbo give in, Joyce put on a grave face.

Men will possibly die, he said.

It's up to you to make sure that doesn't happen.

One of my men is already dead, murdered.

That pig only got what he deserved, said Gobbo, and in that moment, a veil of madness filled his gaze.

Joyce took some time.

I can't decide if I admire you or if I feel pity for you, he continued with a sarcastic tone.

As long as I don't end up owing you anything for it, replied Gobbo with a similar tone.

He feinted as if to move. On the gangway, the men aimed their weapons once more, and the dogs growled with renewed vigor.

I don't think we have anything left to say to one another, he added, before walking out to a stunned look from Joyce.

Lynch was already long gone by the time Joyce walked out of the building in the middle of the night, with his old jacket of cracked leather and his satchel. Two guards rushed over to meet him. He explained that he was stepping out for a moment and that for once he didn't require any protection. He would be back soon. The authoritarian tone that typically marked his voice had disappeared, a voice that in that moment sounded as if it had been broken, and then summarily repaired with something unexpected coming from a man such as he, something left over from childhood.

A dog approached and sniffed the bottom of his pant legs. Joyce crouched down and sat on his heels, like a tracker. He set his satchel on the ground without letting go of the handle and began to pet the dog with his free hand as the guards looked on, speechless. He patted the dog on the head one last time and stood back up, then went off without a glance at the faces staring at him, each painted with amazement. Every time he passed before a brazier, its glow collided first with his face, then spread across his back. Chaotic shadows floated all around, like charcoal-blackened bits of cloth. Once he had cleared the final brazier, his men, who had never taken their eyes off him, saw the leather of his jacket go dark and the shadows fade into thin air. He pushed on into the darkness, swallowed by the mouth of a street that still bore his name, that had become a disused physical wrapper, as if everything that had until that point given him life had been sucked up by the void. The guards remained there a long while, staring at the spot where their boss had vanished. One of them called out to the others, asking where Joyce could possibly be going, alone, in the middle of the night, with a suitcase in his hand.

It wasn't a suitcase, said another.

Close enough.

Maybe that's the last we'll see of him, said a third.

Yet more joined the conversation.

He said he wouldn't be gone long.

He wasn't acting like usual.

He's been through worse.

He won't take this lying down.

The sentries continued the discussion, drinking coffee and smoking hand-rolled cigarettes, the dogs quiet at their feet.

Joyce remained concealed a good moment at the corner of Joyce Main and Joyce 4, from where he was able to observe the crowded Admiral without any risk of being spotted. A deep sadness descended upon him. Despite all the arguments he had prepared to convince himself, he would have preferred to be in there with the workers, to become one with the crowd, to be accepted by these men and share in their human contact. One of these hardworking men, clinking glasses on the other side of the window, with that absent stare one wears the day before a battle. One of these men he could be once again, because he had been such a man in the distant past, and had spent the rest of his life trying to forget it. He tightened his grip on the handle of his satchel and pushed down his weakness. He recognized certain silhouettes. Lynch, his elbows resting on the bar, his hat on his head, who had already by now relayed his desire to meet them at dawn at the plant, to share his proposal with them. When Joyce summoned him, Lynch had wanted to know more, and he had purposefully replied that he was prepared to yield some ground. It was important that the lawman be given the opportunity to make himself seem valuable to the strikers. Joyce had chosen him for his cowardice above all else, the kind of man that he could read without any surprises. He also caught sight of the sailor and the two fellows who had accompanied him to the plant. He looked around for the girl that Snake and Double had mentioned, but didn't see her.

Once Joyce collected all of these different moving images, and put them all back together into one solid picture, he turned back to make his way through the alleys, taking the occasional sharp turn here or there, guided by some mysterious thread. He avoided the occasional puddle of light coming from the odd illuminated window, not out of fear that he would be identified, but so that he wouldn't be tempted to stop and warm himself and end up changing his trajectory, or even turning back. Hidden by the night like this, he moved from doorstep to doorstep, going toward a place from which he would soon be able to contemplate the afterlife of his successes.

The sun was waiting patiently behind the hillside. The dogs raised their muzzles and began to squeak like rats. They could sense Joyce's presence well before he reached the first brazier, precisely at the spot he had vanished the previous night, the newly hatching dawn now spitting him back out. He walked serenely, no longer carrying the satchel. One of the men asked him if he had lost it; he replied affably that he had not, adding that he had given it to someone who would most assuredly need it more than he did. The guards didn't understand what he was talking about, but none of them dared question him further.

Can I have a cup? asked Joyce, indicating the pot of coffee that sat on a grate over the flames of a brazier.

Of course, sir.

The man grabbed a tinplate cup that hung from a nail sunk into the leg of a rocking chair. He filled it to the brim and handed it to Joyce, who blew on it, then brought it to his lips and drank in tiny mouthfuls. After, he handed the empty cup back to the man and said, raising his voice, so that everyone could hear him:

You will all leave for the plant in one hour, I will meet you there.

Why don't you just come with us? asked someone.

Joyce stepped over to the fire and warmed his hands, his face crisscrossed by the dancing flames on either side.

Symbolic force, he said, and as the guards didn't look like they understood what he meant, he added: When the strikers see me arrive on my own, they will know I'm not afraid of them.

We will do as you say, said the man still holding the empty cup.

Joyce pulled his hands away and backed up. With this gesture, it seemed as if he was suppressing the flames, then he moved toward the building and went in. Nobody heard the sound of the bolts being reset.

Martin had forewarned his family that he wouldn't be coming home that night, that he would stay at The Admiral with the striking workers, awaiting their meeting with Joyce at the plant early the next morning. He spoke of solidarity and determination. Martha was surprised at first to hear such words come out of her husband's mouth, then she shrugged her shoulders at the mention of a solidarity that had never truly existed between the people of the valley and those of the town. She felt anxious about this change, brought about by other changes, and about everything her intuition led her to anticipate, but she didn't let it show.

The boys had slipped away as soon as they had eaten breakfast. Elie sat at the end of the table. He asked if there was any coffee left. Martha lifted the lid of the coffeepot to check, then poured what remained into her father's mug.

We could share it, he said.

That's okay!

The old man tossed a sugar cube into his coffee, stirring it with a dessert spoon, and then raised the cup with two hands, the handle of the spoon wedged between two fingers, and, as if he were talking to the wind:

It sounds like things are really starting to happen.

Martha took her time.

You're not going?

I'm too old to be of any use.

Elie lifted the cup to his mouth and took a sip.

How about you, how far are you willing to go? he said after a moment.

Same for me, I can't do much of anything in all this.

He put his cup back down on the table, and the spoon slid into the earthenware vessel with a muffled clink.

I'm talking about your daughter.

Elie pushed the mug back a few inches and sat observing Martha.

I was starting to think that I would invite her more often, he added.

Martha stared at the mug.

If you can tell me when, I'll put her place setting out ahead of time.

Elie finished the coffee, scraping the bottom with his spoon.

It's really very good.

I can make a little more.

I'd like that.

Martha went over to fetch the tin that sat on the hutch. She poured some coffee beans into a grinder, took a seat on a chair, wedged the grinder between her thighs, the fabric hugging shapes that were usually hidden. She began to turn the crank in fits and starts, which produced a rasping rattle. Once the beans had been sufficiently ground, she got up, poured some water into the bottom of the coffeepot, screwed the filter onto the top, filled it with ground coffee, replaced the cover, and set it to heat on the stove. Elie didn't miss any of his daughter's gestures, discerning in them a poetic dimension that he had never noticed before, never considered, as if, for the first time, they didn't cost him anything.

Most people don't know how to explain the world, why they are a part of it, and their inability to comprehend this makes them sad, so they try to force the world to come to them, to remake it with their own hands, and they don't even know that it's the world that they are holding, that it is what creates all the beauty. That the beauty is precisely in the not knowing that they are holding the world in their hands. Elie knew something about this, he had worked on this world, but had never known any of this before part of him was missing, first his leg, then his wife. After those two consecutive tragedies, he had cultivated rage and hatred toward himself, by staying quiet. The entire family had always kept its precarious balance by way of the silence of each one of them, silences that were similar to lies by omission. Only Mabel had had the courage and the strength to rebel against that deathly silence.

As he observed his daughter, Elie understood that without poetry, the world is nothing but constraints; that with it, it grows to become a limitless universe. If he had had the words to translate the fluidity of his thinking, he would have explained to her what he was feeling right then. But his thoughts were moving too quickly, and they were new, and untethered. What did this woman really think, deep down inside? Elie resisted the impulse to ask her, so as not to force her to lie. Because Martha's gestures, well, at least those couldn't lie, because she was unaware that the long series of movements that made up a single simple act were the revelation of her soul laid bare. What could have been no more than a hopeless series of motions that had been passed down instead revealed themselves in all their unconscious perfection. All it took to be convinced of this was to watch her, and up until right then, Elie had never truly watched her. It was time for him to make up for some of the silence as well.

Come and sit for a minute, he said.

I'm going to get dinner started, they're going to be hungry when they get back.

Go on, sit!

Alright, but just five minutes, no more.

As Martha was about to sit down, there was a muffled noise, like the sound of thunder in the distance.

Sounds like there's going to be a storm, said Elie.

Sounds like it, she replied.

The strikers left The Admiral at dawn. No one spoke. Everything had been said during the night; they had talked through all of the possible scenarios, the various maneuvers to be carried out. Gobbo, Martin, and Luz walked at the head of the group. Lynch brought up the rear. On their way down Joyce Main, they heard a cacophony of barking a few streets over. Concern was visible on their faces.

The barking grew louder. The group spilled into the square at the same time that the militia were crossing it on the opposite side. The dogs wore no muzzles this time, and their masters controlled their excitement the best they could by pulling on their leashes and leaning back, as if stubborn animals themselves. The barrels of their weapons rattled and caught glints of the raking early-morning light.

The two streams of men were careful to avoid contact. Gobbo ordered a halt before the statue of the general. He asked the strikers to ready their instruments, and the musicians began to play a festive tune before the dumbfounded looks of the guards, who continued on their route toward the plant. Soon, from the square, it was no longer possible to see the gleam of the weapons, but instead, only the instruments; it was no longer possible to hear the dogs, only the music. Then the musicians fell silent, and the final notes flittered around another moment, like birds leaping from branch to branch before going to sleep. The strikers resumed their rhythmical march. They left the town, made their way along the side of the reservoir, passed the dam, and caught sight of the power plant farther down, with its heavy cables that hung like overstretched jump ropes, the shadows of which traced long rectilinear aisles that grew narrower in the distance, like water lines at the bottom of a basin.

The plant door was wide open. The workers spread out, as if rehearsing in slow motion a choreographed routine that had been learned long before. A circle formed around the three spokesmen. The music rang out again for a brief moment, before ceasing abruptly this time. They could hear the dogs barking inside. Some of the strikers formed a narrow passage in line with the entrance. Gobbo, Martin, and Luz stepped through the bottleneck in single file. They were clapped on the shoulders as they walked past, there were shouts of encouragement and they were urged not to give a single inch of ground in the face of their oppressor. Everyone was counting on them.

Gobbo was first to enter the hall. The guards were stationed along the gangway, like the previous evening; only the spot that Joyce had occupied was vacant.

Where is Joyce? demanded Gobbo.

One of the dogs pushed his head through the guard-rail and snapped his teeth in the air. His master pulled him back and swung the butt of his weapon, striking the animal in the lower back.

He won't be long, replied one of the guards.

This doesn't look good, it might be a trap, we should get going, said Laz, making as if to turn on his heels.

Gobbo grabbed him by the arm.

Stay put!

Feeling uneasiness set in, Martin lifted his head and turned toward the man who had spoken.

Maybe he is afraid, and he won't be coming, he said.

Gobbo looked at Martin like a man who had bet on someone long ago and was finally reaping the rewards.

Him, afraid...? You're losing your marbles, hillbilly, said the guard with a snicker.

My name isn't hillbilly.

We don't give a damn what your name is, you all look the same, you hicks from the valley...

My blood is the same color as yours.

That remains to be seen, and don't tempt me, bellowed the guard, raising his weapon.

Gobbo was still holding Laz by the arm. Martin ran his gaze along the gangway, waiting for the man to lower his weapon.

This is your chance to join us, he won't be coming, he said calmly.

He's right, said Gobbo, doubling down, if you side with us, Joyce will no longer have any way to exert pressure, and everyone will get what is coming to them. Afterward, it will be too late for you.

You're not going to listen to this, are you? We've never had any complaints about Joyce, retorted the same guard, brandishing his gun like a soldier preparing to charge at a barricade.

His warlike posture had no effect at all on his comrades in arms, no more than his words had. Doubt had crept into their minds. They thought back to Joyce's strange walk in the middle of the night, and this missed meeting-time at the plant didn't exactly fill them with confidence, especially considering that this was a man for whom punctuality was a rule of life. Some time went by. People started talking along the gangway, no longer paying any heed to the guard's invectives. Had Joyce fled? Had he been assassinated like Double? Would they, too, be hunted down by the faceless murderer? Without Joyce at their head, they were no more than a bunch of mercenaries without any obligations. The moment had perhaps come for them to rejoin the townsfolk and adopt their ideals, or to at least play along and save their own skins. The debates came to an end, and then there was a long silence. One of the guards leaned his weapon against the guardrail and tied his dog's leash to a post. He made his way along the gangway and started descending the stairs, his footsteps ringing like the pendulum of a clock. Others set their weapons down as well, and the fanatical guard pointed his rifle toward the stairs, shouting:

You get back up there, goddammit!

A hand came down on the gun barrel, the shot rang out, a man fell, and then all hell broke loose, taking all of the others with it.

J ulie White was combing her long hair in front of the
mirror. She stared at her reflection, her eyes like two
little meteorites whirling through the astral void. Since
the strike had begun, Lynch wasn't hassling her anymore. But what would come next? Her thoughts turned
to Mark Volny. Life was most certainly presided over by
some strange machine, far too complex, and over which
she regretted having no control. What was the point
in being attractive if it didn't allow her to accede to her
desire? She didn't think she could handle being Lynch's
plaything for much longer, and there was only one way
for her to break free from that situation. Flight.

She stopped the motion of the brush and began to
meticulously pull free the hairs that were caught between
its bristles, which fell into the sink, mimicking little
scratches in the enamel. She slid her brush back into her
toiletry kit, which she placed in a travel bag along with
the clothing she had packed the night before. Everything
she owned fit in either that bag or in another, smaller one
that contained three pairs of shoes. In that moment, the
two packed bags didn't represent her scant possessions,
but gave tangible form to her departure, her decision to

go against the course imposed by her life. The only way to reaffirm her dignity, and to express her powerlessness.

She wouldn't say goodbye to Mark Volny. She didn't have the time, or the strength. She preferred that he continue to believe he had misunderstood her intentions. It was better for him. It would toughen him up. He was going to need it down the road.

Julie White slipped on her espadrilles, wrapping the straps around her ankles and knotting them. Then she opened the door, sitting down on the steps to smoke a final cigarette. The town was very calm. An emaciated dog crossed the street, holding a rat in its mouth, its limp tail rubbing against the ground like an untied shoelace. The animal picked up its pace when it saw her, and disappeared around the street corner.

The young woman heard the sound of music in the distance, a well-known celebratory melody that for her carried with it infinite sadness. Then the music stopped. As it drifted away, the smoke from her cigarette showed her the direction of the wind. She felt the heavy presence of her bags behind her back. It was time. She crushed the half-finished cigarette and got up to fetch her luggage inside. As she bent down to pick them up, the door slammed shut behind her with the tremendous noise of an explosion.

With water up to his torso, Snake was digging around in the hollows under the bank, beneath the roots of an ash tree. After exploring for a few minutes, he felt a soft and slippery belly against the palm of his hand. Slid his other hand over slowly, from the tail up to the dorsal fin, and squeezed. The fish struggled; Snake squeezed even harder. He pulled the rainbow trout from the water and immediately began to eat it, without killing it or climbing back up onto the bank. He closed his jaws on the quivering, gleaming flesh, spitting out bits of silvery skin, and on occasion pulling a jabbing bone from the roof of his mouth.

Other than Double's presence by his side, he missed nothing about his life before, not even that girl who had so patiently gotten him off while he closed his eyes to forget about the hand and the mouth, forget that a deformed little man wasn't permitted much in the way of sentimental ambitions. The only power he had ever possessed he owed to Joyce, and that had been nothing more than an illusion paid for in full by the death of the giant. His life had been nothing more than an accumulation of subterfuges. He had had no other choice than to submit to them during the time he resided in the town, conscious that without those subterfuges, he would have been at the mercy of his own weaknesses. Nature didn't lie; she had no reason to. Every one of her components had its function, more or less permanently, made up of savagery and discretion.

A flock of birds passed over the river. Snake raised his eyes too late to identify them, and watched them continue into the distance, noting that their plumage had adapted itself to the color of the sky, unless it was the opposite, and this was a beautiful course of thought for him to embark upon, he mused: to seek the unity between beings and things. The sound of galloping echoed along the opposite bank, from behind the curtain of trees, and then died out, quickly absorbed by the noise of the current.

Snake had gone out into nature to become one with that which is, and keep watch over that which was no longer. He abandoned the remains of the trout in the water, then washed his hands and face. A few scales were still stuck to his cheeks, looking like the heads of nails that had been sunk into his skin. He heard cries, and looked over in the direction of the hillside, upon which stood a dozen or so branchless tree trunks covered in a mixture of mud and dried straw, forming the beginnings of a fort. Nobody. It was coming from farther off. The cries died out. He clambered onto the bank.

As he did each morning, Snake went to place a new stone atop Double's grave. His own personal way of erecting a rampart destined to separate that which is from that which is no longer. One of the few things he'd ever been taught: the things that cease to exist must be hidden from those that remain. For the first time, he wondered what the deep reasoning behind this was. Perhaps because death forces itself sufficiently into the things that remain, and that it is easier to find hope for a soul if we're not required to contemplate the rotting envelope from which it has been more or less courageously extracted.

A new barrage of voices, this time more piercing, pulled Snake away from his thoughts. So he hadn't imagined them. He hastily made his way back up the river, passing directly below the fort in progress. The shouts grew more distinct, evidently coming from the viaduct. He came out onto the stony little promenade, just before the great arch. There he discovered four silhouettes swinging in the void, just like excited pendulums suspended above the watering hole. The sun directly in his eyes prevented Snake from making out who it was, and almost completely erased the ropes. After a moment, his eyes grew accustomed to it. He recognized the boy that had thrown the stone at him from the stockade, as well as the waitress from The Admiral, but not the other two. Snake started to shout so that they would hear him. The

Franck Bouysse

four promptly turned in his direction and stopped swinging. Snake imagined, for a brief moment, going up to join them and leaping with them. But it wasn't his place.

Then there was a great noise, which Snake attributed to a different reality. The sound spread, like a wave stretched out by the sky. The silhouettes began to shout again, as if panicked. Their earlier joy had deserted them. Just like that, even these humans were rejecting him. He spread his arms wide, so that the shouts could find him more easily, and turned toward the early sun, like a sunflower seeking the purest light. He saw new flames burn across the surface of the sun. He felt their bite burning his retinas, heard a great blast of air coming from farther upstream, and finally the blood in his veins grew warm once again.

434

Still visible behind the hillside, the sun irrigated the sky and its light deepened from second to second. It was as if the billions of preceding dawns had been necessary for the perfection of this one to be reached, as if it had fed on all the others. Great yellowed ferns varnished with frost swaggered about along the path's edge, like snooty old lady tourists visiting a museum. Autumn was beginning to tint the leaves of the great beeches that were ruffled by the wind. A sonic backdrop, the river sealed over the silence with its monotonous voice. Then the sun appeared, a flamboyant ruin caught in the vegetation, and three shadows spread along the path, like Maasai warriors escorting children.

The fox struggled to walk along at Luke's side, dragging its long, bony flagellum, followed closely by Mark and Matthew, gloomy page boys with clumsy gaits. Luke dropped his hand before the animal's snout, convinced he would feel its cool breath against his palm. He spoke to it inside his head, thanked it for having come down from its den in the sky to accompany him one last time, since after this final walk, he would let it return to the

forest of souls, adding that he would never again ask it
to go against the flow, but that he would keep it always
in his heart.

Seated on a stump near the viaduct, Mabel awaited
her brothers by the path's edge. Spotting his sister, Luke
ran over to meet her, no longer thinking of the fox that he
was abandoning, his face radiating pure joy. He took her
hand. Matthew and Mark joined them, and they all set
out toward the second pillar. Nothing had changed since
they were children. Every gesture came naturally. Words
were useless. They climbed the slope, Luke at their head,
still holding his sister by the hand. Once they reached
the deck atop the bridge, they continued along, following
the railing. Mabel stopped and bent over to look at her
rope, which was still hanging in the void. Her brothers
kept going, then each threw down a rope, attached a second around their waists, and all four of them descended
in concert. Just like before.

Luke started to swing first, with a laugh. The others
followed suit, their shouts largely devoured by the river.
They saw a flock of feral pigeons fly by, leaving the town.
The birds slid through the air, then dove toward the valley before vanishing into the untroubled waters of the
sky. Matthew stopped swinging and shouting.

What's come over them...? They never go that far
out, he said.

Shiver me timbers, look down there, interrupted Luke.

On the right bank, a great stag was hurtling down the towpath. It stopped at the water's edge, but it wasn't thirsty. It swung its head in every direction, as if it wanted to rid itself of some foulness it had picked up in the woods, then spun toward the slope, trampling the stones nervously. Soon, three young females joined it, and the herd promptly scampered off in the terrestrial wake of the pigeons.

Thus had spoken the animals.

They heard shouting and then saw the ludicrous-looking man extricate himself from the plant cover, advance toward the arch, and freeze, watching them. There was a terrifying noise and they turned upriver, discovering a cloud of smoke above the dam, which was split in half, a torrent of water pouring out of the breach. They shouted at the dwarf to run, but he stretched out his arms like a scarecrow without rags. Slabs of concrete broke away from the structure. A wave swelled forth, sweeping away everything in its path. They climbed as quickly as they could to save themselves from the rising waters. By the time they reached the top of the viaduct, the power plant was nearly submerged, and the strands of its web gave under the pressure. When they looked down below the arch, Snake had already been carried away, and the valley that contained the Volny house was transformed into a crazed river, the trees into seaweed.

At that moment, Luke wasn't thinking of his mother or father, neither of whom would escape the disaster. He was imagining the island that would be born of the cataclysm, upon which his grandfather Silver would be waiting to show him where the treasure was located, his parrot obediently stationed on one shoulder.

Epilogue

Joyce unhooked the electric wires from the terminals and slid the detonator into his bag. Knelt down on a sloping ledge on the hillside, he swept his gaze across the valley from the town that was safe above the destroyed dam to the downstream side, drowned below the waters, with the exception of the upper portion of the viaduct, upon which he thought he could make out some movement, though he assumed he must be dreaming. He got up, and his shadow unfurled along the ground, but he didn't see it. He made his way back up the hill, to the precise spot where the first man and the first woman had arrived, but he knew nothing of that. Somewhere on the other side were his wife and child, but he wasn't yet ready to join them. He stopped, and a voice amused itself reciting words in his head, words that he must have learned one day, although he could not remember when, or where, or even who had taught them to him.

And I heard as it were the voice of a great multitude,
and as the voice of many waters, and as the voice
of mighty thunderings…And I saw a great white
throne, and him that sat on it…And the books were
opened…It is done. I am Alpha and Omega, the
beginning and the end…He that overcometh shall
inherit all things…I am Alpha and Omega, the
beginning and the end, the first and the last…

When the voice stopped, Joyce continued his climb.
He turned back one last time before passing over to the
other side, but he had gone too far in his pride to see anything other than a perfect ocean.

Translator's Acknowledgments

Special thanks to Renée Altergott, Santiago Artozqui, Laurie Clarke and Rod Wills, Alexandra Poreda, Lara Vergnaud, Casa de Pablo, and Baguette Loaf Summer Writing Retreat.